Turning Point

Bowering Sivers

W F HOWES LTD

This large print edition published in 2008 by
W F Howes Ltd
Unit 4, Rearsby Business Park, Gaddesby Lane,
Rearsby, Leicester LE7 4YH

1 3 5 7 9 10 8 6 4 2

First published in the United Kingdom in 2005
by Transita

A CIP catalogue record for this book is available
from the British Library

ISBN 978 1 40742 568 9

Typeset by Palimpsest Book Production Limited,
Grangemouth, Stirlingshire
Printed and bound in Great Britain
by MPG Books Ltd, Bodmin, Cornwall

FSC
Mixed Sources
Product group from well-managed
forests and other controlled sources

Cert no. SGS-COC-2953
www.fsc.org
© 1996 Forest Stewardship Council

CHAPTER 1

I'm on a train. I can see through it, carriage after carriage, all empty. There is no driver, no guard, no other passengers, only me. The blare of a siren, a tunnel. We slam into it, lurching from side to side, a long black tunnel with no end. I'm thrown from my seat, screaming . . .

'No! Oh God, no!'

I come to with a start, heart pounding, the words stuck in my throat. Slowly my room comes into focus, the floral wallpaper that matches the curtains that match the duvet. The rag doll I've had since I was two.

I dread that nightmare. It's haunted me ever since I came out of hospital. I lie back on the pillow and take deep breaths. Relax, relax. Everybody has bad dreams. It's just the mind letting off steam. The train is my life and the tunnel is death. Very neat. The wailing siren is the kettle. My mother is already up, making tea.

It's a foul day, grey skies, rain slamming against the windows in gusts. I pull up the duvet and snuggle down. There's something to be said for being an invalid.

Feet scurry down the street, sloshing through puddles. Tyres swish along the wet tarmac. It's a good morning to stay in bed, soft pillows, soft lights, Rob at my feet snoring gently. Smell of toast coming from the kitchen. Sometimes it's nice to be a child again. For a while.

This is a soothing room, all lilac and leafy green. Mother had it repainted it while I was away. It used to be my father's study, dark blue and beige Regency stripe. Mother said it was too austere, not the kind of room to convalesce in.

Rob leaps off the bed when he hears the soft tap on the door, cunning animal. Mother pokes her head round cautiously, the worried frown already in place. She's frightened of finding me toes-up. She comes in with a tray – grapefruit, one thin slice of toast, tea, skimmed milk, no sugar. My new regime. What I'd give for eggs and bacon and half a pint of cappuccino.

'How are you, dear?'

Bright smile masking the worry. My father died of a heart attack, just slumped over the breakfast table one morning. She doesn't want a repeat of that so she's burying me in cotton wool. She'd breathe for me, pump the blood round my body with her own hands if she could.

'How do you feel today, dear?'

She puts the tray down on the bedside table and pours the tea. She moves slowly, her fingers stiff.

'Well, thank you.'

Shall I ever feel well again? Everything is such

an effort, walking, climbing stairs. It would be so much easier to stay in bed.

'Did you have a good sleep?'

Same questions every morning, same answers.

'Yes, I slept like a baby.'

My doctor has given me sleeping pills but I won't take them. Supposing my heart stops while I'm asleep? I lie awake, every nerve taut, listening . . . Is my heart still beating? Am I still alive? Don't let me die yet. Please!

In those long, lonely hours before dawn I'm a little child again pleading with some old gentleman in the sky with the power of life and death.

My first night home I was sick with fear, away from all those efficient nurses, the machinery that held me to life, the constant attention. Mother watches over me but what could she do if I had another attack? The second might be fatal. One in five, they say, I've read the statistics.

Coronary anxiety, my doctor calls it. Simpson's a brisk young man, more like a solicitor than a healer, no waste of National Health time on sympathy. Not that I'm a National Health patient but Simpson doesn't believe in privilege. I get no better treatment than the rest. I'm allowed ten minutes and not a second more. He'd stop me in mid-sentence if I ran over the limit.

'But, Doctor, I'm dying.'

'Sorry, Ruth, go away and die on your own time. Next patient, please!'

The grapefruit tastes bitter. It needs sugar, a lot. I push it away.

'How are you, Mother? You look tired this morning.'

She shakes her head. The arthritis bothers her but she never talks about her miseries, dismissing them with a shrug.

The letterbox clatters and Rob leaps up, barking furiously. I almost drop my cup, spilling a few drops of tea on the beautiful lilac sheet, and Mother lunges at him, grabbing his muzzle to silence him, looking at me anxiously . . . Don't panic, Mother, I'm still alive.

She thinks we ought to get rid of Rob. He's a Springer Spaniel, aptly named, a noisy, bouncy animal, but that's what I love about him. I reach out in the night and feel him lying next to me on the duvet, warm body, silky ears. Dear Rob.

'Two letters, both for you,' says Mother, slitting them open for me. She won't allow me to do anything that might tire me. Simpson said I should get up, do a few gentle exercises, go for short walks, start to build up my strength but Mother would strap me to this bed if she had her way. She's convinced overwork killed Daddy, the demands 'they' made on him, 'they' pushed him too hard. She's determined 'they' are not going to get her daughter too.

She sits on the bed waiting for me to read the letters out loud. I've always shared everything with her. We're more like sisters than mother and daughter. I've never quarrelled with her, not even when I was a teenager, that supposedly rebellious time in everyone's life. We seem to have led a very tranquil existence, just the two of us in this comfortable house, bolstered against the world by Daddy's money, a couple of sloths at heart, too lazy to squabble.

The first letter is from my cousin Delphine. She's as daft as her name. She enquires after my health, assures me there's nothing to worry about, lots of people have heart attacks and get over them, modern medicine is so wonderful, isn't it, the things they do today? Then she tells me about her neighbour, Trevor, prime of life, picture of health, dropped dead of a coronary last week, leaving a widow and three small – Mother snatches the letter from my hand.

The second is from an old school friend who moved to Bristol a few years ago. We were close once. Now she has a husband, three warring teenagers and a huge dog of uncertain breed which persists in jumping on visitors, playfully suffocating them. She would like me to go and stay with them when I'm well enough. Mother pulls a face.

'Ruthy,' she says, smoothing the lilac duvet. She is building up to something. Her hands are always busy when her brain is scheming.

Ruthy. I do wish she wouldn't call me that. I'm forty-four, a middle-aged woman. I have no delusions about myself. Ruth the Moabite. Loyal, obedient, stodgy Ruth.

5

'Matthew phoned last night,' she says. His bi-monthly call. Funds must be low. 'He'd like to come for the weekend. I told him I'd speak to you first.'

'Why? It's your house.'

'Don't be silly, dear. He wants to bring a friend.'

'Doesn't he always? Matthew couldn't get through the weekend without a girl in his bed.'

'Oh, Ruthy.'

Mustn't criticise our baby boy.

Poor old mother, she hasn't had it easy. It was thoughtless of Daddy to pop off like that, face down in the cornflakes. He left her well provided for though, big house in the stockbroker belt, money well invested. Merchant bankers are such sensible men.

Mother married in her early thirties. She had always lived at home, never had to work. There was always a man to look after her, a daddy then a husband to earn the money, pay the bills. My father died in the fifties when I was twenty, Matthew only five. Matthew was a mistake.

It had been a peaceful house for years, no voices raised in anger or passion, then Mother got pregnant – 'fell' she said – and nothing was ever the same again. I was embarrassed by her swollen belly and huge breasts, felt a fool walking down the street with her, praying we wouldn't meet any girls from school. My mother and father were far too old for that kind of thing. It was ridiculous. To this day Mother and I never discuss things sexual.

We kind of skirt round them. Anyway, it's not part of our lives any more.

It was a difficult pregnancy. Mother was on her back for a lot of the time, especially towards the end, so I ran the house. I felt a strange mixture of devotion and rage looking after Daddy, feeling very proud and at the same time furious. It was his fault she was so ill.

They were both pleased it was a boy. And Daddy looked very smug. 'Takes a man to make a boy, Harold,' his friends chortled, raising their glasses to him. 'So there's life in the old dog yet, eh?'

You would have thought he'd just climbed Everest.

Matthew started the way he intended to carry on, screaming day and night, his face scarlet, fists clenched, screaming for food, for attention, for the sheer cussed fun of it. Colic, said the nurse. Bad temper, said Daddy, who was clearly beginning to wish he hadn't been quite so potent in bed. I saw Mother feeding Matthew once. He was tugging on the nipple, his fingers digging into her breast as if he were trying to squeeze out every last drop.

'He'll only be here for one night, Ruthy,' she says. 'He has to leave on Sunday evening.'

I've grown very philosophical about Matthew. What choice do I have? He'll come for the weekend whether I agree or not. He'll bring a girl, one of those wannabe actresses he works with or somebody he picked up at a party. They'll go out on Saturday evening, get sloshed, come in at two or three in the morning and thump around in his room, giggling, too drunk to do anything but giving it a good try.

Sunday lunchtime he'll wake up with a sore head, throw a tantrum and drive off with or without the girl – quite a few of them have had to take the train. Like all bad actors, his greatest scenes are offstage. Somewhere in all that he will ask Mother for money just to 'tide him over'. It's become a tidal wave over the years.

'It's a horrible morning, Ruthy, why don't you stay in bed, dear?'

She tucks the lilac duvet under my chin, moulding it round my neck like pastry round a pie funnel.

'Oh, Mother, please, I'm so sick of bed. I've spent the last six weeks in this damned bed.'

She gets up quickly and takes the tray.

I've upset her again. She does so much for me, I think she'd rip the heart out of her own body and give it to me if I asked and all I do is snap at her. I never used to be like this, never swore, never raised my voice. Good old Ruth. Whatever happened to her?

CHAPTER 2

I'm going on a cruise in the spring. Antigua, Guadeloupe, Grenada, Martinique – magical names, magical places. I'm sailing on a clipper, she's called Ariel. There's a shot of her on the cover of the brochure, scudding across the water, her white sails billowing like clouds.

I've chosen my cabin, the ultimate in luxury, with a king size bed and a jacuzzi. It's utterly immoral to spend that kind of money on a holiday but I don't care. I've never spoiled myself like this before. Daddy taught me to be very careful with money but he didn't teach me how to live. I'm going to make up for lost time. The places I'll see, the people I'll meet . . . There's nothing like a coronary to frighten the life into you.

I had a lot of time to think lying in that hospital bed. I've let the years slip by and here I am middle-aged with nothing to show for it. I've always lived with Mother. It seemed easier . . . Well, it didn't seem anything really, it just happened that way. I was always going to do something with my life but I just kind of drifted and it's led me – Where? To this house, this room, this bed.

The cruise starts in May, six months away. Should I book now or check with Simpson first? I'll be well enough to travel in May – won't I?

I keep the brochure on my bedside table along with a stack of books and magazines and read it before I fall asleep. 'Turquoise seas – Sunlight glinting on the waves – Gala dinners – Dancing under the stars – Twinkling harbour lights – Idyllic – Romantic . . .'

I know it's only advertising, the reality will be quite different, but it gets me through the night.

Afterwards, when I get back to England, tanned and fit, I'm going to find a small flat in town. No more damned trains morning and night, no more getting up at six, waiting on draughty platforms, plodding home in the dark, too tired to do anything but eat, sit in front of the television and fall into bed.

I want something around Russell Square, walking distance from my office. It doesn't have to be big. One bedroom is all I need. Mother will be fine here on her own. She has good neighbours, loads of friends, lots of hobbies. And I'll come back and stay with her at the weekend.

I'd like to take courses in art appreciation, art history. Most of all I'd like to do something in the theatre. No, that's nonsense, it's too late for that. But I could become a friend of The Old Vic or the National. At least I'd be involved in a small way.

I ought to do some kind of exercise as well. I'm no good at sports, too heavy, too slow on my feet.

And I've let myself go. 'Something for the fuller figure,' they say, pointing Madam unerringly at the size 16 rack. I've got fuller and fuller over the years, witness to a lifetime of Mother's cooking.

I've lost quite a bit of weight in the past couple of months though. Simpson says I have another stone to go. I'll do it. I will. I'm not going to waddle around the deck of the *Ariel* like a pregnant penguin. I'll buy a whole new wardrobe for the cruise, slinky skirts, silk tops, high-heeled sandals . . . Dear God, there's so much to live for.

I'll get up now. Take it slowly, remember what Simpson said, build up gradually, regain your strength a little more day by day. Mother's in the kitchen. Oh, those delicious smells – almond tarts, sponges, gingerbread. Forbidden, all of it, forbidden for me if I want to go on living. I wish I could smoke. Sometimes I think I'll go out of my mind if I don't have a cigarette . . . Mustn't think about it. It's only a habit.

I'll do my exercises now. Right leg up to waist level – if only I'd done this years ago. Left leg up – I wouldn't be in the poor shape I am now. Right leg up – 'You eat too much fat, too much sugar, Ruth.' Left leg up – 'You lead a sedentary life and you smoke – How many? *Forty a day*? Good grief, woman, you were asking for trouble.' Right leg up – 'And your father died of a coronary, didn't he?' Left leg up – 'Yes, Doctor, and my father's father too. The Websters have probably been filling their lungs with smoke and dropping dead for centuries.'

Right leg up – that's enough of that, I'm breath-
less again.

'Goodness, Mother, you have been busy.' It's her
turn to entertain the bridge club today and a
matter of principle to outdo the other ladies, to
bake bigger and better. 'I think I'll go for a walk.
Do you want anything at the shops?'

'Oh, Ruthy, do you think you should? The
weather's so –'

'Do you want anything at the shops?'

'Wrap up warmly, dear. Put on your –'

'It isn't cold.'

'It's still raining. I'll go and get your –'

'I can get my mac, thank you.'

'Don't tire yourself, dear. You know what the
doctor said.'

'He said I should get some exercise and walking's
very good for me.'

'Don't go too far though.'

'Why don't you follow me with the wheelchair
in case I collapse?'

She flushes and turns away, she doesn't know
how to cope with sarcasm. It's a vice I inherited
from my father, he had a very sharp tongue. His
staff got the full benefit of it, now Mother's getting
the full benefit of mine. I know she doesn't deserve
it but she did buy a wheelchair for me. It was in
the hall when I got back from the hospital, the
first thing I saw when I opened the door. It was
all I could do not to burst into tears. I know she
meant well but . . .

The rain's almost stopped so I won't have to take an umbrella. Good, that's something less to carry. Seeing me dressed to go out Rob leaps for joy, but I can't manage him any more. He's not a big dog but he made it clear from a young age that walking to heel was out of the question and he tugs on the lead, lunging from one lamp-post to the next.

'Sorry, Rob.'

He looks at me with sad eyes. Be patient, Rob, I'll soon be strong again. We'll walk for miles, you and I, miles and miles. He stands at the garden gate, head down, watching me go. He thinks he's being punished for something. I can feel his mournful eyes boring into my back.

It's great to be out, to be moving again, however slowly.

'Hello, Miss Webster . . . Hello, Ruth . . . Hello, my dear, lovely to see you up and about again. How are you?'

I'm stopped every few yards. We've lived here forty years. We still call it the village, Mother and I, though it's grown too big for that, it's almost a suburb of Guildford. New money has moved in – stockbrokers in their unassuming mansions set well back from the road, four acres, three cars, two children.

There are a few colonels' widows still rattling around in their six-bedroom houses, living with their housekeepers now husbands dead, children long gone. They don't fit in any more don't know what's wrong with the world, not like it was in their young day.

I should have left this place years ago. I have nothing in common with anyone here. Girls I was at school with have all moved away. We meet up once a year in London. It's funny to remember them when they were skinny little things, all knees and elbows. Now they have high-powered jobs. Many are mothers, one already a grandmother.

The trick is not to walk too far or coming back can be hell. I'd like to have a cup of coffee at The Rat and Parrot but it's a long trek. I'll just go as far as the florist and buy some flowers for Mother. She deserves them, poor wretch. She's given and given these past few weeks and received nothing but snarls in return.

There aren't many flowers in the shop. November's a dreary month. Everything's dying, trees, flowers, me . . . Oh shut up!

'Ruth!'

'Hello, Mrs Dalton.'

She hurries forward, arms outstretched, her kind old face wrinkled in a smile of welcome.

Daddy loved gardening. It calmed him after a week of haggling over million-pound loans to some foreign government. Back in the days when the Daltons had a market garden he used to chat with them for hours about repotting and pruning. I'd tag along just to be with him, I was his shadow. The market garden got too much for the Daltons so they bought this little shop. They do a brisk business though, especially on Friday evenings, all the husbands popping in on their way home. They buy roses and carnations by the cartload. Love or guilt?

'It's so nice to see you again. We missed you. How are you, my dear?' She holds me at arm's length, peering into my face. 'Arthur, bring a chair. Arthur!'

Good God, do I look that bad? I dressed so carefully too, floral scarf, peonies rampant on an azure field, bright lipstick. Mr Dalton rushes in with a chair, nearly tripping over a Boston fern in his haste. He thinks someone has fainted in the street, one of the geriatric set.

'Ruth?' He stops short, staring at me. The grave has opened. 'Well, well, well.'

His wife snatches the chair from him, rams it behind my knees, pushes me down.

'Can I get you anything, Ruth?' A wreath? 'A cup of coffee?'

'I'd love one, thanks.'

'Arthur!'

Mr Dalton hurries away but she hovers over me, the same expression in her eyes I see in Mother's.

'How are you, dear? Getting over it, are you?'

'I'm fine, thanks. I'd like something for Mother, some roses.'

'She was so worried about you, Ruth. I thought she'd go off her head, poor thing. I met her in the street the day after it happened and she said you were –'

'Yellow.'

'Pardon?'

'Yellow roses. They're her favourite. And put in something for contrast.'

'A few of these green carnations?'

An abomination.

'Irises, I think.'

'You should take it easy, Ruth.' She keeps glancing at me as she fiddles with the flowers, afraid I'll fall off the chair if she doesn't keep a close watch. 'Don't overdo it.'

Overdo what? I've barely raised a finger for seven weeks.

'I'm much better. In fact, I'm going back to work soon.'

You'd think I'd told her the queen mother was pregnant.

'Oh, Ruth, don't go and do anything rash.'

I've never done anything rash. That's the trouble. All my rash times are ahead, I hope.

'You deserve some time off. You've worked so hard all these years. I see you hurrying by every morning, regular as clockwork. I said to my husband I wish there were more people like Ruth Webster, she's so conscientious.'

Conscientious.

They used to put that on my school report every year. I looked it up in the dictionary. 'Influenced by conscience; governed by a strict regard to the known or supposed rules of right and wrong; painstaking; careful.'

Dull.

'You never missed a day.' She's still rabbiting on. 'Twenty years now, isn't it? I don't know what that firm would do without you. They won't begrudge you taking some time off, Ruth. You enjoy yourself while you can, dear. Stay home and have a good long rest.' And to think I walked a mile for this. 'I only wish Arthur and I could retire. I'd love to give up all this.' She spreads her arms to indicate the vast extent of her empire. 'I've give it up tomorrow if I could.'

'I'll buy it.'

'What?'

'I'll buy this shop from you.'

'Oh, well now,' she laughs nervously, 'I didn't quite mean . . .'

It's shut her up, anyway.

Mr Dalton comes back with the coffee. 'And a nice piece of fruit cake,' he says, beaming.

His wife shakes her head at him and tries to push the plate away.

'Thank you, Mr Dalton. It looks delicious.' I gulp it down. I'd eat the whole damned cake if he offered it, plate too.

'It's home-made,' says Mrs Dalton doubtfully, not sure whether that's in its favour or not, thinking of all the brown sugar, treacle, butter and dried fruit clogging up my arteries.

'Well, I'd better be going.'

Her hands move to help me to my feet. His hand is under my elbow. Between them they practically carry me to the door. I can't shake them off, not without being rude, and I'm too Home Counties for that. Anyway, it would be round the village in no time. Mother would get a full report.

'Now, you take my advice, Ruth . . .'

I wrap the scarf tightly round my ears, blocking out the barrage of 'Stay home, Ruth, take it easy, Ruth, don't overdo it.'

I give a cheery wave and stride off determinedly, the stride of a strong, healthy woman. The pain in my chest is back. It must be that wretched fruit cake. Walk fast, faster! I can drop dead when I turn the corner but not in front of the Daltons watching me from their shop doorway like Mummy and Daddy watching baby's first steps.

'Ruth!' Footsteps pattering behind me. She's going to tell me not to walk so quickly. 'You've forgotten these, dear.'

The flowers. How stupid of me. I fumble in my purse.

'No, no, take them.'

'No, really, I couldn't. Thanks all the same but I'd prefer to pay.'

'Please. Take them as a get-well gift.'

CHAPTER 3

Mother's in the garden when I get back, pretending to weed a flower bed. It just happens to be by the gate so she can pop up every few minutes to see if I'm coming. I wonder she didn't push the wheelchair down to meet me.

'Ready for lunch, dear? I've made a nice salad.'

'I'm not hungry. I had some fruit cake at the Daltons and it's ruined my appetite. Sorry.'

'Oh, Ruthy, you shouldn't . . .'

'I bought these for you.'

I put the bouquet in her arms. It's good to see the frown leave her face for a moment. She loves flowers. When my father was alive this garden was full of them. We were quite a show house in those days. An old man does the gardening for us now. He keeps it looking neat but not much more.

'Go into the living room, dear, and put your feet up. Mrs Humphreys has laid a fire.'

She downs tools, follows me in and fidgets round me while I make myself comfortable in an armchair, lifts my feet up and places them gently on the footstool. In a moment she'll wrap a blanket round my knees.

19

'Mother, why don't you go and put the flowers in water?'

'Yes, I will. Now, can I get you anything? A cup of –'

I snap open the newspaper and hold it up in front of my face. I remember Daddy doing that, shutting us all out. The door closes softly. Mother has gone back to the kitchen to make yet more sandwiches for the bridge club. You'd think they were all going on a forced march instead of driving half a mile in their highly-polished Rovers just to sit at little green tables all the afternoon, bickering.

The paper is full of strikes and strife. I escape into sleep and wake as the clock strikes two. I must have slept for an hour or more, I who used to laugh at people who had a nap in the middle of the day now fall asleep over the paper like some dozy old gentleman in his London club, my head lolling, mouth open. I hope I didn't dribble.

The bridge brigade will be here in a minute. I really don't feel up to them, not yet, Henshaw braying, Mrs Pryce gushing, the Fussels, Major Fordham. Mother hoped I would start playing now that I'm home all the time. I used to be very good but there's no way I'd take up bridge again, the small victories, the never-ending squabbles – he shouldn't have led an ace, she should have bid two clubs. I don't want to be part of it any more.

I walk slowly up the stairs and remember half-way that my bedroom isn't up there. Mother converted the garden room for me, my father's sanctuary, French windows giving on to the patio, no stairs to worry about. The perfect room for an invalid.

I think I'll stay there this afternoon and do some reading. I've got a mound of books, they must have cleaned out Smiths for me when I was in hospital. Light romances were the favourite, no horror, no sex, nothing to get the old heart beating madly. Books, magazines and grapes. Scent, talcum powder and grapes. Flowers, pot plants and grapes . . . I could have made my own wine.

My aunt Kitty brought me Turkish Delight. Mother nearly had a fit. Turkish Delight, marrons glacés, pistachio halva . . . all my old vices, banished for ever. I'm allowed to drink in moderation, Simpson says. That means one Scotch a day or a glass of red wine. But no cigarettes, the unkindest cut of all.

Ah, there's the bell. It must be the Henshaws, always first. Yes, I can hear him bellowing his usual greetings. You'd think Mother was standing at the other end of the high street. Clive Henshaw long ago took on the mantle of the village character, mildly eccentric, a touch deaf, what?

He uses his deafness to shout down any opposition to his entrenched opinions. And we all dive under the table when he gets started on 'that woman'. He has nightmares about her becoming prime minister. *A woman prime minister?* He doesn't know what the country's coming to . . .

21

That's Mrs Pryce now. With her two daughters, by the sound of it. Twins, Jane and Jean. Jean's the one with the moustache, that's the only way we can tell them apart. She shaved it off once. We were all very confused.

I can't go in. I have a perfectly good excuse, Mother will make my apologies. They'll be disappointed, it's a long time since I had a game with them and they like fresh blood. The thought of them all chattering, arguing, scoffing Mother's egg and cress sandwiches, scones, cakes, gossiping, doing the same thing, saying the same thing week after week after week . . . No, damn it, I've had enough. I'm too young to be buried in bridge and brandy-snaps.

'Some people use a coronary to escape from their responsibilities. They see it as an opportunity to withdraw from life.' I've read a lot on the subject during the past few weeks, technical books by doctors explaining how the heart works and why it fails, get-well books by people who've been there and come out the other side, religious books. I'm a living authority on the heart.

I think, in a way, my attack was a good thing. It's jolted me out of my comfortable rut. I hadn't even noticed I was growing older, fatter, duller, plodding back and forth to the station every day. I'd no idea people set their clocks by me – poor old Ruth Webster, there she goes again, the clockwork mouse.

'You were an obvious candidate for a coronary,

Ruth,' said Simpson with magnificent hindsight. 'Behind that complaisant exterior I suspect you're a bit of a perfectionist.'

Me, Doctor? I've never done a perfect thing in my whole life. I just try to keep twenty restless girls up to scratch. I try to keep their minds on their work, no matter how they're longing to discuss their boyfriends or the disco or what they saw on the box the previous night. I try to make sure that everything that leaves my department is neat, free of errors, a credit to the company.

It's not an exciting job but what else could I do? I was twenty-two. I had no qualifications, no experience. I left school at sixteen, a convent, with a handful of O levels in useless subjects. I could make a superb sponge, dissect a frog, in theory never in practice, patter along in French, provided the conversation never got much past the weather, and stumble through a Chopin nocturne – all very jolly but not the kind of skills that impress a personnel manager.

Not that I even considered a career. I was good at art, the school wanted me to stay on and do A Level, there was even talk of going to college, taking some kind of diploma. But my father was adamant, fiddling about with easels and brushes was for Bohemians. He didn't want his daughter mixed up with people like that. I never even mentioned the theatre. He'd have put me in a straightjacket till I came to my senses. So I did a little voluntary work, helping out here and there while I waited for the right man to come along.

23

A lot of the girls went to finishing schools in Switzerland – more sponges, more French, laced with skiing and art appreciation. Daddy was against my going to Switzerland, probably because it was full of foreigners. Anyway I'd had enough of school. I was impatient for life, whatever that was, to begin.

When I was twenty-two I took a shorthand typing course like most other girls. I threw myself into it, working at college all day and practising at home in the evenings. I graduated with honours, the fastest typist they had ever known, and as for my shorthand – I believe my name is still mentioned with reverence. Of course, if Daddy had been alive he would have insisted I work in his bank, the most honourable and ancient house in the City. But then if he had still been alive I would have married Anthony.

There is a soft knock on the door.

'Come in, Mother.'

She steals into my room, looking over her shoulder as if she is engaged in some conspiracy, closes the door, sits on the edge of my bed, leans towards me and whispers, 'It's tea time, dear.'

'Well, I promise to keep it a secret,' I whisper back.

'I've told them you still need a lot of rest and visitors tire you but they'd like to see you all the same, just for a moment, just to say hello.'

'I'll come in.' I start to get off the bed.

'No, no!' She almost rams me back into the

pillows. 'They'll come in here, one at a time. They won't stay long, they understand.'

'Mother, I don't want them in here.' Forming an orderly queue outside my door, filing in one at a time, standing by the bed the way they used to at the hospital, shuffling from one foot to the other, not knowing what to say after they'd said, 'How are you?' and 'You're certainly looking a lot better. Soon be out of here.' Unless it was Henshaw. He invariably bellowed, 'Can't stand these places, always stink. And what's the food like? Usual muck?' The nurses looked forward to his visits.

'Oh dear, I wish now I'd said you were asleep.'

Poor wretch, she's done the wrong thing again. I must be the most awkward of invalids to care for.

'Tell them I'll be in in a minute, Mother.'

I sit at the dressing table, turn on the light, not the soft light that glows flatteringly through the pink silk lampshade but the neon strips down the side of the mirror. I want to see the truth.

Sister Anne was always accusing me of being vain. She'd make me say Hail Marys ten to the dozen because she thought I was admiring my reflection in the window. I wasn't but I didn't dare contradict her. Nobody contradicted Sister Anne and lived.

'God made you pretty, Ruth, so that you could learn to overcome the sin of vanity,' she said. God's a cunning old devil, isn't he? After a time I wished I had blonde hair instead of black, I wished I had green eyes instead of blue, I wished I had an oval face instead of heart shaped . . . She did a good job on me, Sister Anne.

I must get my hair permed again. It looks dreadful like this and – Oh no, there's another grey one. If I pull out any more I'll go bald. My eyes are my best feature. Wicked eyes, Anthony used to say.

I was what is known as a bonny baby, breastfed for a year, weaned on steak pies and suet puddings. 'Take off all your clothes,' said a woman doctor when I was twenty, thinking about a wedding dress, a filmy negligee, a bikini for my honeymoon in Greece. 'Take off all your clothes and look at yourself in the mirror every day. If you don't like what you see . . .' I don't. I inherited my mother's body and my father's temperament. Unlucky for me it wasn't the other way round. Daddy was a spare fellow, long and lean. When he was at home he was always thinking about the bank and when he was at the bank he phoned Mother a dozen times a day to see if we were all right.

He was a tightly-coiled, hair-trigger kind of man, a terror to his staff. Even we were a bit afraid of him. Only Mother could gentle him. But then she could gentle anyone. If it weren't considered an insult I'd say she resembled a cow. It's a pity the word has taken on such a derogatory meaning. Cows are beautiful animals, sweet-natured, most of them, and they make wonderful mothers, so I'm told.

There are photos of Mother all over the house, on her wedding day, on her honeymoon, with me, then Matthew, always the same gentle smile. She was lovely when she was a young woman. And she's ageing well. Her skin's clear, her hair's silky white and though she's never been sylphlike she carries her weight, as Daddy used to say, with dignity. She had several proposals of marriage after he died. Major Fordham was one of them. Not a direct proposal, he's too shy for that, but he hinted that if she ever felt she could bring herself to remarry . . . I think he's still in love with her. I tried to talk to her about it one day, suggesting none too subtly that he and she should get together but she just laughed.

There are cries of delight when I go in and they all get to their feet. You'd think they hadn't seen me for years whereas they plodded to the hospital regularly, clutching their frankincense and myrrh.

Mrs Pryce presses me to her large bosom and we strain to touch cheeks and peck at the air. One of the twins has shaved off her moustache again . . . Panic! No, wait a minute, at closer range I can still see that luxurious outcrop. She's bleached it. In an odd way it's almost attractive. Blond moustaches could become the in thing this year. Thank goodness we're not on kissing terms. Anthony had a moustache. He promised to shave it off when we were married.

'You've lost a bit of weight, Ruth,' barks Henshaw, our musical comedy character.

'You certainly have,' echoes his shadow.

'Don't lose too much.' He waves a nicotine-stained finger in my face. 'Don't want to end up looking like one of those half-starved models, do you?'

Yes.

He reeks of tobacco. He has been persuaded to give up smoking while he's here. The stale smell of his clothes stirs my senses like some exotic perfume.

'I'm so glad you're better,' says Mrs Henshaw, taking my hand in her small, dry claw.

'Where are the Fussels?'

'Wolf phoned to say they wouldn't be coming today. His mother's got a cold.'

'Don't want her bringing her germs here,' snaps Henshaw with a sidelong glance at me.

The Fussels haven't missed a game of bridge since they moved to this village from Austria thirty years ago. The old lady has struggled here through hail, sleet and snow, sweating with fever.

'She must be close to death,' I joke. There is an awkward silence. 'Well, at least Wolf could've come.'

'He's afraid he might be a carrier.'

'A cup of tea, Ruth?' Mrs Pryce adroitly changes the subject.

'Yes, thanks.' I get to my feet but she's faster. The cup is in my hand before I am half-way up and Mrs Henshaw creaks to her feet and offers me shortbread, rich, golden, buttery. Mother frowns.

'Oh no. Oh dear, I'm so sorry, I quite forgot.' Mrs Henshaw steps back, flustered, not knowing what to do with the offensive shortbread. For one moment she looks as if she's going to stuff it up her sweater. 'I'm so sorry,' she apologises endlessly. 'You can't, can you?'

'Course she can,' bellows her husband. He looks like a rabbit that man, all teeth and ears. 'Lot of rubbish talked about food. It's *not* eating what you want to eat and *not* doing what you want to do that makes you ill, that's what I say.'

Out of the mouths of babes and rabbits.

Sadly, his words fall on deaf ears. The rich offerings are withdrawn and I'm left with one thin slice of brown bread, meagrely buttered. Not even butter. It's margarine, high in polyunsaturates. Mother's been watching the commercials.

'You're really looking very well, Ruth.'

I do wish they'd shut up. Just get on with the eating and drinking and bridge, that's what they came for. The tea break is traditionally the time for discussion and recrimination. Mother usually wins. She's a cunning player. She looks as if her mind is off with the fairies, then she trumps your ace. I can't believe such a sweet old lady is capable of such guile.

'When do you go back to Cambridge, Jane?'

I hope I've got the right one. Jane's the bright twin, reading something terrifying like bio-medical engineering, all set for a brilliant career. Jean works in a day nursery. No career, no hope of

29

catching a husband either, not with that broom on her lip.

'I *am* back,' Jane says.

Stupid of me. It's November. I seem to have stopped my mental clock at September the thirtieth.

'You must be near the end?'

'The end?'

'I mean . . .' Have I got it wrong again? 'You'll be taking your Finals next summer, won't you?'

'But I've got my BSc, Ruth. I'm doing my Masters now.'

Of course. There was a celebration garden party in June, champagne and strawberries. Half the village went. Has it affected her brain as well, she's thinking, smiling at me sweetly.

'Nitro-glycerine,' announces Henshaw. I can't think of an answer to that. It's a real conversation stopper. But at least he's got everyone's attention again. 'Completely cured Roger, didn't it, Amy?'

He turns to his little wife crunched up in her chair, birdlike claws curled round the handle of her teacup. She crumbles under his stare. 'What did, dear?'

'Nitro-glycerine,' he snaps irritably. He's given her eight children and what has she given him in return? She doesn't listen to anything he says, never laughs at his jokes, won't play bridge the way he tells her to . . . 'Roger took nitro-glycerine and it cured him. He's fit as a fiddle. Doctor said he wouldn't last till Christmas, not a hope, and look

30

at him now. Eats like a horse, drinks, rides to hounds, chases Bunty round the bedroom every night. Some doctors say you should give it up after a coronary. Absolute nonsense! Bunty says Roger's like an old goat, can't get enough. Said *I* should get some, didn't she, Amy?'

Mrs Henshaw blushes hotly, staring into her teacup. I think all her children must have been virgin births.

'You ought to get some, Ruth. Tell that fellow Simpson I think he should give you nitro-glycerine.'

'I take anticoagulants actually.'

'My mother died from a blood clot, started in her leg, went up to her lung. She was dead before the doctor got there. Course, we lived right in the country then, Berkshire, great big house set in twenty acres. It wasn't so easy for tradesmen to get to.' We've heard it a hundred times before, the 'great big house', it gets bigger with every telling, the orchards, stables, servants. 'By the time we got a message through to the doctor my mother was –'

'Of course a stroke is much worse than a heart attack,' says Mrs Pryce, interrupting him in an absent-minded way.

He glares at her, cups his hand to his ear. 'What?'

'A stroke I said a stroke is much worse than a heart attack.'

'My mother didn't have a stroke.'

'I didn't say she did. I was only saying –'

'Cancer's the worst of the lot.' Henshaw steamrollers her flat. 'Worse thing you can get, cancer. Horrible, lingering death. All Amy's people died of it. At least with a heart attack you drop dead on the spot –'

'Shall we start playing again?' Mother rises quickly, collects plates and cutlery, crashes them on the tray, nearly breaking one of her Doulton cups.

'Just finish my tea,' says Henshaw, straining it through those big, yellow teeth. 'Very refreshing, tea. I read in the paper yesterday it's bad for you. Load of rubbish. They say everything's bad for you. Too much red meat gives you cancer. Too much fat gives you a dicky heart –'

Mother whisks the cup from his hand, nearly disjointing his finger.

'Load of rubbish,' he rumbles on. 'Eat what you like, that's my opinion. Eat, drink and be merry for tomorrow we –'

Mother knocks over the milk jug. The creamy fluid flows across the table. The whole room rises like a flight of Canada geese, flapping at the wet patch with napkins and handkerchiefs. Only Henshaw stays in his chair, watching the performance with disinterest, sucking his teeth thoughtfully.

He sees me looking at him and gives me a little smile. We're both above such menial tasks, he for the obvious reason, I because I'm now an invalid, exempted from domestic service by my 'dicky heart'.

I go back to my room. In the midst of such confusion they'll never notice. There's a scratch at the door, Rob wants to escape too. We snuggle down on the bed together. When I wake, hours later, the room is in darkness, the house silent.

CHAPTER 4

I see Simpson twice a week. He's such an irritating young man, barely in his thirties but
already he has that condescending attitude
that should have gone out with Mother's gener-
ation – clean sheets, clean nightie, sit up straight,
dear, the doctor's coming.

Nobody reveres doctors any more. We all know
they're just ordinary people who chose medicine
instead of maths. Or art.

'Hello Ruth.'

I keep plucking up the courage to say 'Hello
Martin.' 'Ruth' is meant to make me feel at ease,
put our relationship on a friendly, informal basis.
It's something he was taught, patient psychology,
only the way he says it reminds me of the Mother
Superior at my school, forbidding expression,
steel-rimmed glasses, a hair shirt under her
habit . . .

'Good morning Ruth.'

'Good morning Mother Teresa.'

I could no more say 'Hello, Martin' to him than
I could have said 'Hello Terry' to her.

He reads through my notes. My whole life is

there for all to see, every itch and twitch I've ever had. While I'm waiting I look at the photos on his desk. He seems too young to have a wife and two children but they're a mandatory accessory for doctors. After a certain age bachelors are probably struck off.

'How are you?'

'I'm fine, thanks.'

He cocks his head to one side, quizzing me.

I have automatically slipped into the standard reply reserved for friends and relatives, quite forgetting he's not fooled by my jaunty confidence. He knows very well how I am, the niggling pains that frighten me, the palpitations, the breathlessness.

'I keep getting this feeling . . .' I put my hand on my chest, just above the left breast.

'Feeling?'

'Pressure.'

'Persistent?'

'It comes and goes.'

'Try this.'

He scribbles a prescription, pushes it across the desk to me. Nitro-glycerine. But, Doctor, I've nobody to chase round the bedroom.

'Next time you feel that pain take one immediately and let me know how long it is before it goes away. Phone me.'

'What if it's the middle of the night?'

'I'm on call.'

He's short on humour, this young man. If he

laughs, God forbid, he might lose some of his authority.

'Sleeping well?'

'I keep waking up.' I tell him about my nightmare.

'Take a sleeping pill. It won't harm you. Better to get a good rest than lie all night listening to your heart ticking.'

It's a relief to talk to someone who knows what I'm going through. At least I don't have to pretend with him.

'Any other problems?'

'My mother . . .'

Foolishly I blurt it out before I can stop myself. It's so much on my mind and I don't have anyone else to talk to. There's a woman at work, Deirdre, who loves the theatre as much as I do so we see everything together, opera and ballet too, but I'm not close to her. We chat about work mostly. I've not confided in anyone since Anthony, and in those days I had no secrets anyway, no fears, no nightmares.

'Worrying about you all the time, is she? Coddling you?' There's the supercilious smile again. Silly little women. Well, I did ask for it. 'Thank your lucky stars you have someone to take care of you, Ruth. You could be living in a bedsit on your own like some of my patients.'

Some of his patients? There's nobody living in a bedsit around here . . . Oh, he's talking about his London practice. He has a clinic in Whitechapel once a week.

36

He listens to my heart, makes me say 'Ah', peers into my eyes, takes my blood pressure, checks my wrists and ankles.

'All right, get dressed.'

He goes back to his desk while I put on my blouse, modestly screened from his view.

'You're doing very well, you know.'

I feel a great surge of relief. Reprieved.

'Do you think I'll be able to go back to work soon?'

'I don't see why not. Come and sit down.'

He's reading through my notes again. For goodness sake, why do I always have to have a conversation with the top of his head? I'll bring my notebook next time and sit here scribbling in short-hand while he's talking to the top of *my* head. Better still I'll bring my typewriter, I've got a portable.

'When did you have the cardiac arrest, Ruth? End of September. Yes, you should be thinking of getting back to work now. Just a couple of hours a day to start with. You work in London, don't you? Pity. The travelling's probably more tiring than the job. Couldn't you find something local?'

'There's nothing to do round here.'

'Surely you could get work in a small company or a shop?'

And I could kick you in the crotch, you insulting bastard!

'Actually I'd like to go away. I was thinking of a cruise.'

'Excellent. When?'

'The end of May.'

'Somewhere warm?'

'The Caribbean.'

'We'll cut down the checks to every other week from now on.' He leans back, gives me his professional smile. 'Keep up the good work.'

Two gold stars and a merit badge, Ruthy. I wish I hadn't told him about Mother though. I feel I've betrayed her and to Simpson of all people. Suppose he mentions it to her? Of course she's worried. I'd be exactly the same if it had happened to her, probably a lot worse.

I buy chocolates for her on the way home. Her eyes light up. 'Daddy always used to bring me Bendicks.'

Yes, I remember. He didn't approve of lavish gifts but chocolates were acceptable.

'Mother, I'm sorry I've been so crabby lately. I know I keep snapping your head off but it's just that I feel so . . .'

'I know, dear, I understand. It's been a hard time for you.'

She puts her hand over mine, a warm, comforting hand, not like Mrs Henshaw's dry little claw. 'All I want is for you to get better, Ruthy. Your happiness is the only thing that matters to me.'

There are tears in her eyes.

'Simpson says I'm making excellent progress.' I can't bear to see her cry. 'I've just booked a holiday, a cruise.' I say it quickly to cheer her up before the tears start to flow. I've always done that, ever since Daddy died, told her jokes, silly things that happened at work, anything to stop her from crying. 'I've got a lot of holiday time due to me. I'm sure they won't mind if I take a few weeks in the spring. After all they told me to take as long as I needed to get over this.'

She doesn't look as pleased as I thought she would.

'Boats are such noisy places, Ruthy. Daddy and I went to America on the *Queen Mary*. Do you remember, he was getting over bronchitis? The doctor said it would do him the world of good and we thought we'd have such a nice, relaxing time but it was nothing of the sort. The boat creaked, you wouldn't believe how a boat creaks and groans all the time. And there was always something going on, games and parties and people rushing about, up and down the corridors day and night, shouting and laughing.' It sounds wonderful.

'What about that nice little hotel we found in Brittany? Or you could go to Aunt Mildred. She'd love to have you.'

My father's sister, a desiccated twig who lives in a mausoleum in Eastbourne. She goes to bed at nine o'clock and has three neurotic dogs, Yorkshire terriers, that never shut up.

'You must be joking. I couldn't stand one day with her. Anyway, I've already booked the cruise.'

'Speak to Doctor Simpson before you put any money down, Ruthy.'

'He thinks it's a good idea.'

'Well, I don't know –'

'It isn't up to you.'

'Don't jump down my throat like that, dear. I'm only trying to help you.'

'I think I'll go and lie down.' Before my blood pressure starts rising.

'Remember Kitty's coming this evening,' she calls after me.

All the more reason for taking a long nap now.

Kitty is Mother's half-sister, twelve years younger, a funny, sweet, infuriating little chatterbox. She'd stay up half the night, prattling about nothing if we let her. Mother usually finds a way of pushing her back in the box and closing the lid around ten o'clock.

I'm back in bed again. It's like being a toddler – a little nap, a walk, a little nap, a meal, a little nap. But Simpson is pleased with my progress. That's comforting, a nice thought to hold on to while I drift off to sleep, one hand imbedded in Rob's thick golden coat.

Kitty's high-pitched, excited voice brings me back. She comes to dinner once a week, arriving by taxi, laden with parcels. Since her husband died time lies very heavily on Kitty. She has a small flat in Maida Vale, no children, no hobbies. What does a woman like that do when she's widowed? For someone like Mother it's different. She has plenty of friends, lots of interests, her life will always be full. But Kitty?

She brings expensive presents, jewellery, perfume, pillboxes, crystal paperweights, leather purses, things that can easily be slipped into a pocket. Mother's so worried about her. She asked her outright if she was stealing. It wasn't easy, accusing her own sister. Of course, Kitty denied it, was most upset that Mother should even suggest . . . 'Can't I bring you a little prezzy without you thinking I'm a thief?'

I think Kitty should go somewhere for treatment. It's such an obvious emotional problem, you read about it every day, the old lady screaming for attention, but Mother is wary of psychiatry. We don't tell family secrets to strangers. So what do we do about Kitty?

She's been very busy as usual, so many friends, so much to do . . . Mother and I nod, playing the game.

'And how are you, darling?' She gives me a big hug. She's a very affectionate woman, like a puppy, needing to be stroked all the time, giving unquestioning love and devotion in return. 'I've got something nice for you.'

No more gloves, I hope, no more stockings. Not another bracelet – I've got a whole armful in my bedroom, it makes me feel guilty just looking at them. If the police were ever to search this place . . . Wonder of wonders she draws from her shopping bag a large box. I exchange startled looks with Mother. She couldn't possibly have stuffed that in her pocket.

Kitty's very excited as I untie the string and snuggles up to me. Under the Chanel Five, courtesy of Harrod's perfumery when the saleswoman's back was turned, I can smell moth balls. I think she buys her clothes, if she buys them, from second-hand shops off the King's Road. They're all bits and pieces, frilly skirts and fringed shawls that somebody has kept at the back of their wardrobe for years. Lately she's taken to matching her eye shadow to her outfit, somebody told her it was chic. Mother and I dread her purple days.

'Hurry up, Ruthy.' She's like a little girl at a birthday party.

I unwrap my present. It's a box with a picture of Windsor Castle on the front. Chocolates by appointment? Good grief, it's a jigsaw puzzle.

'I thought it would be something for you to do, Ruthy. Jigsaws are such fun. And this is a really big one.' She puts her arm around me and squeezes my shoulder. 'Look, four thousand pieces. We could start tonight, if you like. We could spread it out on the table in your room. The sky's going to be a problem, isn't it, all those clouds? Remember the trouble we used to have with clouds?'

It's just like my baby days, little Ruthy and Aunty Kitty sitting at the table doing jigsaws, drawing doggies, playing with plasticine.

'I don't want any dinner, thanks, Mother.' She's made something special. She works so hard to make interesting meals out of my Spartan diet.

'I've got a pain, just here.' I put a hand over my heart. It's a cruel thing to do, their faces are contorted with anxiety, but I must get away.

'I'll help you, dear.' Mother gets up and puts her hand under my elbow, Kitty takes the other.

Back in my room, in the darkness, I lie on the bed, staring at the ceiling.

Jigsaws. Good God!

CHAPTER 5

Mrs Fraser wakes us up at eight o'clock. So sorry, so early, a vicar's wife is always on the go. She just wants to confirm that Mother will be manning one of the stalls at the arts and crafts fair next Saturday. The church roof is falling in and the ladies of the village are sewing, painting, baking to shore it up.

Mother has embroidered six cushions, Mrs Fraser can't stop exclaiming over them, and I have painted some thimbles, a hobby I started at school. They always seemed so dull, those little white thimbles we used in the needlework class. I couldn't resist covering them with roses and pansies. Now I'm doing abstract art, intricate patterns in brilliant colours. Silly little things, but people love them. I'm quite famous for my thimbles in these parts. Collectors' items, so they tell me. I've done about twenty for the sale.

Mother and I are always first on the list of willing helpers. Jumble sales, church suppers, cricket teas, we've never said no. Why should we? Our Saturdays are always free. There are no men, no children to clutter up our lives.

'Of course, Ruthy won't be able to.'

'Oh no, no, Mrs Webster. I didn't think for one minute that she would.'

'Of course I'll help. I always do.'

'But, dear, it'll be very tiring.'

'Mother, you know you can't handle that stall alone.'

'It's true,' she smiles apologetically at Mrs Fraser. 'It's all those people, picking things up and asking the price, shouting at me, and then I get mixed up with the change. I still miss the old money, you know.'

There is a brief discussion about 'dear old three-penny bits and half-crowns' and then the vicar's wife is on her way. 'It's very kind of you both to help, very kind. I don't know what we'd do without you.'

Matthew arrives just after two o'clock. He was supposed to be here for lunch at one. Mother insisted I eat, my usual cottage cheese and fruit, and I didn't argue with her. I hear his car racing up the road, screeching into the driveway, crunching to a halt on the gravel. A sports car, of course, ages old, held together with string, but it looks glamorous – at least he thinks so.

I always have a strong desire to hide in my room when Matthew comes and now I have a perfectly good excuse. I'm not afraid of him but I am afraid of the feelings he brings out in me. I don't want to get worked up. It would be ridiculous to have a second attack because of something he said or did.

Mother has put him and his girlfriend in the guest room. I think it's pretty broadminded of her. There are still matrons in this village who wouldn't let their children sleep with someone of the opposite sex 'under my own roof!' and Mother's an Edwardian lady, after all, convent educated like me.

There's a pink and beige flowered quilt on their bed, matching frills on the dressing table and stool, deep pink velvet curtains, my flowers, the yellow roses I gave her, clashing nicely on the bedside table, and, of course, a profusion of cushions she has embroidered in pastel shades.

Matthew sneers at our taste in furnishings. Little women, he calls us, Marmy and Ruthy. But it doesn't stop him coming back every so often to cadge a couple of hundred from Marmy, clean out her larder, drink all her booze.

He bursts in, throws his arms around her and swings her round, no mean feat for such a slight man and she must be all of fourteen stone. It's an impressive entrance. As usual.

'Hello you.'

We always start off well with a hug and a kiss.

He never came to see me in hospital. I didn't mind, I know illness frightens him. 'But he asks about you all the time,' Mother said.

'Ian! What the hell . . . Ian!' he shouts. 'Come on in. What's the matter with you, gone all shy, silly sod?'

Mother and I are taken aback. We were expecting

46

one of Matthew's little girls in a skirt up, or down, to her crotch. He's never had men friends. He discovered girls early and he's never been without one since, very young, wrapping themselves around him adoringly.

'Mum, this is Ian Trevelyan. Remember the name because he's going to be famous one day and then you can stick a sign over the door saying he actually slept here. Ian, meet my dear old mum. And this is my sister Ruth. She always looks that fierce but don't worry about it, we pulled her teeth out years ago so she can't bite.'

Ian Trevelyan is tall and thin. He has nice eyes and a huge Adam's apple. Even the cravat, artfully swathed, can't hide it. He's dressed in jeans and sweater, like Matthew. Another actor, I suppose. Matthew has no friends outside the theatre. This one's a bit more successful than my brother from the look of him. He has a certain confidence about him, real confidence, not Matthew's loud bluster.

'Hello.' He stoops to greet us. He must be well over six feet. 'I'm sorry to barge in on you like this. I'm sure you weren't expecting me.'

He has a beautiful voice. What a pity he doesn't have a face to match. And he's so thin. Anthony wasn't tall but he was sturdy. Rugby was his game. This man looks more like one of the goal posts.

Mother in her own special way immediately puts her unexpected guest at ease. She was a little flustered at first, two men, so much maleness in this feminine sanctuary, but she will tame them. In no time she has them sitting at the table, napkins on their knees, while she heaps their plates with chicken and ham pie, roast potatoes, carrots, peas.

'It's rather dry,' she apologises. Cunning old thing, she knows she's a marvellous cook and nothing that comes out of her oven could ever be less than perfect.

'It's absolutely delicious,' says Ian as she knew he would.

'The vegetables are fresh, they're from our garden, Mr Trevelyan. May I help you to more?'

I can see she's going to build him up, she has that look in her eye. She turns all men into little boys sooner or later. In one weekend she intends to put some flesh on Ian Trevelyan's spare frame and, judging from the way he's tucking in, he's a willing accomplice.

'I'm so sorry about the time.' He glances at his watch. 'I didn't realise we were supposed to be here for lunch.'

'For Christ's sake stop apologising,' says Matthew. 'Mum, got any beer?'

'There's some in the fridge, dear.'

We always get in a good supply when Matthew comes. From the amount he eats and drinks he should be a lot fatter than me. It's an unfair world.

'Want one, Ian?'

'Yes, thanks.' He begins to get up.

Mother puts her hand on his shoulder. 'No, no, finish your lunch. You've had a long drive.'

Matthew lets out a loud guffaw, one of his stage

laughs, back arched, mouth wide open. They should be able to hear that in the gallery. 'Mum, you're unreal. You'd think we'd driven down from Edinburgh. I live in London, darling, Ealing. It's a breeze getting here on a Saturday.'

'Have you found a nice place this time?'

Matthew is always changing. He says he gets fed up living in the same place. I say he gets kicked out.

'I've got a nice little pigsty, if that's what you mean.'

'And do you live in Ealing, Mr Trevelyan?'

'Please call me Ian, Mrs Webster. And I live in Hampstead, a small flat, the attic actually, in my uncle's house.'

'Oh, Hampstead, such a lovely place,' says Mother, who hasn't been there for years, 'and so handy for working in London. Are you in the theatre too?'

'Ian's a fringe man,' Matthew butts in before his friend can open his mouth.

'I'm not sure what fringe means,' Mother frowns. Her knowledge of theatre doesn't go much further than the local amateur dramatic productions.

'Social relevance, political issues, and all that.'

That doesn't help her either.

'Are you in a play at the moment, Ian?'

'I'm not an actor, Mrs Webster. I'm a director.'

'Artistic director,' says Matthew, though the distinction is lost on us. 'He's doing a very naughty play at the moment, full of lewd bedroom scenes and four-letter words.'

He's cleaned one plate of pie and is half-way through the second, ramming it in. Matthew always eats as if there's a famine in the offing.

'You make it sound like trivial rubbish,' says the artistic director. He says it quietly, with no trace of anger. How on earth does he manage all those stroppy actors with a gentle voice like that?

He has an odd face, very sensitive and yet the outline is hard and angular. The eyes are soft, the jaw stubborn. He's had an awful hair cut, a kind of long crew cut, neither one thing nor another. And it's thin hair. Not like Matthew's. He has enough for both of them. And of course he wears it long even though it's no longer in fashion. Actors are above fashion.

'Tell us about it, Ian.' I'm interested in fringe theatre but Deirdre finds it heavy going so we only go to what she calls 'mainstream' productions.

He puts down his knife and fork and gives me his full attention. 'It's set in a typical seaside conference town. You know the kind of place I mean.'

I do. Mildred country.

'It shows the other side of the annual political party jamboree, the pols back in their hotel rooms, wheeling and dealing.'

'Fiddling,' Matthew explains for Mother's benefit.

'The bedroom scenes are juxtaposed with scenes from the convention itself, fine speeches, noble sentiments, the kind of rubbish pols force feed us.

50

It's a play that has a lot to say . . .' He stops and frowns. 'No, that makes it sound boring. What I really meant was it isn't an excuse for a lot of smut and –'

'Although there's plenty of that,' Matthew chirrups. 'A juicy seduction, a couple of gay MPs caught shagging. Not the kind of thing you should see, Ruthy Wuthy.' He leans over and pats my hand. 'You stay with *The Mousetrap*.'

I can feel the blood rising in my face. Ian sees it too.

'It's an interesting play, Ruth, despite what your brother says. It sets you thinking – at least it ought to. I'd like you to see it.'

'She isn't allowed out yet,' says Matthew. 'She had a heart attack a couple of months ago. Got to take it easy for a bit, haven't you, old girl?'

'I'm sorry,' Ian says. 'My father had a coronary . . .' Here we go. Everybody's father, brother, cousin has had one. We shall now hear all the details about Mr Trevelyan Senior's, especially the part where he fell to the floor, clutching his chest . . .' But he got over it. He's in good shape now.'

Is that it? No deathbed scene?

'Another beer?'

'Not for me, thanks, Matt.'

'Are you in Ian's play, Matthew?' says Mother hopefully.

She would have liked her son to be a banker, a solicitor. If he had to be an actor he could at least

51

be a successful one, somebody she could point to on the television. I often wonder what would have happened if Daddy had lived. 'My son, an *actor* . . . ?' I'll bet he's turned over in his grave so many times he's giddy.

'No, 'fraid not, darling. He turned me down flat,' says Matthew, 'but I live in hope.'

So that's why Ian Trevelyan is here. I catch Matthew glancing at him, an oddly vulnerable look. One more chance has slipped away. Then the mask is back in place.

Ian says nothing, just smiles, refusing to be drawn into apologies or promises. His expression in repose is thoughtful, almost sad. I wish I could take my eyes off that huge Adam's apple. The cravat has slipped a bit.

'That was an excellent lunch, Mrs Webster. Thank you. Matt told me you were a superb cook.'

I'll bet he didn't say anything of the sort, never even mentioned Mother or me, but Ian Trevelyan is a bit of a smoothy. He uses that lovely, choco-laty voice to advantage. I can tell he's going to play the gallant with Mother and be very gentlemanly with me, as befits my age and indisposition.

'Let me help you with the washing up.'

'Bless you, no.' Mother is falling in love with him already. 'You stay right where you are.'

'She's got a dishwasher but she won't use it. T'ain't natural,' Matthew grins.

'It seems such a waste to run it for a few dishes,'

she says. 'And I have to rinse them first, anyway. I can't see the point.'

Matthew wraps his arms around her waist and buries his head in her apron. The baby boy again. 'She's the bestest Mum in the whole world,' he gushes.

What will he be calling her this time tomorrow, I wonder? He has a theatrical vocabulary. It gets a full airing when he's in one of his moods.

I have such mixed feelings about my brother. He's lovable, hateful, charming, churlish. I remember him as a baby. Such a dear little face, but it could change in a second to rage, venom pouring from that rosebud mouth in torrents. He's still the same.

'Oh, I thay, Ian, ithn't thith jutht lovely?' They've gone upstairs to put their things in the bedroom appointed for them. Matthew always makes fun of Mother's pretty pillows and pouffes. 'And a double bed too! Oh darling, we'll be sleeping together at last.'

There are guffaws, a lot of banging around. Matthew never moves quietly and his friend is a big man. It's good to hear laughter in the house again. Matthew bounds down the stairs, pouting. 'Ian won't let me sleep with him, Mum. He says he's still a virgin.'

'You can take the small room, the bed's made up. Just don't make any noise, Matthew. It's right over Ruthy and I don't want her disturbed, do you understand?'

She reverts to the tone she used to use when he was a child. 'Don't stay out playing too long, do you understand? Don't leave your toys all over the floor, do you understand?' I was her little echo in those days, bearing down on him in her absence, always scolding. I can see the rebellious look in his eyes still. Him against us.

'I promise to be very, very good, Marmy,' he says in a falsetto voice. 'I will not disturb Ruthy, cross my heart and hope to die.' An unfortunate expression. He casts a sideways glance at me. 'Come on, Ian, move your arse, Chrissake!' he shouts up the stairs. 'It starts at three.'

'What does?' Mother asks.

'A play, something one of the local theatres is putting on. I want Ian to take a look at Nightingale, she's got the lead.'

Nightingale is probably his current girlfriend. The last one was Antigone. He never brings home an Ann or a Mary.

'Ruthy and I enjoy going to the theatre,' says Mother. She's angling for an invite. 'Is it a comedy?'

'Hardly. It's about the Russian invasion of Afghanistan.'

No, that certainly won't get them rolling in the aisles.

'You should go and see Ian's play. It's very funny and very sexy,' Matthew says. 'Nothing like a bit of funny sex, eh, Marmy?' He runs his fingers up and down her spine, paddling them in her neck.

'Oh, Matthew . . .' She laughs and scolds. Now he has her where he's always had her, in the palm of his hand. Soon that hand will close, start to squeeze, draw blood. It infuriates me that she falls for it every time.

'I thought it was a serious play,' I say. 'Your friend is obviously an earnest young man with an important message for the world.'

He bridles. 'A prig, you mean?'

'You said it.'

'He's just trying to make small-minded people think. He doesn't have much time for politics.'

'Ah, a little anarchist, one of the "down with them" brigade.'

'At least he hasn't swallowed the whole fucking package like you – church on Sunday, stand up for the Queen, ride to hounds, lunch with Lady Tina Tightbottom.'

It's ridiculous. I haven't been to Mass in ages, I never learned to ride properly and certainly not to hunt, God forbid, and my closest friend is Deirdre Winterton who lives in a two-bedroom flat in Catford.

'You're giving me pretensions well above my station, Matthew.'

'True. You're only a second-class snob. You'd like to be first class but we're not quite in that bracket, are we?'

'Now, please, you two!'

Our disagreements distress Mother. She likes playing happy families.

'Ian is worth a hundred of your kind.' Matthew likes to have the last word.

'My goodness, what a paragon.' So do I. 'But what if he doesn't give you a part in his next production, will he still be Mr Wonderful?'

Matthew blows himself up for a full-scale explosion. How dare I see through his devious little scheme?

Ian clatters down the stairs, making a lot of noise. Naturally he hasn't heard a word we've been bellowing.

'Would you like to come with us, Ruth?' he says.

'What, three of us in that little car? You must be joking,' Matthew laughs. 'My sister is hardly sports-car size.'

'I've lost a stone.' I wish I could stop rising to the bait.

'And you could do with losing another one here.' He slaps my bottom. 'And here.' A resounding slap on my thigh.

Ian is clearly disturbed that Mother and I aren't going. It's obviously not in his code of conduct to leave the hostesses quite so abruptly after arrival but Matthew doesn't abide by the same rules. If we go who's going to stay home and cook his dinner?

CHAPTER 6

I always sleep in the afternoon, my best sleep of the day, no nightmares. When I wake I'm still on my back, my chin tucked in, arms folded piously across my breast like the marble effigy of Lady Vere de Vere in the parish church.

There's no more room in our churchyard. Daddy's there, Mother wants to be buried alongside him. I want to be cremated. Mother's horrified. I'll be excommunicated, cast into outer darkness. Where will they scatter my ashes, I wonder, along the Guildford to Waterloo Line?

Mother comes in with a cup of tea, sits on the bed and smiles. She's so pleased I'm home all the time so we can have lots of little chats. 'Ian seems a very nice boy, doesn't he?'

I suppose when you're her age anyone under forty must seem young.

'A nice man, Mother. He must be well into his thirties.'

'He's only twenty-nine.'

'How do you know?'

'I asked Matthew.'

'Nosy old devil.'

57

'Matthew says he's known him for quite a long time. They met when they were both working on that comedy thing in Oxford.' That 'comedy thing' best describes it. If that's an example of Ian Trevelyan's work . . .' Though Ian was only a stage manager in those days.' Exonerated. 'He's done very well for himself since then, Matthew says.' Better than my son, she's thinking, though she'd never say it. 'He's nice looking, isn't he?'

'A bit gaunt.'

'Yes, he's dreadfully thin, but he'd really be quite handsome if he filled out. And he's got lovely eyes.' Good heavens, what are Ian Trevelyan's eyes doing to my old mother? 'And he's beautifully mannered.'

'Unlike your son.'

'Oh, Ruthy,' she sighs. 'You're so hard on that boy.'

'No, Mother, I really don't think you can get away with calling Matthew a boy. He was twenty-eight in August.'

'Well, he's boyish.'

'He plays the part well, I agree.'

'Poor Matthew.'

She's been saying that for years. 'Poor Matthew' when he was thrown out of one school after another. 'Poor Matthew' when he hung around the house for years, not knowing what to do, tormenting us with his noisy despair. 'Poor Matthew' when he failed auditions.

She reaches out and touches my cheek. Mother

loves to touch. When Matthew and I were small she was always hugging us.

'We're very contented here, aren't we, Ruthy?'

Of course, Mother. We fit together like sugar and spice. The sound of a key in the lock disrupts our contemplation of all things nice.

'There they are, back earlier than I expected. I'd better go and put the potatoes on. Are you getting up for dinner, dear?'

'Of course.'

'Don't overdo it, Ruthy, just because someone's here. You do just what you want.'

'I always get up for dinner.'

'But you look rather flushed this evening.'

'It's the excitement of meeting a new man. My heart keeps going boom-ti-ti-boom-ti-ti-boom.'

She is not amused.

'Today's been a bit of a strain for you.'

'Mother, do stop fussing over me.'

It's a word she dislikes. On the rare occasions they had a disagreement Daddy would accuse her of fussing, although he was just as guilty of it in his way.

Ian and Matthew are sitting in front of the fire. Ian gets up when I go in. 'Sit here, Ruth.'

'No, I'm quite comfortable here, thank you. I don't like to sit right on top of the fire.' Liar, I'm like a cat about fires but I won't have him treating me like some fragile old woman.

'Did you enjoy the play?'

'It wasn't bad.'

Damned by faint praise.

'And what about the actress?'

'Not quite as good as she was cracked up to be,' says Ian.

Hardly surprising. Nightingale was only live bait. Now Matthew's got his artistic director on the hook – or has he? I've a feeling Ian Trevelyan can't be gaffed that easily.

'May I get you a drink, Ruth?'

'She's not allowed,' says Matthew.

'I'll have a Scotch, thanks.'

'Naughty girl.'

'Water?'

'A little.'

Ian moves slowly, as if he were on stage, conscious of his every action. I can't imagine this man doing anything that wasn't well thought through.

'To your speedy recovery.' He raises his glass, leans back in his chair, looking at me intently. I can tell he's going to talk to me now about my heart attack . . . 'What do you do?'

'Well, I have special exercises I'm supposed to do three or four times a day although they're so boring I skip them now and then.' Out of the corner of my eye I see Matthew raise his eyes to the ceiling in stagy despair. 'And I go for walks. I still have to rest a lot though. I get tired so easily and –'

'I meant what work do you do?'

'Oh . . . Oh, I work for an insurance company.'

'She's a dragon,' says Matthew, pouring himself another vodka. 'She sits at a big desk glaring at rows and rows of pathetic little creatures all bashing the hell out of typewriters.'

If you take out the exaggeration I suppose that is what I do.

'Sounds very boring,' says Ian. I'm stunned by his rudeness. 'I thought you'd do something far more interesting than that. You don't look the type for such a dull job.'

It's so neatly turned into a compliment I can't help laughing. 'It isn't that bad. Anyway, there's nothing else I can do.'

'You paint thimbles,' says Matthew. 'Show Ian.'

'Excuse me.' I get up quickly. 'I must see if Mother needs any help in the kitchen.'

'Is there anything I can do?' He's on his feet again.

'Sit down, Ian, Chrissake,' says Matthew. 'You're up and down like a jerk-in-the-box.'

For once I have to agree with him.

My brother dominates the conversation at dinner as usual. As a child he'd tell us how successful he'd been at school that day, how the teachers had praised him, how popular he was with the other boys, how skilled in sport, how gifted at arts and crafts, and when his end of term report came it was quite obvious to Mother and me that the only thing Matthew was good at was pretending.

He always loved dressing up, playing make-believe, as long as he was the hero. He's still frontstage centre in his own mind, a star, and then the end of term report comes in.

'Matthew Webster seemed very impressed with himself. It's a pity he didn't impress the audience as well . . .' 'Never have I seen a more promising pupil in the art of coarse acting . . .' 'With dedication and perseverance Matthew Webster might one day become an inspiring second spear carrier . . .'

The reviews have been devastating.

This evening he's telling us about a part his agent is after for him, an absolute plum. I can't imagine why anyone took him on but I suppose there are dud agents just as there are dud actors. Mother and I pretend to believe every word. It is the least we can do for him. He hasn't worked for almost a year, not even as a third spear carrier.

'Of course, the theatre's going through a stinking time at the moment, like everything else in this God-forsaken country.'

He leans back, glass in hand. He is about to give us a lecture on the state of the arts in Britain. The same one he gave the last time he was here. Ian catches my eye and smiles. He's barely said a word since he sat down. A pity, I'd like to hear something new. I have all Matthew's opinions and prejudices off by heart.

'What's for pud, Mum?'

Mother always makes something special for him. 'Fresh fruit salad.'

His face falls. 'Oh come on, love, there must be something decent to eat, a cake or a trifle.'

Mother puts the fruit salad on the table and a bowl of spiced yoghurt. It's for me, of course. She comes back with a huge Black Forest gateau, a heart attack of a cake. Just looking at it is clogging up my arteries.

Matthew's eyes light up. 'I knew it!' he cries.

'Will you have a slice, Ian?'

'No, I'll have some of the fruit salad, Mrs Webster.'

'Oh, come off it! Have a bit of Mum's cake. I'll bet you've never tasted anything like it. Eh, love?' Matthew beams at her.

'Perhaps Ian will have a slice afterwards with his coffee.'

'I'm afraid I'm diabetic.'

Matthew frowns. Two invalids in one house are more than he can cope with. Mother looks concerned, someone else for her to worry about, this poor young man. I am delighted. It's like meeting another member of the club – Sickies of the World unite!

Ian glances at me and grins. I raise my spoonful of healthy fruit salad to him. Cheers! Afterwards he insists on helping Mother wash up. No, no, she won't hear of it, whatever next . . . She tries to bustle him out of the kitchen but he's more determined than she. Finally she assigns him my job, the wiping up, despatching me to the living room.

I catch snatches of their conversation, he's telling her how he got started in the theatre. Matthew has exhausted himself at the dinner table. The performance over, he falls asleep on the sofa. Ian comes in with the coffee tray, followed by Mother carrying a plate of home-made florentines and the chocolates I gave her.

Cooking for me is such a waste of her talents. But Matthew is here now. She can stuff him with puddings and cakes and biscuits until he sinks down on his little webbed feet. And, of course, there is the spare-framed Ian Trevelyan. Pity about his diabetes though.

'I think I'll pass up the coffee, thanks. I'm off to bed.'

'But it's only ten o'clock.'

'I feel rather tired.'

I see a look of panic in Matthew's eyes. Don't be ill, big sister. Don't die. You're tough old Ruthy, indestructible.

'Good night, dear,' says Mother. 'Sleep well.'

I leave my bedroom door ajar. Eavesdropping. It's a stupid thing to do and conceited to imagine they will talk about me – but they are.

'She's been so ill,' says Mother. 'There were times I thought –' I can't hear the rest but I can imagine it. 'And now she looks so drawn. Poor Ruthy, she used to be such a pretty girl.'

'She still is. She's very attractive.'

Oh thank you, Ian Trevelyan, thank you.

'She's let herself go,' says Matthew, his voice a petulant tenor to Ian's soft bass.

'It wasn't her fault.' Mother rushes to my defence. 'You can't blame her –'

'I was only saying –'

'How old is she?' asks Ian.

'Oh . . . er . . .' Mother is taken aback. Gentlemen don't ask a lady's age. I'll bet Ian Trevelyan just went down a notch or two. 'She's still quite young.'

'Forty-four.'

Thank you, Matthew.

'She's a perfectionist, that's her problem. Daddy was the same. They're as alike as two peas in a pod. They got on so well too. He thought the world of her, his little Ruthy. He had such plans for her.'

She's talking about me as if I were already a corpse.

'She smoked too much, that's the real trouble,' Matthew says.

'Everything she does she does well,' Mother goes on as if she hadn't heard him. 'She was always top of her class, winning all the prizes. Daddy was so proud of her. Of course it was a terrible blow to her when he died. She seemed to lose all heart –' She stops short, suddenly realising what she's said.

Ian asks a question but his voice is so low I can't hear it.

'Just over two months ago,' says Mother.

Another murmured comment or question from Ian.

'As long as she takes care of herself. The doctor said the first attack is just a warning.'

I feel like screaming at them 'I'm not bloody well dead yet!'

'Ruth . . . ?'

They look up, startled, when I go in. The ghost of Banquo has appeared at the feast.

'I've just remembered *The Sweeney* starts at half past ten. Anybody want to watch it?'

CHAPTER 7

In the morning the sun streams through my windows. I lie in bed for a while, remember with a sinking feeling what Mother said the night before, but in the morning sunshine her words have lost their power. I don't believe Simpson told her I might have another attack. He'd have told me. He thinks people should know the truth. Anyway, anybody can have a coronary. I read about a football coach who dropped dead, one of those up-at-dawn-and-jog-round-the-park-twenty-times men. But you can have a second, third and fourth attack and still live as long as Rip Van Winkle. It's just Mother. She's talked herself into believing the worst . . . Ruthy almost died, Ruthy's going to have another attack, the next one might be fatal. No wonder people treat me like Dresden china if she's spreading rumours like that.

I didn't hear any noise in the night, no crashes or yells from upstairs, so Matthew must have gone to bed sober for a change. Ian doesn't seem the boozy type, anyway. But then I'm not sure what type he is. Definitely not pipe and slippers, not a prima donna like Matthew, too down to earth to be really arty. I like to identify people as quickly as I can, stick a pin through them, put them in a glass case and close the lid. But I'm having difficulty with this one.

Mother brings me breakfast on a tray.

'But why?' I've been getting up for breakfast for the past week. Meals on wheels have lost their charm.

'I just thought you might enjoy it, dear.'

'But . . .'

'You looked so tired last night. I think it was very sil . . .' she stops herself in time, 'very unwise to have stayed up so late.'

So now I'm in detention. I remember other girls being kept in for misbehaviour and now I'm being kept in bed. Oh well, take your punishment with good grace, Ruthy, and eat your grapefruit. Good grief, it's bitter. I'd rather do a hundred lines than eat this.

Ian's in the kitchen chatting to Mother when I go in. They're sitting at the table, heads together, sipping coffee like a couple of old cronies.

'Good morning, Ruth.' He pulls out a chair for me. It makes me feel like Queen Victoria.

'I took Matthew a cup of tea but I couldn't wake him,' says Mother. 'He was always a heavy sleeper, wasn't he, Ruthy? Do you remember how we used to get him out of bed for school? I'd pull all the blankets off him and you'd . . .'

Mother has got to the stage in her life where she can recall all the trivia of our childhood and recounts them over and over.

'I'm going for a walk.'

'Mind if I come too?' says Ian.

'I walk very slowly.'

'So do I. Shall we take the dog? Want to go for a walk, old fellow?'

Rob rolls onto his back and puts on his adoring act.

'He'll pull you over,' Mother warns. Hardly likely. Ian Trevelyan may be thin but there's still a lot of him. 'Ruthy . . .' she turns to me. I can see she's about to tell me to wrap up warmly, put on a hat, scarf, gloves. I'm out of the house and away before she can smother me in wool.

It's a magnificent day.

'Isn't it wonderful?' I lift my face to the sun. Isn't it wonderful to be alive.

'Yes, it's on days like this I wish I lived in the country too,' says Ian.

The country? Surrey? He makes it sound like the Orkneys.

'So why don't you? You could work for one of the reps, surely?'

'The gin and tonic circuit, Ayckbourn and Stoppard?' He shakes his head. 'No, I don't think so.'

'I see. It has to be London or nothing.'

'It has to be worthwhile or nothing.'

'Meaning that Ayckbourn and Stoppard are rubbish.'

'Meaning that I think Brenton and Poliakoff and Keeffe would go down like a lead balloon here.'

He's right. Mother and I go to all the local productions, they're invariably Ayckbourn and Stoppard with a little Shakespeare now and then, but it irritates me to hear him say it.

'You don't strike me as a very theatrical type, actually.'

He looks at me, amused. 'And what is a theatrical type *actually*?'

'Well . . . Someone like my brother.'

He chuckles. 'There's no one like your brother.'

'I'm surprised that you and he are friends. I mean you're – you seem so different.' I haven't said anything disloyal, have I? It's all right to talk to Mother about Matthew but I would never run him down to strangers.

'We're not friends. Acquaintances would be nearer the mark. I've known him on and off for the past four or five years but only to have the occasional beer with. Until last Friday I hadn't seen him for, oh, about six months or more. I was in my local and Matt just happened to drop in.'

Just? I doubt it.

'And he invited you down for the weekend?' I shouldn't have sounded so surprised, that wasn't very courteous.

'I wanted a change of scene for a day or two and I thought we were coming to some bachelor hideaway, Ruth, some derelict old barn where Matt holes up at weekends. He didn't tell me it was his mother's place until we were practically on the doorstep. I'd never have come if I'd known.'

'Oh, don't worry, Mother's delighted you're here. You could come every weekend –'

'I'd love to.'

'– as far as she's concerned.' I didn't intend it as an open invitation. 'Is your play doing well?'

'It doesn't open till Tuesday.'

'Shouldn't you be rehearsing?'

On the rare occasions Matthew has landed a part in a play the few days leading up to the opening night have always seemed to be fraught, one disaster piling on top of the last. Or maybe that's just because Matthew's involved.

'You can rehearse till you're stale. It's good to get away from it and forget about the whole thing for a few days.'

'Well, this is the perfect place for you to get away from it all, isn't it? Quiet house, quiet people, a perfect retreat from the glitter of the London stage.'

Why does everything I say to him come out in such a snide way? Am I jealous? Yes. I envy him his health, his strength, his freedom. Most of all I envy him his job . . . No, it isn't a job, it's his passion.

'The theatre I work in hardly qualifies as the London stage, Ruth.'

'Where is it?'

'Clapham.'

He's right, that has none of the glitz of Shaftesbury Avenue.

'Do you live there?'

'No, Hampstead.'

'Oh yes, of course. Do you live alone?' Look, I'm old enough to be . . . Well, his big sister, anyway, so I can ask these things.

'I do now. Up until last Friday I lived with a girlfriend but we had a hell of a row and she walked out. That's why I was in the pub when Matt came in.'

'Drowning your sorrows.'

He shrugs. 'Not really. This is the second time Tasha's left in three years.'

'Perhaps she's trying to tell you something.'

'Like – ?'

'You should marry her.'

And you should mind your own business, his expression retorts.

'Why don't you bring her down here some time?' What is the matter with me? The last thing I want is this man and his temperamental girlfriend hanging round the house. 'Is Tasha an actress?'

'She works in wardrobe. Costumes.'

'Yes, I do know what it means.'

'She's absolutely first rate. She's done some of the big musicals.'

'How interesting.'

I loathe musicals. Deirdre loves them. I go just to keep her company.

'No, I don't like that kind of thing either,' he smiles, acknowledging my ill-concealed disdain, 'but it's better than working in insurance, isn't it? I'd say anything's better than that.'

I know I deserved it, I've been pretty obnoxious to him, but that hurt.

'Oh, I'm sure you think it's very mundane but somebody's got to do it, haven't they, somebody's got to do the serious work? We can't all frolic around in never-never land, sewing bows and beads on bits of taffeta!' I pull up my collar with an angry gesture, blocking him out.

'Why don't you leave the mundane work to mundane people?'

'Because I'm no different from them.'

'Bollocks! You're an attractive woman, Ruth. You're lively, you're witty, you've got character, you've got – Oh sorry, I forgot, we Brits can't cope with compliments, can we?' He glances at my face and laughs. 'But I think behind that tight-arsed Home Counties lady act there's a real woman struggling to get out, so why don't you try living in never-never land for a change, Ruth? I think you'd enjoy it.'

I would like to say something really cutting, surely I can get under this man's thick hide with my sharp tongue, but my eyes are full of tears and I have a lump in my throat. How dare he see the futility of my little life? How dare he show me the stars when I have no way of reaching them?

'I think we should turn back now, I've gone far enough for today.'

'Do you usually go this far?'

'Yes.'

'So why not push yourself a bit further?' He

points at The Rat and Parrot. 'Down to that pub, say. It's only a couple of hundred yards.'

'Is it my health or your thirst that concerns you, Mr Trevelyan?'

'Oh, there's no contest, a pint of good British ale ranks higher than any woman in my estimation. Come on, Miss Webster.' He grabs me round the waist and pulls me along, 'let's get pissed to the eyeballs!'

CHAPTER 8

We get back at half past two, late for lunch. Mother is po-faced. My own is flushed, it was so hot in the pub, and I burst into silly giggles every time I catch Ian's eye.

It's not that I've been drinking. I only had my daily allowance – well, two Scotches, small ones, but it was so good to be out again among people who didn't keep asking me how I was and telling me to take it easy. For a brief time I forgot about my heart. It just ticked away happily. This morning has been wonderful. I've thrown off the invalid mantle at last.

I must start getting out again. There are loads of cosy little pubs around here. But whom could I go with? Mother doesn't approve of them. They're for people with nothing better to do with their lives, she says, though I can't imagine why embroidering cushions or painting thimbles is a more worthwhile pastime. Deirdre would come with me but she lives in south London.

If only Ian lived nearer. He's so easy to talk to, I feel as if I've known him for . . . Oh, don't be ridiculous! He's a young man, fifteen years younger than me. He lives in a totally different world. And he's got a girlfriend, a live-in lover, who wouldn't take kindly to his being a . . . what do they call it, an escort? No, a walker. He was obviously upset when she left, despite his pretence of not caring, and they've been together for three years. She'll be back. Anyway, he must work with lots of attractive girls, all fawning on him, the great artistic director. He can take his pick.

I must get myself a boyfriend . . . Now there's a coy expression for a lady of my maturity. I suppose someone in his fifties or sixties would be right for me, a divorcee or widower. Apparently most of the people on cruises are old. Oh well, I might find my ageing lover on *Ariel*.

Goodness knows what Ian's been saying to Mother, they've been closeted in the kitchen for the past ten minutes, but when they come out she's her old self again. She puts her arms around me and kisses me. Now what honeyed words has that cunning gentleman been pouring into her troubled ear? He winks at me over her shoulder and I giggle. She pulls back, offended.

'I was just thinking of a joke Ian told me,' I lie.

She turns to him, already smiling, ready for a good laugh. Mother loves jokes, though she doesn't always get the point.

'Tell me,' she says to him eagerly.

I turn away, giggling like a fool. Though we laughed a lot in the pub it wasn't because of any jokes he told. He's just a droll fellow when he gets going. But now I've really put him on the spot.

'Which particular joke did you have in mind, Ruth?' he lobs over my head.

'Er . . .' I can't think of anything. 'The one about the Englishman, the Irishman and the Scotsman.'

'Oh no.' Mother is disappointed. 'I've heard it.'

She can't understand why we all fall about laughing.

'Well, it's no good telling you a joke you've already heard,' says Ian, 'but do you know the one about the Israeli who bought a Palestinian parrot?'

He tells it well, his face poker straight. Mother and I clutch at each other, tears in our eyes. Even Matthew, who doesn't like playing audience to someone else's act, bellows with laughter.

Lunch is a very jolly affair. Ian suddenly remembers a lot of jokes, most of them about the theatre, some a bit risqué, but he has Mother round his little finger now, she'd laugh at anything, forgive him everything. I can see she's decided to adopt him. She'll be telling him to call her Marmy any minute.

All too soon it's over. He and Matthew stand in the hall, their overnight bags packed and stowed away in the boot of the car, Matthew anxious to be off, Ian going through the formalities in his gentlemanly way, thanking Mother profusely, praising her cooking, her hospitality. She is enchanted. Time and again she tells him to come any time, it doesn't matter if Matthew is coming or not. If she were forty, fifty years younger she'd be sitting by the phone all week waiting for him to call. And if she were forty, fifty years younger I think he probably would.

'Good luck on Thursday,' I say briskly when it's my turn. 'Hope it's a huge success.'

He takes my hand, holds it against his chest and looks deeply into my eyes. I know he's in the theatre, they love these gushy 'parting is such sweet sorrow' kind of gestures, but it's a bit over the top for a tight-arsed home counties lady.

'Keep your fingers crossed for me,' he says.

'We'll be thinking of you, won't we, Mother?'

'You must come and see it. I'll send you tickets.'

'We'd love to.'

He's still holding my hand. I don't want to pull away, that would be impolite, but I feel horribly embarrassed standing front stage centre with Mother and Matthew watching my performance.

Ian seems totally unaware of them, as if we were quite alone, he and I. 'Take good care of your-self, Ruth.'

'Yes, thanks. You too.'

'Well, goodbye, Mum.' Matthew has had enough of my starring role. 'See you soon, old love.'

'Don't come out,' says Ian. 'It's too cold.'

'No, I'm fine.'

'Put your coat on then, dear.' Mother wraps it round my shoulders.

It's comic to see see Ian cramming his long legs into that tiny car. It reminds me of the time

Matthew found a grass snake in the forest. He brought it back and rammed it in a jam jar. It was dead the next morning, suffocated in its own coils. I cried for a long time. Quite ridiculous, of course, it was just a snake, a creature with no feelings, no thoughts, but it had a right to life, a right to slither through the dewy grass, to mate, to produce its young . . . And Matthew took that away.

'Cheer up, old girl!' he bellows, misinterpreting my expression as self pity. 'They're doing marvellous things with transplants these days.'

It's meant to be a joke.

'How much did he rip you off this time?' I ask when the tail lights of his car have disappeared into the misty night. Mother doesn't understand. 'How much did you give him?'

She turns away. 'I like to help him out.'

'It's about time he stood on his own feet. It's ludicrous, someone his age taking money from his mummy.'

'Acting's such a difficult profession, it isn't easy to find work.'

'Especially when you can't act.'

'What are you going to do now, dear?'

Abrupt change of subject. She'd rather not think about Matthew too closely or she'll have to admit the truth to herself.

'I'm going to read for a bit. I got a good book out of the library.'

'Shall we have a game of cards? We haven't

played for such a long time and you used to love to.'

'No, I don't feel like it, thanks.'

Not cards. Marmy and Ruthy sitting at the little green table in front of the fire, whiling the hours away. Marmy and Ruthy, the perfect bridge partners, defeating the Henshaws, the Pryces, the Fussels . . . No!

'You are looking rather tired, dear,' she agrees, although that isn't what I meant. 'Why don't you take your book to bed and I'll bring you some hot milk?'

'I'd rather stay up for a while.'

'It's been a long day for you, Ruthy.'

'Mother, I said . . .'

'All right, I'm sorry.' She goes out. She's going to work on her cushions. They're softer, more amenable companions than me.

CHAPTER 9

Simpson says I may drive again. It's one of the things I've missed the most, buzzing around in my little Fiat. I'm probably a potential hazard on the road, I might have a heart attack at the wheel and crash into another car or flatten a pedestrian, but so might anyone. At least I know what the warning signs are. And Simpson says I'm okay to drive. The news has really cheered me up.

'So I think I'll do some Christmas shopping before the rush starts.'

'Yes, that's a good idea. Just let me pop this casserole in the oven. I can leave it on a low heat and –'

'Mother, I can hardly buy your present if you're with me.'

'I won't look.'

I want to go alone. We've been together, almost every hour of every day for the past twelve weeks. Whenever I opened my eyes in hospital she was there. She's a dear, she's been marvellous to me and I love her but I want to be on my own for a bit.

Guildford on a Friday morning, people rushing around, frowning. One woman dragging a whining toddler bumps into me, almost knocks me off the pavement, no word of apology. I'm elated by it. It means I'm normal again, just one of the crowd to be pushed and shoved.

I've never enjoyed shopping, especially for presents. I can never make up my mind and I'm getting sillier with age . . . Is this too showy for her or too dull? Am I spending too much, embarrassing him, or too little, being stingy? Today I'm determined not to work myself into a state about it. Whatever I buy will be used up, thrown away or stuffed in a bottom drawer and forgotten before January's out anyway.

I pick up a cashmere sweater for Matthew, a velvet dressing gown and matching slippers for Mother, a bottle of 'Arpège' for Kitty, her favourite perfume, although she's probably filched the entire Lanvin range from Harrods or Fenwicks anyway, and some aftershave for Uncle Geoffrey, a bachelor cousin of Mother's. He's a sweet old gentleman who arrives every Christmas morning and disappears into the heart of the Cotswolds on Boxing Day not to be seen again for another twelve months. What he'll do with the aftershave I can't imagine. Drink it, probably. Or pour it over his pigs.

I'll get him a pipe as well, another one for his collection. I know I shouldn't encourage him, he'll wander round the house tapping its vile contents into any convenient holder while Mother follows, mopping, deodorizing, but he loves a pipe almost as much as he loves his pigs and I can't pass up the pleasure of hearing him say, 'Oh, a pipe. What a lovely surprise!' as if I hadn't given him one every Christmas for the past twenty years.

The odds and sods for other relatives and friends I'll pick up next week.

Ian Trevelyan suddenly pops into my head. Stupid. Of course I'm not going to buy him a present, I hardly know him.

Time for coffee. And a cigarette, says a little gremlin in my head. I don't mind the boring exercises and the dull food but, oh, what I'd give for a cigarette. I'd give my – my life? My life for a few tobacco leaves wrapped in paper?

My favourite restaurant is crowded. I enjoy this place so much, it's one of the few left in Guildford that has any charm or character but I can't be bothered to join the queue and wait for a table. I turn to leave and am riveted to the spot by a bellow from the far corner of the room.

'Ruth!' Even before I see the pointed ears and big yellow teeth I recognise that strident voice. 'Over here, m'dear. Plenty of room.'

By a stroke of bad luck there's a spare place at their table. Mrs Henshaw starts shuffling plates and cups to make room for me. It's a tight squeeze getting in but Henshaw rams my chair back, forcing the people at the next table to move theirs, completely impervious to their hostile glares.

'All by yourself, are you?' he booms, raising his voice above the restrained chatter around us. 'How did you get in? Bus?'

'I'm driving again.'

'Now don't go overdoing it, girl. It's all very well to be up and about again but –'

'Ruth knows what's best for her, Clive,' a small voice interrupts him. 'I'm sure she takes her doctor's advice.'

Having said its piece the little creature crawls back into its shell, its tiny eyes darting from Henshaw to me, fearful of some terrible reprisal. Now where did it find the courage to contradict its owner? Is there brandy in the fruit cake? Is the coffee laced with heroin?

'Yes, Simpson's given me a clean bill of health.' I rush in before he can stamp on her. 'I can go for walks, drive, do anything.'

'Anything?' His watery eyes twinkle. He's going to tell me about his good friend Roger, the nitro-glycerine goat.

'As long as I don't push myself too hard.'

'Exactly. Everything in moderation.' He jabs a nicotine-stained finger in my face. 'That's my motto, everything in moderation. What are you going to have, m'dear?'

'A cup of coffee.'

'Have some of their teacakes, they're delicious. Waitress!' His command stops her in her tracks. For a moment she hesitates, she was about to take someone else's order, but he's been here before, many times, and she knows it's better to serve him quickly than risk alienating the other customers with his imperious bark. 'Pot of coffee and a plate of toasted teacakes for this young lady, if you please.'

'Just a cup of coffee, thanks. Black.'

'She's had a heart attack, you see,' he shouts in the waitress's ear, though she's only standing a foot away from him. 'Nasty business.' The people at the surrounding tables stop talking and listen with great interest. 'Has to watch what she eats and drinks, everything in moderation, that's what her doctor said.' The waitress looks at me with polite interest. She would like to get on with her job. 'Made a marvellous recovery though. Look at her. Blooming! You'd never think she was at death's door a few weeks ago, would you.'

Everyone turns to look at this wonderwoman.

'Well, well,' says the waitress.

'Blooming!' bellows Henshaw.

I'd like to tip this table, the plates, cups, cutlery, the whole bloody lot into his lap.

Damn him! Damn him!

I'm in a rotten mood when I get home and it's some time before I notice how quiet Mother is. She's a tolerant woman, enduring other people's failings more easily than I. Although she agrees Henshaw can be a pain she's usually quick to spring to his defence, or anyone else's, if I get too acid, but today she listens to my tirade, saying nothing.

'What's the matter?'

She turns away from me, puts her head in her hands and sobs.

'Mother, what's wrong?'

I put my arms around her. I feel strong again, strong old Ruthy, the rock on which her mother leans.

'It's Kitty. They've arrested her.'

It was bound to happen. They caught her in Selfridges piling expensive little baubles into her shopping bag. She went the whole hog and bristles this time apparently, a silver egg timer, a manicure set, apostle spoons, napkin rings, things she doesn't want, doesn't need. Perhaps it's best they've stopped her in the minor league before she moved on to diamonds and furs. At least we can do something for her now it's out in the open.

'Where is she?'

'She's on her way back to the flat. The police are taking her.'

'Did she phone you herself?'

'No, a policewoman.'

'How long ago?'

'About an hour, a little more, I don't know.'

We drive to Kitty's place in Maida Vale. The police have gone. Fortunately Mother has a spare key. I've never seen my aunt so distraught. She's like a little doll, broken, her make-up streaked, her hair a tangled mess. The police have looked through her flat, drawer by drawer.

'Did they have a search warrant, Kitty? Did they take anything away with them?'

It's no use, I can't get through to her. She sits on the edge of a chair, staring into space, her body convulsed by nervous spasms as if she were connected to electrodes.

Mother cleans out the refrigerator and writes a note for the milkman while I pack a case for Kitty. The clothes in this bedroom! Dear God, I've never seen so many scarves and gloves, most of them still in their wrappers with the price tags on. If the police saw all this . . .

We bundle Kitty down the stairs into the car. Mother sits in the back, her arm around Kitty's shoulders. She has got over her tears now. She's white-faced, tense, but in control again.

When we get home Kitty breaks down completely, screaming, throwing herself about. Mother tries to grab her arms, she's twice the size of her frail sister, but madness gives Kitty strength and she breaks free, lashing at us. I've never hit anyone, it's a repulsive thing to do, but I steel myself and give her a swingeing slap around the face. She falls back, stunned, then hides in Mother's arms, clinging to her, sobbing. When she has no more tears we help her upstairs.

I look at her lying in the big double bed, a tiny figure overwhelmed by the bunches of blowsy, overblown roses that cover the sheets and pillow case. What's left for Kitty? She's too weak, too childlike to look after herself any more. But then she never could. All her life she's had a man to take care of her. Now when she needs him most he's abandoned her.

'Poor Kitty,' murmurs Mother, pulling up the rose-pink blanket and gently tucking it round her.

'She'll be all right,' I say, trying to sound optimistic. But Mother only shakes her head.

'Poor Kitty. What can we do?'

Simon Fairfax has been the family solicitor since the beginning of time, a dear old gentleman, good for wills and probate but quite out of touch with the cut and thrust of the real world. A sharper brain is called for on this occasion. One of my distant relatives is a lawyer, a very bright young man, going places, so they tell me. I give him a call.

'They searched her flat, James.'

'Provided they had her permission they didn't need a search warrant.'

'What will they do to her?'

'Serve a summons. She'll go up before the magistrates. Is this her first offence?'

'Yes. They won't send her to prison, will they?'

My fragile aunt in her Liberty prints and tasselled shawls crouching in the corner of a bare cell, like an old dog in an animal shelter, confused, condemned. They wouldn't do that to her, would they? Surely they'll see she's sick, she needs help.

'Has she been at it for long?'

'I don't know. Well, I suppose ever since Uncle Julian died. That's three or four years ago.'

'It depends on the magistrates really. They've got to hammer these people. Shops are losing millions of pounds every year to petty thieves.'

I think of all the expensive little 'prezzies' Kitty

has given us. You'd hardly call her a petty thief. And what about us, Mother and me? We knew what she was doing, we're accessories to her crime.

'I think Kitty'll be all right,' says James in his flat, unemotional voice. 'Dithery old lady, first offence, they'll probably slap a fine on her, give her a good talking to, something to frighten her into giving up her little hobby. Won't make any difference though, she's obviously a nutter.'

'I was hoping you'd be able to help her.'

'How?'

'Well, defend her.'

'Don't be daft, Ruth, she was caught with the stuff.' There's nothing in this for him. He's only concerned with the big cases, high court drama that will put his name in the papers. 'Tell her to plead guilty, throw herself on the mercy of the court.' I get the feeling he'd defend the Yorkshire Ripper if he thought it would help him up the ladder. 'Recently widowed, grief and distress, that kind of thing.' That kind of thing . . . Widowhood, loneliness, grief and distress mean nothing to him. 'Oh, and keep an eye on her for the next few weeks. They often try to top themselves. By the way,' talking of death, 'how are you? I hear you had a spot of bother recently.'

Mother thinks we should get someone to defend Kitty. 'You know she won't be able to say a word in court, Ruthy. She'll be so frightened.'

'I think close relatives are allowed to speak for her.'

'But what on earth would we say? We don't know the law.'

And we might incriminate ourselves. No, better to get a lawyer on the job. The less Mother and I say the better. Dear old Simon Fairfax is our man.

CHAPTER 10

Today is the anniversary of my heart attack. Exactly three months ago this morning I woke up, stretched, kicked Rob off the duvet and got out of bed. I felt fine, no pain, no palpitations, nothing to warn me of the horror in store. Today I've decided to celebrate. I'm going up to The Trust to tell them I'm ready to get back into harness. I've enjoyed pottering around the house, reading, painting my thimbles, playing the piano, watching the box, catching up on my letters, zipping in and out of Guildford on shopping trips, taking Rob for walks – but enough is enough. Stop the world, I want to get on.

Kitty has been a blessing in disguise. Mother is so worried about her she's stopped flapping around me. I shall creep back to work without her even noticing.

'Will you be back for lunch, Ruthy?'

'No, I'll have it in town.'

Deirdre and I always go out for Friday lunch. Our staff restaurant serves the kind of food you've forgotten the minute you've swallowed it. Friday is celebration, real food day.

'How's Kitty?' I ask Mother.

She sighs by way of answer. One day my aunt is brittle and gay, dressing up, pancaking her face, chattering on until I could throttle her, the next day silent, wandering around the house in her dressing gown, staring vacantly at us when we speak to her.

She mutters to herself like an old bag lady, sings snatches of songs that were popular when she and Mother were young. 'A touch of the Ophelias,' said Matthew last time he was here. 'Keep her away from water.' It was meant as a joke but I couldn't laugh.

The summons came yesterday. We weren't going to tell Kitty about it until much nearer the time but the policeman came to the door and, sod's law, it just happened to be Kitty who opened it. She started to put her coat on when she saw him, thinking he'd come to take her away there and then. He was such a nice young man too, you'd have thought he was delivering Christmas cards. She had a terrible attack of nerves afterwards. We had to phone for Simpson. Now she's heavily sedated. Mother sits by her bed hour after hour stroking her hand and watching over her like a guardian angel.

I don't usually pay much attention to what I wear. I buy skirts and blouses and jackets that are smart in a safe, low-key way. But today I must make an effort. Everyone at The Trust will be expecting a pasty-faced invalid in shades of grey.

Well, I'm going to surprise them. I have a coat that I bought in a sale at Dickens & Jones some years ago – goodness knows why, it isn't me at all. It's beautifully cut, very straight, but the colour's a bit overwhelming, a particularly shocking pink. I've never had the courage to wear it. Today's the day.

I've never used make-up, nothing on my skin or eyes, just a little lipstick. I find one that almost matches my coat and apply it more liberally than usual. Mother's a bit startled. 'You look very nice, dear,' she says doubtfully.

I walk to the station. My season ticket's run out so I've got to buy another one.

'Hello there!' A familiar face peers at me through the grille. 'Long time no see.'

'I've had a bit of time off.'

'Holiday?'

'Hardly,' I grimace. 'I haven't been very well.'

'Sorry to hear that. Better now though?'

'Much better, thanks. I feel fine.'

And I do. I've lost weight and it shows, I've got stretch marks on my breasts, stomach and thighs. I'm exercising more and I take Rob for long walks. We went three miles yesterday.

I'm as excited as a kid on a school outing. I'm going to London again. Big train to the city, lots of people, Christmas lights, excitement . . . Oh boy, Ruthy, isn't this fun, isn't life a precious, marvellous thing? To think I've treated it with such indifference all these years.

Holborn. It seems ages since I walked along this grimy platform, stood on this long, draughty escalator. I pass the man selling papers. He's been there for years and I've walked past him every day for years but, of course, he doesn't remember me. Why would he recognise me out of the hordes that file past him every day? He gives me a nod, a smile. I couldn't be more surprised if Prince Philip had flashed at me from the back of his Daimler.

For twenty years I've walked out of this station, crossed this road, up Southampton Row, right at Theobald, left . . . The pavements of London feel good beneath my feet. It feels odd being out midmorning though, like playing truant. It's quite different from the rush hour, the bustle of lunch time. There isn't the same feeling of urgency about High Holborn at ten-thirty.

I should stop for a cup of coffee, calm myself. I'm almost sick with excitement. I'm going to see them again, all my old friends. It's like a school reunion. Better, in a way. I've nothing in common any more with the girls I went to school with but I've grown up, grown old with the people at The Trust.

So many of them came to see me in hospital, making the long trek in the evenings from all over London. All my girls came too. There was a huge bouquet with a message from Mr Bridgewater, the managing director, and Valerie Pierce from Personnel phoned several times to find out how I was getting on.

'Such a nice woman,' said Mother. 'She says you're to take all the time you need to get well again, Ruthy. She says you're very special to them. Wasn't that sweet of her?'

Valerie comes on rather strong at times but when you're flat on your back expecting to die a bucket of gush can be very comforting.

Provided all goes well, and why shouldn't it, I'll be back full time by the end of January. I've hardly ever taken sick leave before. No matter how awful I felt I always battled in through toothache, neuralgia, flu. I thought the place would fall apart if I wasn't there. When he'd relaxed a little after a gin or two at Tim Conway's retirement party, the managing director took me to one side and told me I was one of the most reliable, conscientious people they'd ever employed. 'I don't know what we'd do without you, Ruth.'

If it had come from somebody else I would have laughed, but Bridgewater? Deirdre couldn't believe it either. 'Bridgey paid you a compliment? He must be going through the menopause.'

Well, here's the old place. I remember the first time I pushed through these swing doors, a very nervous young woman in a navy blue suit, white blouse and court shoes as we called them. There was a commissionaire, lovely old fellow, used to show me snaps of his grandchildren. Today there are two stern-looking men behind the desk, obviously ex-policemen. They nod a greeting – almost.

The lift doors open and Deirdre steps out. She

almost bowls me over, hugging me so hard I can hardly breathe. Visitors with briefcases, young messengers with parcels, look at us askance. We British don't like letting our hair down and certainly not in the august halls of a major financial house. But Deirdre doesn't care. She keeps squeezing me and saying, 'Oh Ruth . . . Oh Ruth . . .'

We arrange to meet for lunch. Bridgewater's going to a meeting at twelve, one that's sure to go on for several hours, so Deirdre will have time for a good blather.

'And you'll come to the Christmas party, won't you?'

I hadn't thought of that. I'm not keen on office parties but I've always had to go as a head of department. This year will be different, though. This year will be a real celebration.

I suppose I should go and see Valerie Pierce first. She's the one I have to talk to about holidays and sick leave. I can do the rounds later. If I go and see my girls now I shan't get away till midnight.

'Ruth!'

More hugs.

'Hey, look who's here!'

More kisses.

This is turning into a triumph. They'll be lifting me on their shoulders next.

'Come and see us.'

'I will, I will.'

Everyone greets me warmly, people I hardly

know, women in Accounts and Legal, I've never done more than chat with them briefly in the loo.

'What about lunch?'

'I'm meeting Deirdre.'

'What time?'

'Half twelve, usual place.'

'See you there.'

There won't be room for all of us in that little restaurant but who cares? We'll sit on each other's laps.

Personnel is on the second floor . . . at least it was three months ago.

'They've moved,' says a boy unloading files from a red crate. 'They're up on the fourth floor now.'

We play musical departments in The Trust. The point of the game is to wait until everybody's settled in and then move them again. Maximum disruption, maximum points. Marketing are the winners to date. In three years they've gone from the first floor to the fifth to the ninth to the fourth and back to the first again.

When I started this was an old-fashioned, old family business but three or four years ago a predator loomed out of the deep and gobbled us up. Now we're just another big company, part of a group, making all the big company mistakes.

I've grown so used to this place. It's like a second home, with all the comforts and irritations of home. My girls are fun, most of the time. They tell me about their boyfriends, the parties they go to, the arguments with their parents. They ask my advice, cry on my shoulder. I'm known as the old hen – behind my back, of course – the maiden aunt. It didn't use to bother me, but now . . .

Valerie Pierce has been given a plush office, as befits her position as Personnel Manager. There are armchairs for cosy chats with staff about personal problems, stiffback chairs for reprimands and warnings. I pause before I go in, patting my hair, collecting myself after all the hugs and handshakes. I always feel slightly uneasy with Valerie, as if I'm not quite up to the mark in her eyes. I shouldn't care, of course. But I do.

I know exactly what she'll be wearing, Gucci sweater, Jaeger skirt, Rayne shoes. Very expensive, very understated. She would blend perfectly into the grace and favour apartments at Kensington Palace. Her nose never shines, her hair never needs washing, her nail polish, palest peach, is never chipped.

Unlike her I'm decidedly dishevelled. I'm sure my lipstick's smudged, if there's any left at all after all that kissing. But I don't give a damn. It's the teddy bear on the bed with one eye and no fur that's loved, not the one sitting on the shelf with the shiny new bow. A daft saying of Kitty's. I like to think there's some truth in it.

'Come in!'

She's writing. With one of those very expensive pens, Daddy had one, a Mont Blanc. You'd never find a biro in her hand.

'Hello, Valerie.'

98

She looks up, professional smile in place.

'Ruth!' For one moment the smile is lopsided, but she rallies, moves quickly round the desk, gives me a perfunctory hug and points to a chair. 'What a lovely surprise!'

I've always avoided her, dealt with the problems in my department in my own way. She resented it at first. Some rather catty memos went back and forth, copies to Bridgewater, then we reached a truce, I would do what I wanted with my girls but keep her informed.

I think she must have been born a personnel officer, the mark of the beast stamped on her little forehead long before she composed her first application form. She's respectful to superiors, attentive to inferiors, the perfect channel for what Bridgewater calls 'the effective flow of communication.' In all the years I've known her I've never heard Valerie give an opinion about anything. It's not for personnel ladies to plump for one faction or another, although in any serious disputes between management and staff Valerie knows exactly which side of the fence she should be cowering behind.

'You're looking very well, Ruth.'

She is looking superb in a beige suit and burgundy boots. I'm beginning to regret my shocking pink coat. I look like a stick of rock.

We exchange gossip for a few minutes. A lot of people have been made redundant, although she doesn't put it as crudely as that. Our people are 'selected out'. Some of them were due to retire anyway but it's sad for the others. Now they've got to look for a company to select them in.

'I thought we'd had the last of the cutbacks. That's what Bridgewater said –' in his anodyne address to the troops in the blatant piece of propaganda we call a staff magazine. I only said it to wind her up. It's the long, sleek, burgundy boots.

'Oh well, Ruth . . .' here comes the party line 'Mr Bridgewater couldn't foresee the way the economy would turn in recent years.'

Recent? The rot set in six years ago when the whole country was blacked out by the miners' strike. Even a blind bat could have seen we'd end up in this mess.

'Have there been any other changes?'

'We have a management consultant working with us now.'

'But we've had them before.'

'Ah, yes, but this one is . . .' Different. The answer to all our prayers, the bringer of solutions to all our problems. She is clearly impressed. She can see that I am not.

'He's made a number of useful recommendations. He's improved our overall performance tremendously.' They used to be called time and motion men and were thoroughly despised. Now they've given themselves a more impressive title, charge a thousand a day and are revered. 'There have been changes in your area, too.' Her smile is positively dazzling. 'I was going to write to you about it. I'd no idea you'd be back this side of Christmas.'

'Well no, I'm not back, not yet. But I will be in the new year, just for a few hours a day at first. The doctor said I should start gradually and build up.'

'Of course.' She picks up her pen – it's silver with gold trimmings, real silver, real gold – and fiddles with it. That's not like Valerie, usually she's so composed. I'm the one who tortures paper clips or doodles while I'm working out what to say. 'Ruth,' she says, 'in the interests of strengthening our entire operation, Miles Bentink . . .'

The name is new to me. 'Oh, the consultant.'

'Yes. Miles has dismantled Office Services.'

'With a spanner?' I can't help laughing. And then the full impact of what she has said hits me.

'Each girl has been assigned to a departmental head.'

'What?'

'Miles thinks it's a much more effective use of our employees.' People, Valerie, people. Call someone an employee and you stop thinking of them as a human being. You can insult them, 'select them out' with no qualms. 'Each girl will get to know her own specific area.'

'You mean they've gone back to being private secretaries?'

'Oh no.'

Oh no. You don't get a thousand a day for recommending something as retrograde as that. Unless, of course, you wrap it up in consultantspeak. 'The intention is to make them more involved, more motivated.'

'But my girls were involved, they were motivated.'

'Of course, Ruth, we all know that and we appreciate the way you have . . .'

'And what do they think about it?'

'Mr Bridgewater is very –'

'I'm talking about my girls.'

'Oh, well, we . . . er . . .'

'You didn't ask them.'

'They all seem to have settled in well and in time I'm sure they'll –'

'It all sounds very underhand to me.'

She flushes. 'Oh now, Ruth, that's hardly fair. After all, you weren't here to –'

'Precisely.'

'It was a top management decision taken in the light of expert advice.' The personnel manager is loyal to the death. In this case, it is clearly mine.

'So where does that leave me?'

'Oh, there's no cause for concern.' She is her bright self again. 'I have very good news for you. That's why I was going to write to you. You've been promoted –' I feel rather sheepish now. Trust me to jump to the wrong conclusions '– to Administrative Officer Grade Five.'

'To what?'

'You'll be in charge of the Client Care and Communication Department.'

'I didn't know we had one.'

'It's recently been set up at the instigation of . . .'

Miles Bentink. Yes, it sounds like one of his ideas, especially the title. That must have earned him a yacht or two.

'How many people work in this wonderful new department?'

'Just you.' Her smile is pasted into place. 'For the moment. Of course, it will grow as the volume of work increases.'

'And what am I supposed to do?'

'For the most part, at least at the beginning, you'll be dealing with customer complaints.'

'But they're always dealt with by the departments.' Every manager guards his area jealously, fire, accident, motor, pensions, life assurance, all in their separate boxes. There's a near riot if one dares encroach on the other.

'I don't mean specific complaints, Ruth. I'm referring to those of a more general nature. You'll be a kind of ombudsman for the company. And initially there'll be other duties.'

I can't wait to hear about them. What little jollies has Miles Bentink lined up for me to while away the twenty years till retirement, I wonder? I'm a dab hand at making tea. And as for cleaning loos . . .

'Like what?'

'Filling in for people.'

'Acting as a temp, you mean?'

'I wouldn't call it that, Ruth.'

'Oh? What would you call it, Valerie?'

'You'll just be helping out until your new job begins to pick up momentum and then –'

'What you mean is I have been promoted to an Administrative Officer Grade Five Dogsbody, Valerie, only you haven't the guts to say it.'

'Now, Ruth, don't be . . .'

Silly? Hasty? Ungrateful? After all, they've been very generous. They could have selected me out like the other rejects.

'I've given twenty years of my life to The Trust –' Good God, I sound like a pensioner giving her gold watch speech 'and the minute I'm ill, the first time I've ever stayed away, you stab me in the back.'

'Ruth, please, calm down.' She thinks I'm going to have another attack.

'I'm absolutely disgusted. I'm . . . I'm . . .'

'You're being quite unreasonable, Ruth.'

She gets up and moves round the desk towards me. I'd better leave before my stupid heart does give out. I don't want her giving me the kiss of life with that expertly painted mouth. I slam out of her office and blast down the corridor, ignoring the cries of 'Ruth, how lovely to see you!' Hypocrites. They all knew and not one of them had the guts to tell me, coming to the hospital, smothering me with flowers, stuffing me with grapes . . . Bloody cowards.

The lift door opens and the luck of the devil is with me. Bridgewater himself steps out. He looks momentarily taken aback – did he think, hope I was already ten feet under? – but pulls himself together and puts out his hand.

'Ruth. How nice to see you again.'

'Sod off!'

I have the exquisite pleasure of seeing his mouth open and his eyelids flicker as if he's squinting at a very bright light. People stop and stare. Heads poke nervously round screens. The whole building seems to hold its breath.

'Sod off, you bastard!'

CHAPTER 11

I walk and walk, pounding along. To hell with the lot of them! But that place was my whole life, I thought they cared, I thought . . . More fool you! 'She's been here twenty years? That's a big redundancy payout, let's give her a rubbish job, humiliate her, she'll resign, then we're off the hook.' But surely they wouldn't . . . Naïve, Ruth, you're too old to be so naïve.

What shall I do now? I feel like Kitty, abandoned, afraid. They've taken my job away, my girls. I have nothing left.

'Hello. Hey . . . Ruth. Ruth!'

A hand on my shoulder swings me round. A very tall man stands there, smiling at me. Where am I? Covent Garden, isn't it?

'Oh,' I think I know him, 'hello.' He works in Marketing. Or is it Accounts? 'Hello, Steve.'

'Ian. Ian Trevelyan.'

'Yes, I meant Ian. Sorry, I was miles away.'

'I know, I've been shouting at you all down the street. What're you doing here? Are you back at work?'

'No, I'm . . . I'm just shopping.'

'Good, come and have coffee.' He looks at his watch. 'On second thoughts make that lunch. There's an Italian restaurant just near here that makes really good –'

'No thanks.' I don't want to make small talk over a bottle of Chianti.

'Well, how about one of the wine bars? They serve salads and stuff.'

He thinks it's the rich Italian food I object to. I search for an excuse, late for an appointment, have to meet a friend, but I'm too slow, too obvious.

'Come on.' He's a very forceful young man.

The wine bar is a noisy place, oak tables and benches, horsy prints, sawdust on the floor, lots of bright young people impressing each other, the girls in their 'dress for success' trouser suits. Advertising people. There are a lot of small agencies round here. I feel very out of place, a suburban matron up for the day, dressed to shock in pink.

'What?' He cups his ear.

I must have said it out loud. I'm getting as vague as Kitty, muttering to myself. 'I said this coat's awful. I wish I'd worn something else.'

'Mm,' he nods. 'I'd give it to Oxfam if I were you.'

'Thank you.' The way he's looking at it you'd think it was a horse blanket instead of one of Dickens & Jones' finest.

He chuckles. 'That got you going.'

'You have a right to say what you think.' He has no right at all but everybody else has had a turn at kicking me today so why shouldn't this arrogant young man?

'Exactly,' he says. 'I don't see the point in lying, it's a waste of energy. Come on, let's get something to eat. I've been here a couple of times and I recommend . . .'

I don't give a damn what he recommends. Just to be cussed I choose the opposite.

'Red wine or white?'

'Neither.'

He puts a large carafe on his tray and one glass, pulls out his wallet. 'For both,' he says to the girl at the till, indicating his tray and mine. I open my purse hastily, draw out a couple of notes – I'm not going to let him patronise me – and thrust them at the girl.

'It's okay.' He waves my hand away.

'No, I wouldn't dream of it.'

Without another word he picks up his tray and goes looking for a table. I am left to pay for both of us.

'Nineteen pounds and sixty-five pence,' says the girl. It's a ridiculous amount but I suppose someone's got to pay their rent.

I look longingly at the door. I'd like to leave him with the two plates of food, the wine and the bill but he's a friend of Matthew's and . . . 'Come on, please, there are people behind you.'

He's sitting, chin resting on his hand, a bemused look on his face. 'Why are you in such a filthy mood, Ruth?' He runs his eye up and down me like a trainer assessing a new filly for his stable. I suppose he's going to tell me everything that's wrong with me now, starting with the coat. Well go on, Mr Trevelyan, enjoy yourself, have a go at me, everyone else has.

'Ruth,' he reaches out and takes the knife and fork from my hands, 'don't eat when you're angry. It'll ruin your digestion.'

'Now look here!' I try to snatch them back.

'What's wrong?'

'How dare you do that? I will not be treated like a –'

'Ruth,' he says very quietly, 'what's wrong?'

'Nothing.'

'Don't give me that crap. You're close to tears.'

'I am not.' Damn it, I will not cry in front of this young man. His self-composure infuriates me. 'It has nothing to do with you, anyway.'

He shrugs, hands back the knife and fork. 'Please yourself. It's your stomach.'

Right. It's *my* stomach and *my* heart, so why the hell don't people leave me alone and let me do what I like with them? I'm sick to death of . . . He looks up from his plate and sees me glaring at him.

'Christ, you look like an old maid who's just been goosed by the vicar.'

'I am an old maid.' I grab the carafe of wine in a rage. God knows what I'm going to do with it. I haven't a glass but the damned thing's mine, I paid for it.

He cowers from me, shielding his face with his hands. 'No, Ruth, don't, don't! I apologise. I apologise for everything. You're not in a bad mood, you're in a wonderful mood and . . . and I love your coat, it's my favourite colour.'

I start to laugh but it all goes wrong and I'm crying, sobbing. I'm aware of his hands on my head, big hands, shutting out the stares of other people.

'I'm sorry.' I shuffle through my bag for a tissue 'Sorry.'

Anyone else would be horribly embarrassed, there would be mutterings of 'there, there, dear' and wads of Kleenex thrust at me, but Ian Trevelyan is quite unperturbed. Of course he's used to it in the theatre, emotional scenes. Matthew says every rehearsal ends in screams and tears, mostly his.

'Sorry, I'm so sorry.'

'For God's sake stop saying you're sorry. Here,' he pushes his glass towards me, 'have some wine.'

I feel hungry now but my plate looks like something you'd find in a trough, an unappetising mess of macaroni, cabbage salad and onion rings.

'Your fault,' he says. '"I'm not going to eat what he tells me . . ."' He mimics my voice. 'Silly bitch.'

He picks up my plate, takes it to the counter, returns with stuffed aubergines, mushrooms à la Grecque, risotto, another carafe of wine and a glass for me.

'Don't diabetics have to watch what they drink?'

I'm in my 'Tut! Tut!' maiden-aunt mode with him again.

'Who said I was diabetic?'

'You did.'

'Only to keep you company.' He winks. 'I thought Matt and your mother were giving you a hard time – "Poor little Ruthy's sick so she can only eat dry toast and semolina." You looked as if you needed some moral support.'

'I thought you said you couldn't see the point in lying.'

'Not white lies, Ruth. Sometimes they can be more helpful than the truth.'

'So wouldn't it have helped me just now if you hadn't agreed that this coat makes me look like a stick of . . . of . . . ?'

'Rhubarb? No. Because there's nothing you can do about your heart. You have to eat and drink sensibly if you want to go on living and that's all there is to it. But the way you look, you can change that in a minute.'

'Well, this is hardly eating sensibly, is it?' I point at my loaded plate. 'There are lots of things here I shouldn't even sniff let alone put in my mouth.'

'Ah, but you see, Ruth, there are times when it's permissible to break the rules in the greater interest of the body corporate.'

'What *are* you talking about?'

'I've no idea.'

'Well, you sounded just like old Bridgey.'

'I've never heard of old Bridgey.'

'I wish I hadn't either.'

'Ah, therein lies a tale, methinks. But eat first and talk later. I'll go and get us some strudel.'

I should say no. 'And coffee, please. Black.'

The crowd is thinning out now, the noise dying down. The wine has gone to my head, taking away some of the pain of rejection, the rage and resentment, leaving me feeling more philosophical.

He comes back with the strudels and coffee, sits down, leans back, crosses his arms. 'Well?'

'I've been sacked.'

'Don't believe it. You're not the kind to get booted out.'

'I booted myself out.'

'Great! So you're free at last. This is indeed cause for celebration.' He raises his cup. 'To the end of a boring job and the start of something better.'

'It wasn't that bad really. I've had a lot of happy times there. And I'll miss some of the people. At least The Trust was . . .' Safe. Secure. If I say that he'll really despise me. 'They offered me another job but I didn't take it.'

'Total crap?'

I tell him about my interview with Valerie, about 'dismantling Officer Services in the interests of strengthening our operation', my promotion to Administrative Officer Grade Five.

'*Grade Five*? Wow!' he laughs. 'Move over, Jehovah.'

'Grades are very important at The Trust. Fives don't fraternise with four's and fours wouldn't be seen dead with threes . . .' It all sounds so ridiculous now, so petty. When I tell him about my parting shot to the managing director he's doubled up. 'You should write a play about people like that.'

'Oh, it's been done, Ruth, many times. But they never see themselves as they really are, little plastic people, the chairman of the board, the company secretary, the personnel officer – I'd like to put them all on a desert island, no titles, no offices, no executive desks –'

'No separate dining rooms according to rank.'

'Little plastic people. They'd melt in the sun. I wonder if you'd find anything worthwhile in the little pools they left behind.'

Was my father plastic too, the merchant banker, strutting around in his pin-stripe suit, a carnation in his buttonhole? Am I?

'I'll find something else.'

'Of course you will. Only for Christ's sake take your time. Don't rush into another graveyard. You don't have to sit watching rows of girls bashing typewriters for the rest of your life.'

Painting thimbles is my only talent but I don't think there's a career in it.

'Have you got enough money to tide you over for a while, so you can look around?'

Never tell anyone about your financial situation, not even your closest friends – my father's advice, the wise banker. I've always stuck to it. So why do I open my mouth and say, 'I've got about eighty-five thousand in bonds and things and I'll get whatever's in my pension fund from The Trust.'

I've never had to pay Mother for my keep. She wouldn't accept anything from me so most of the money I've earned I've invested, safe investments, 'bonds and things'. I'm going to blow a chunk of it on my cruise though.

'I could give up work tomorrow if I wanted to. Mother would be delighted. She didn't want me to get a job in the first place.'

'No, Ruth, don't do that. You might as well dig a hole in the ground and jump in.'

I tell him about my plans, the cruise, the flat in town.

'You should have done that years ago.'

'I know. I just kind of . . .'

'Gave up.'

'No. I just didn't realise time was passing so quickly. This illness, this heart attack has made me stop and look at what I've – what I haven't done with my life.'

'You never wanted to marry?'

Anthony. We met at a friend's party. He was good looking, very fair, blue eyes, quite the opposite of me. We used to say our children would all be ginger-tops. He was an architect, only in training then but good at it, everybody said so, obviously destined for success. I was bowled over that first evening and so, he told me afterwards, was he. Within two weeks we were talking about marriage. On Christmas morning he put a ring on my finger, a pearl set in diamonds.

'Pearls for tears,' said Kitty in her silly, unthinking way.

Daddy was pleased. The wedding was set for April, a honeymoon in Greece. We started looking for a house. West London, we thought, Kew, Richmond. It was to be Daddy's wedding present. Anthony's parents bought us a car.

On a bitterly cold morning in February my father died. He'd been shovelling snow out of the driveway. Stupid really, the bank would have sent a car for him, he could have left the shovelling to the gardener, but he was such an impatient man. Everything had to be done there and then. And snow in his driveway annoyed him. It had no right to be there. He came in for breakfast, sat down at the table and it was all over in minutes, Mother said. When she came back from phoning the doctor, Daddy was dead.

She was sick with grief, wouldn't leave her room, wouldn't eat, wouldn't talk to anyone, not even me. She couldn't see any point in living without him. I nursed her, fed her, washed her, watched over her day and night. And just when I thought the worst was over she tried to kill herself.

I'd been out with Anthony, the first time in weeks. We'd been to a concert. It was such a relief to get out of the house, to be with him again, to sit, holding his hand, listening to Vivaldi's *Gloria*. When I got home Mother was in bed fast asleep – at least that's what I thought until I saw the empty pill box on her side table.

I wanted Anthony to move in with us, it seemed such a logical solution, just for a little while until

Mother was better, but he refused. I don't blame him because Mother, who had seemed to like him at the beginning, turned against him after Daddy died. She was sullen, finding fault with everything he said and did, behind his back at first, then to his face.

'She's upset, she's not herself. Mother isn't like this, Anthony.'

He was only twenty-three. How could such a young man begin to understand the terrors of a middle-aged woman, widowed? She clung to me. I couldn't cast her adrift.

We postponed the wedding until September, November, January . . . Finally Anthony gave me an ultimatum. He'd been very patient but he'd had enough of waiting. Either we got married right away and moved into a flat he'd found or . . . I begged him to understand. 'Suppose she tries to take her life again. I couldn't live with the guilt.'

'Ruth, darling, this could go on for –'

'No, no, it won't, Anthony. Give me time, just a little longer. Please.'

He got married two years later. To a girl in his office, so I heard. They live in Primrose Hill, lovely old house, four children, all boys. Anthony would be very good with children. He had such a sense of fun. I can imagine him romping with them, playing football in the park. Four little gingertops.

I haven't talked about him for years. I honestly thought I'd got over him. But it seems it has all been lying there, deep inside me, like a stagnant pool, and I'm crying again. This time I don't keep saying sorry.

'I've never been the sweetest person in the world, not gentle like Mother, but these past few months . . . Everything upsets me. I snap at people all the time. God, I feel like a rat in a maze. I can't seem to . . . I can't get out.' I've never talked to anyone like this. The loneliness, the frustration, the anger are all pouring out now. It's like being in a confessional. 'I ought to be grateful I'm still alive and yet all I feel is bitterness. All those years, just frittered away. I've wandered around like a . . . like a cabbage on legs. It's such a waste.'

'So you're taking it out on yourself. And everybody around you.'

'I know, I know, it's despicable. But I just want to live, Ian. I want to get out and do things and meet people, interesting people and . . . Look at you, you're only twenty-nine, you're doing what you want.'

'Nothing's stopping you doing what you want. You're only forty-four.'

'*Only*? That isn't exactly young.'

'It isn't exactly old either. Come back and weep on my shoulder when you're sixty-four. And if you waste the next twenty years the way you've done the last I'll give you a good kick up the arse. You won't get any pity from me.' If Simpson weren't a doctor he'd probably talk to me like this. 'Tell me, where is Matthew in all this?'

'He was only five when Daddy died. Mother

tried to make it up to him by spoiling him. He was never refused anything. I tried to tell her but . . .'

'Strong Ruth. Weak Matthew. Possessive Mum.'

I suddenly realise I've been spilling family secrets to a stranger, letting the side down. 'You don't understand what it was like for Mother. Being kicked out of a job after twenty years is bad enough but to lose a husband like she did, and so suddenly . . .'

'What makes you think I don't understand?' he frowns. 'You think you've cornered the market in compassion?'

'I'm sorry, I didn't mean it that way.'

'Anyway, I'm looking at it from your point of view, Ruth, not hers. Why did you let her blackmail you?'

Blackmail? Can a sick, frightened woman be accused of such a crime? It took her ages to get over the shock of Daddy's death but when I felt I could leave her alone, at least during the day, I decided to get a job. I did six months' training at a secretarial college and worked as a temp.

The Trust was one of the jobs I took on for a month while a senior secretary was off sick. They asked me to stay, offered me a decent salary. In time they promoted me. I didn't think I'd be there long. I didn't think anything really, just drifted from one day to the next, a walking cabbage . . . 'About the only interesting thing that's happened to me in the past twenty years is my heart attack.'

'How did it happen?'

'I was coming home . . .' I feel as if there's a huge weight on my chest, I can't breathe.

'Sorry. Let's talk about something else.'

'No, no, I'm all right.' Take a deep breath and let it out very slowly, the way Simpson told me. 'I was coming home from work. I'd stayed late that night . . .'

CHAPTER 12

I always stayed late. There always seemed to be something extra to do after five o'clock. I'd walk around all the work stations, making sure everything was orderly in my little world, typewriters turned off, paper filed away, nothing on the desks, no work overdue – I'd have done it myself before I'd let that happen.

'We were about ten minutes from Guildford when I suddenly felt a piercing sensation in my chest, here, like a red hot needle. I thought it was indigestion at first but it got worse, a really cruel pain. It spread up into my shoulders, my neck, even my jaw . . .'

'Take it easy, Ruth.'

He puts out his hands and I clutch them. Dear God I wish I'd had these hands to cling to that night. I was frightened but too embarrassed to ask for help. The man opposite kept looking at me over his newspaper, hoping I wouldn't do anything silly before he got out. But he was quite safe. I wouldn't have made a scene.

I tried to look out of the window but it was too dark. All I could see was my face staring back at me. I looked terrified. Then I started to count, very slowly, anything to take my mind off the pain.

I got a taxi from the station. The driver kept looking in his mirror and saying, 'You all right, love?' I was doubled up when I got home. Mother phoned Simpson, her voice trembling so much she could hardly get the words out. Another heart attack in the family, another death . . .

I'm crying again. Poor Ian Trevelyan, I'm drowning him in tears. He comes round to my side of the table and puts his arm around my shoulders. It's such a relief, I've cried so much these past few months and always alone. I would never let Mother see my grief, she has enough of her own to bear.

My face is a wet, blubbery mess. People passing the window stare at me. 'I'm sorry.'

'Don't start that again.'

'You'd make a marvellous psychiatrist.'

'Really? And I haven't said a word.'

'That's what good psychiatrists do, they just listen.'

'Sounds like money for old rope.'

'Ian, I'm so –'

'If you say sorry one more time I'll throttle you.'

It's almost five o'clock. The waiters are piling the chairs on the tables.

I've talked for hours, sitting in a wine bar some-where in Covent Garden, telling this young man things I've barely admitted to myself. I hope he doesn't tell Matthew . . . No, he and Matthew aren't friends and somehow I don't think he's the kind of man who would betray a confidence. He'll say a few comforting words, walk away and never think of me again.

A chill wind has sprung up. We huddle together on the pavement, his arms around me. Like Mother he's not afraid to touch.

'Did you drive in, Ruth?'

'No, I don't bring the car into London unless I have to.'

'I've love to take you home.' He laughs. 'I meant I'd love to *see* you home but –'

'Oh, don't be silly.'

'It's just that I've got to go to a reading. I can't duck out of it.'

'Of course not. I'll take a taxi to Waterloo.'

'Look, could you come to the play on Saturday? I think you might enjoy it.'

I turn all shades of scarlet. I've been with him all afternoon, chattering non-stop, and I haven't asked, haven't even thought about his play.

He laughs at my contrite expression. 'It's going very well, not yet up to my standard but the audiences obviously like it. Will you come?'

'We'd love to.'

'Not the whole dynasty, just you. Come for a drink at the flat first – no, come for dinner. I'm no Galloping Gourmet but I'm not bad. Make it about six so we have time to eat in comfort. Take the train to West Hampstead. Here's my telephone number. Give me a call just before you leave Guildford and I'll meet you at the station, okay?'

He helps me into a taxi, pokes his head through the window and looks at me critically, surveying me from top to toe with mock solemnity. 'To be honest I think you look good in pink,' he says. 'It matches your eyes.'

I take aim with my handbag. The last view I have of him through the back window is a long, lean fellow standing in the road, laughing.

I'm half-way home before I remember I was supposed to be having lunch with Deirdre.

CHAPTER 13

Mother is not at all put out by my news. 'I'm disappointed they've treated you like this, especially as you've always been so conscientious.' That word again. 'It's very shabby of them. But I do think it's for the best.'

'That I'm out of work?'

'Did you get a golden handshake?' says Kitty, whose thoughts never stray far from all that glitters. She's sitting on the sofa, her feet tucked under her like a kitten, listening intently to our conversation. She's become an old woman these past few weeks, nodding her head as we talk, mouthing the words after us.

'All I got was a slap in the face.' The anger's coming back now, all the things I should have said welling up inside me. I'll write a letter, a real stinger, and send it to Bridgewater with a copy to that bitch Valerie and anyone else I can think of. I want my girls to know what they've done to me. I want everyone to know. 'They offered me another job.'

'That was nice of them.'

'Nice? It was crap.' I don't usually talk like this

in front of Mother and Kitty but I'm in such a strop I don't care.

'You'll find something else, Ruthy, something much nicer than the silly old Trust, you see.'

'She doesn't have to work at all if she doesn't want to,' says Mother.

She's embroidering a cushion, a gift for Mrs Pryce, water lilies exquisitely worked in silver, but her hands, once so deft, fumble now. The arthritis gives her a lot of pain, though she'd never admit it.

'But I do. I'm going to start looking right away – when I get back from my holiday, I mean.'

'Are you going away, darling?'

Kitty wants to know all about the cruise. I bring the brochure and we sit close together on the sofa looking at it. 'Tobago . . . Isn't that Robinson Crusoe's island? Oh and Barbados, that's where we went for our honeymoon, Ruthy. It was so beautiful.'

Mother stays silent, her hand moving methodically back and forth, piercing the ice blue taffeta. I don't know why she doesn't approve of the cruise. It can't be because I'm going alone, I've been on holiday without her before.

'Oh, Ruthy, it's so exciting,' says my aunt, looking at the pictures longingly. 'Lucky you. I wish I could come too.'

'Well, you and Mother should go,' I say brightly. 'There're lots of wonderful cruises.' I flick through the pages. 'You could go to the Mediterranean. Look at this one, Lisbon, Gibraltar, Nice, Pisa . . .'

'Could we, Ann?' Kitty looks more animated than I've seen her in weeks.

'I don't think so, dear.'

'Why not?'

Mother shakes her head.

Kitty turns to me hopefully, like a child waiting for a grown-up to fight its battles, but from the look on Mother's face I know the battle's already lost.

'I bumped into that Ian Trevelyan fellow in town. We had lunch together in Covent Garden.'

'What was he doing there? I thought his theatre was somewhere in South London.'

'I don't know.' I didn't ask. I was much too busy talking about myself. 'There are lots of little theatrical places around Covent Garden, costumiers, make-up people, that kind of thing. Anyway, I don't suppose he's tied to the theatre all the time. The play's running now. I imagine his part in it is virtually over.'

'Who is he, Ruthy?' Kitty, intrigued, links her arm through mine and draws me close. 'Is he a boyfriend?' She loves romance. I think she's read every Barbara Cartland, all those happy, pappy endings.

'No, darling, he's a friend of Matthew's. They came down a couple of weekends ago. He's rather an odd-looking fellow, isn't he, Mother?' I quite forgot to stare at his Adam's apple this time. I only noticed those lovely, gentle eyes, the comforting hands. 'He's in the theatre. You know the type . . .' Brash, vain, self-centred, all the things Ian is so obviously not. 'I promised I'd go and see his play on Saturday.'

'Is it a success?' says Mother.

'Yes, at least he thinks so. I'll let you know when I've seen it.'

'I love the theatre,' cries Kitty. 'Julian and I used to go all the time. We saw everything, all the musicals and reviews. What's the play called?'

I'm stumped. I think he did tell me.

'*Who's a Pretty Pol?*' says Mother.

Kitty blinks. 'What, dear?'

'It's a pun,' I explain. 'Pol is short for politician, you see.'

'Oh.' Kitty doesn't see. 'Is it a comedy?'

'I think it's supposed to be funny, but not in the way you mean.'

'Not like *Dry Rot?*'

Kitty loves all those Whitehall farces.

'No.'

'Who's in it?'

'I don't know. Probably nobody we've ever heard of.'

'Is it the matinee you're going to, Ruthy?' says Mother.

'No, the evening performance. I'm going to have dinner with him first.'

'Oh, where?' Kitty is agog. She and Julian were always eating out, usually at Italian or Spanish places, guitars strumming, tenors warbling, a rose for the beautiful señora.

'At his flat.' It's out before I can stop myself. But why shouldn't I tell them? I doubt he's planning to ravish me.

'Oh.' Kitty is disappointed.

'I hope you won't make it too late, Ruthy.'

'I am over twenty-one, dear.'

'I didn't mean that. I'm just thinking of your condition.' Mother bends her head to her embroidery again. 'It would be a mistake to overdo it, just when you're beginning to get back on your feet.'

'Condition' means only one thing to Kitty. 'Ruthy,' she says wistfully, 'wouldn't it be nice if you'd had . . .'

'Goodness, I do feel tired.' Yes, Kitty, it would have been nice if I'd had four little gingertops but I'd rather not think about what might have been. 'It must have been all that wine at lunchtime.' Mother purses her lips. 'And the dreadful morning at The Trust. It really upset me.' Unkind of me but I deliberately punched the right button. Mother gets up immediately.

'Would you like me to bring you dinner in bed, dear?'

'Oh yes, that would be lovely. Would you mind?'

'What a strange thing to say. You know I never mind doing anything for you.'

It's been a wearing day, so much anger, so many tears. My whole life seems to have changed in just a few hours. I'm out of the rut now, whether I like it or not.

CHAPTER 14

I'm like a young girl on her first date. I've been through my wardrobe, tried on everything, paraded in front of the mirror. My clothes are eminently suited to the lifestyle of a middle-aged spinster. I'm going to give the whole lot to Oxfam, all the dresses in muted colours, the sensible suits, the blouses and skirts, the comfortable shoes with low heels in exciting shades of black and brown.

Even my evening dresses are dismal. A lime green taffeta with puff sleeves. How could I do that to myself? A full-length beige affair, swathed around the bust. I have a lot of formal clothes which get their annual outing at this time of year, The Trust dinner dance, the Conservative Association Ball, New Year's Eve at the Henshaws.

I've lost weight and nothing fits me any more. Out with the lot.

I drive over to Guildford. I'm trying to pretend that I'm buying new clothes for the cruise, not because I want to find something dazzling for Saturday night, something that will really make him . . . Oh stop it, you idiot. Stop it! You're forty-four, fifteen years older than him. Anyway, he's only being kind, he wants to cheer me up. That's hardly surprising after the sob story I gave him yesterday.

I'm going to buy something stunning, sweep into his grotty little attic on Saturday in my magnificent new outfit, make a complete fool of myself. And I don't care.

His girlfriend will be back in residence, they obviously have the kind of on-off relationship that means they can't live without each other, and she'll be wearing jeans and a scruffy old sweater. She'll still look gorgeous though. She's probably blonde, long silky hair down to the waist, perfect skin, no make-up. And they'll laugh about me. I'll hear them in the kitchen, sniggering – 'Poor old thing, mutton dressed up as lamb. Wherever did you find her, Ian? She's really tarted herself up for you. She's got her eye on you, darling . . .' No, it isn't that, my little loves. It's just that this is the beginning of my new life and I'm celebrating. Anyway what does it matter what they think of me? What does it matter if they laugh?

It matters.

I'll play safe, buy something nice but discreet. No short sleeves, no low necks, no bright colours. Oh no, play safe with the pastels, Ruthy. Another lime green, so tasteful. Another lilac to match your bedroom wallpaper. And what about one of Kitty's little girl Laura Ashley prints to add to your collection? And since you're going backwards in time, why not go right back to your childhood – pink satin roses on organza? Remember how Mother embroidered it for you, dozens of tiny roses, each one perfect?

There's a smart new shop in Guildford. I'm told their clothes are very sophisticated, aimed at the Surrey jet set.

'For day or evening, Madam?'

'Evening. I'm going to dinner and then on to the theatre.'

She thinks I mean the Ritz followed by Drury Lane.

'What size?'

'Sixteen.'

'Oh no, I don't think so.' She measures me. 'You're only a fourteen. In fact, I think you could probably get into a twelve.'

A twelve? Happy Christmas, Ruthy!

'If you'd like to sit over there,' she points to a chaise longue in blue and gold brocade, 'I'll bring something to show you, Madam.'

Madam has never been in a shop, boutique, like this before. It's the kind of place you shouldn't be in if you have to ask the price.

Madam seats herself, trying to look the part. What should I say? 'Oh no, not Givenchy, he's losing his touch . . . I adore Ungaro but I have so much of his stuff . . . How very Lagerfeld . . .' Would I even recognise a Lagerfeld? Maybe I'd better just keep my mouth shut.

The saleswoman – is it right to call such an elegant creature by such a lowly name? – returns with an armful of froth, tiers of purple chiffon, scarlet and gold stripes, a huge off-the-shoulder frill, a sequinned bodice. I explain that it is not that kind of evening. Ian's flat will be draughty. We'll probably sit on huge cushions that pass for chairs and eat off our laps. As for the theatre, it's bound to be a leaking warehouse in some bleak back street . . . I don't put it quite that bluntly because I'm afraid she might show me the door but she gets the message anyway.

'How about something like this then?'

She comes back with loose-fitting trousers and a matching top in chocolate and a long straight coat – 'It's a duster, Madam' – a coat that falls just below the knee in a pinky coral piped with chocolate. 'It's very soft and easy to wear. Try it on.'

I can't stop staring at myself in the mirror. It makes me feel like a different person. How much is it? I daren't ask. There don't seem to be any price tags. Oh well . . . 'It's very nice.'

'It's beautiful,' she corrects me. 'With the right accessories, of course.' She returns with a chunky pendant and earrings that reflect the coral and brown.

'I'll need some shoes to go with it.' I am entirely in her hands now.

'What size?'

I wonder if my feet have shrunk as well?

She flips through a line of white boxes on the wall, holds up some shoes for my approval, very high heels, one fine strap diagonally across the instep. I put them on, wobble a bit, I'm not used to these dizzy heights. I need a handbag. 'This little clutch purse?' Why not? All my bags are sensible holdalls for carrying a compact, lipstick, cheque book, pen, diary, cigarettes, a novel to read on the train – the working woman's pantechnicon. This silly, utterly beautiful little purse will hold nothing except a tissue and loose change.

'You look splendid,' she says.

'Thank you.' I almost blush. Nobody has said that to me in years.

'Is there anything else I can interest you in?'

I am at her mercy now. If, in five minutes, she can transform me from a dowdy duckling into a, well, not exactly a swan but . . .

'I need a coat.'

'Ah, I have something I think you'll like.' Not in shocking pink, please, I've already given one of those to Oxfam. 'It will go perfectly with that outfit.'

I leave an hour later with half a dozen bags. Tomorrow I'll make an appointment with the hairdresser. My hair's too long and I'm fed up with this style. Toni has grown so used to giving me the same cut once a month, the same perm twice a year, she's in the same rut that I am – that I was. Time for a change. Maybe I'll try that new place. I'll have a facial too.

CHAPTER 15

I phone him from the station.

At least a dozen times today I've changed my mind about coming. I even got as far as dialling his number but hung up when I heard his voice. Finally I poured myself a stiff whisky and got dressed, all the regalia. I'm shaved and deodorised and perfumed. I've sucked enough breath fresheners to sweeten the Salvation Army hostel. I'm ready for my big date. No schoolgirl, no dizzy teenager ever tried harder.

Am I out of my mind?

I have a lot of time to think, waiting here at this dismal station. He's fifteen years younger than me – I've been through this a hundred times already – when he was still a schoolboy in short trousers I was wearing an engagement ring and buying a trousseau. He's in the theatre, a world so different from mine. I long to be a part of it but what do I know of actors – real actors, not amateur hopefuls like my brother – directors, designers, musicians, unconventional people who live by their own rules?

My life is bounded by a barbed-wire fence of

convention that seals off a little world as suffocating as his is open and free. Can a domesticated
animal, trained to sit and jump and defecate on
command, jump that high fence and survive in
the dangerous world outside?

He has a lover. He's probably had many. Anyway,
why am I getting so agitated, he has no intention
of adding me to the notches on his walking stick.
He thinks of me, if he thinks of me at all, as a
middle-aged woman he feels rather sorry for . . .
I wonder if he'll like my outfit?

'Hello.'

I didn't expect him to come by car. It's a battered
Triumph, the same vintage as Matthew's . . . I think
it is Matthew's. Is my brother coming to dinner
too? Oh God, I never thought of that. The minute
he sees my clothes, the new hairdo, the makeup,
he'll know. He'll take one look at me and . . . No,
I can see now underneath the grime it's a green
car. Matthew's is grey.

Ian greets me with a hug.

'I didn't think it was you for the minute. You've
done something marvellous with your hair. It
really suits you.'

'Do you think so?' I can't help touching it,
pushing it self consciously all the time.

'It looks fabulous.'

Marvellous, fabulous . . . theatrical exaggera-
tions but I love them.

'And you're a lot taller.'

My new high heels. He hasn't missed a thing.

But then he's used to auditioning people, weighing them up, noticing all the details . . . Wonder if I'll get the part?

He opens the car door and strides round to the other side leaving me to lower myself gingerly into the passenger seat. What happened to the elaborate old-world manners? 'It's a friend's car. I borrowed it for the evening. It's bloody cold, isn't it? Not the kind of weather to hang around in waiting for London Transport.'

'Do you think we'll be back very late?'

'There's a cast party afterwards. I thought you might like to go.'

I'd love to but of course I won't. What would I do, what would I say to them after I'd said 'it was wonderful, you were wonderful'?

The car is dirty and it stinks of cigarette smoke. I wish I could develop an aversion to cigarettes. Perhaps I should take one of those hypnotism courses.

I don't know Hampstead. We used to come here years ago when I was a child, a school friend of Mother's had married an artist or musician or something. I'm sure all the arty bohemians have given way to solid wealth now. Today's beautiful people equate creativity with money. To hell with starving in a garret.

He pulls up in front of a huge gingerbread house, all towers and turrets, in a quiet side street. I can't help smiling.

'No, it's not Surrey Tudor,' he says, mistaking

my smile for a sneer. But I love all those odd-shaped windows and balconies and flying buttresses and Lord knows what.

Our house was designed by a geometrician, if that's the right word. The front door is in the centre and leads into a big square entrance hall with two big square rooms to the right, two big square rooms to the left, an oblong kitchen at the back alongside an oblong conservatory which looks on to a big square garden. Even our flower beds are square and laid out with military precision. Daddy liked them that way.

This house will be full of surprises, full of crooks and nannies, as Kitty says. I can't wait to see inside.

'My uncle's out. I'd like you to meet him later.'

Our entrance hall is lined with rural scenes, the Downs at sunset, a meadow full of buttercups, a churchyard full of flower-strewn gravestones. This entrance hall is lined with paintings of nude males, dozens of them, all colours and sizes, in various postures. It's like a life class, the kind I went to once, only our model was a woman, and discreetly draped at that.

'Is your uncle an artist?'

'No, he just likes boys.'

I must be broad-minded. After all they can't help it, it's in their genes. Matthew says almost everyone in the theatre is gay.

'He likes girls too, the younger the better. I suppose he's what's known as a dirty old man.' He grins.

I smell sin, orgies and decadence. This is a do-what-you-damned-well-please house. Not one room will be big and square and filled with wholesome sunlight. I'm horrified. And thrilled.

'I'm sorry about the stairs.' Three flights, steep too. 'Take them slowly.' He puts his arm round my waist and helps me up, but still I have to pause for breath on the second landing. 'Just one more flight, okay?'

My heart is fluttering when I get to his door. The stairs or stage fright?

The flat is a surprise. There's so much white, such a feeling of space – shining white ceilings and walls, gleaming wooden floors, huge windows, no doors, lots of sofas, white and beige, and mobile units, I think they're called, pieces that can be pulled apart to make separate seats or beds. Huge paintings on the walls, not paintings really, not landscapes or people, just odd shapes and figures.

It must be like living in an art gallery, a very elegant one to be sure, a lot of money has been spent here. His girlfriend's? The director of a struggling fringe group couldn't afford all this, could he? Maybe his family's rich. Obviously his uncle is.

'Throw your coat on the bed. I'll get you a drink. Scotch?'

His bedroom is part of the open plan. It's utterly bleak. A huge double bed – king size, emperor size? – on a raised platform. He certainly likes to be on stage, this man, even when he's asleep.

There's an evil cactus in one corner, spines as thick as nails, I wouldn't like to back into that in the middle of the night, white louvered blinds over the windows and a painting that covers one entire wall, except that it isn't a painting, it's just white paint in a blue frame. Weird.

I know what Mother would do with this room, there would be chintz covers and frills and embroidered cushions everywhere. How he must have loathed our house.

'Hey!' He stands back to get a better look at me. 'Turn around. That is stunning.' He emphasises every word. 'And you're so slim.'

'I've lost quite a lot of weight but I think it's probably this outfit. My other clothes made me look a bit . . .'

'Yes,' he laughs. And so do I. 'They certainly did.'

'Mm, what a lovely smell.' I edge towards the kitchen. I'm dying to know if she's there, slaving over a hot stove, her long blonde hair drawn back in a ponytail, silky tendrils curling about her face. I think she's probably tall – no, she's definitely tall with long, slim legs that go on for ever.

'It's a soufflé. Not too rich, I promise. Well,' he raises his glass, 'Cheers.' This is my second Scotch of the day, my last, or it should be. I feel very cold and very tense. I could down ten of these and it wouldn't make a scrap of difference. 'Would you like to see the rest of the place?'

I want to look in every corner. I've a feeling

she's hiding in a wardrobe, crouching behind one of those sliding doors . . . What nonsense. Why would she hide from me?

He takes my arm. 'This is the spare bedroom.' It certainly is, like everything else in this flat. 'The kitchen.' Everything's hidden – cooker, sink, fridge, all discreetly out of sight. 'And this is the dining room.' In an alcove, austerely elegant, a glass-topped table, black candles in crystal holders, the whitest, finest china, mirrors from floor to ceiling. He pulls up the blinds and I gasp. A world of tiny lights sparkles beneath us.

'I hadn't realised this house was so high up.'

'Best view for miles. That's why my uncle bought it.'

How lucky Ian is to live at the top of this house at the top of a hill. There's such a feeling of lightness here, of freedom . . . Freedom. It's a word that keeps coming into my mind of late.

'My uncle lets me have this place rent-free in return for a game of chess now and then. The furniture is his too. I chose it, he paid.'

I ought to say something polite now, about how attractive it is, what good taste he has, but I can't bring myself to tell such a whopping lie, not even in the interests of courtesy.

He chuckles. 'You hate it, don't you?'

'Well, I . . .'

He wags a warning finger. 'Be honest or say nothing.'

I'm not used to telling the truth, not the whole,

140

ungracious truth, and saying nothing is equally rude.

'I wouldn't care to live with it myself.' I've changed my mind about his girlfriend. She isn't the casual, beautifully scruffy creature I had imagined. If she can live comfortably here she's an ice maiden; platinum hair swept up in a severe chignon, eyes as grey as a winter sky. But where does he fit in, this lean, easygoing fellow, in his chunky sweater and jeans? 'I think my taste is somewhere between yours and Mother's. I don't like all the . . . well, the buttons and bows but I do like to be cosy.' My favourite word. Log fires and chestnuts, a soft bed, rain pattering on the window-pane. Sometimes I think I've never left the womb.

'Oh, he's rather nice.'

A small Buddha, a beautiful piece of jade, its fat belly at odds with this lean room.

'My uncle brought it back from Shanghai for me. I must have been about four or five. Cheerful bloke, isn't he? I never go anywhere without him.'

'Your mascot?'

'Let's just say a close friend.'

He's a laughing Buddha, chuckling so hard he's clutching his huge belly with podgy little hands. Even his toes are curling. I start to giggle myself.

'He has that effect on everyone, even the most miserable git ends up laughing.'

'I think he's got the right attitude.'

'I think he's got the only attitude. Come on, let's eat.'

I haven't eaten all day, too frightened. He pulls out my chair, tucks it under me, leans over my shoulder. 'Smells good. Wonder how it tastes?' He kisses my neck. 'Wonderful. What is it?'

'Vent Vert.' I fiddle with my napkin.

'Ah, James Bond.'

'What?'

'All James Bond's women wore Vent Vert.'

That's me all right, a James Bond woman from the top of my blue-rinsed head to the toes of my woollen stockings.

'Will you have some wine?'

'Please.'

I shouldn't but I need all the Dutch courage I can get. A woman of my age should be absolutely in control of a situation like this. A situation like what? I'm just having dinner with a nice young man. He's pleasantly attentive, flattering, but thats his style, he's like that with everyone. Look how he handled Mother. I suspect he's a wily old schemer behind that urbane exterior, a man used to getting his own way. The theatre's his first love, his only love, that's obvious. The rest of us, family, friends, middle-aged ladies with failing hearts have to fall into place behind.

This is killing me, I've got to ask – 'Where's your girlfriend?'

'Tasha? She cleared out. I told you.'

'I thought she might've come back.'

'No, it's finito this time.'

Why do I feel such relief?

'Does your uncle live alone?'

He nods. 'Except when he has some young thing in his bed. He's a lecherous old bastard but very charming. You'll like him.'

I hope I don't meet him. Musgrove in Accounts was a lecherous old bastard. He used to come into my department on some pretext but we all knew he just wanted to stare at my girls' breasts, dribble on their mini skirts. I took him aside one day and told him if he ever came anywhere near them again I'd go straight up to Bridgewater and . . .

'Don't you like it?'

'Sorry? Oh, the soup, yes, it's excellent.'

Avocado soup, cool and tangy. The soufflé is perfect and the wine is beginning to work its magic. I look up and catch him staring at me.

'You look great this evening, Ruth, you really do.'

I keep stealing glimpses of myself in the mirror. Sister Anne would be mortified. I've never worn my hair this short. The hairdresser said it showed off my wonderful cheek bones, which ensured a handsome tip.

The eye make-up looks good in the candlelight, not as dramatic as I'd feared. 'But lilac brings out the blue of your eyes . . .' I tried to copy what the girl at the cosmetic counter did, smudging the eyeliner, blending it into the shadow. I had to wipe it off twice and start again but I think I've got the hang of it now.

'You're a very good cook. You must give me the

recipe for the soup. Mother would love it.' A nice, safe, girly conversation.

He refills my glass. I've already had more than three times my daily allowance. The candles are reflected in the mirrors that surround us, lights twinkle beneath the window. We're in a fairyland, cut off from the world, far above it, floating . . . This wine must be a lot stronger than I thought. I'd better slow down.

'Have you seen Matthew lately?'

Safe subject number two.

'No.'

'He came over last week. Apparently he didn't get that part his agent was after for him. They wanted someone better known. He thinks television's the answer, the only way to get your face in front of casting directors, so he's going to try and . . .' I rabbit on, punctuating details of Matthew's career, or lack of it, with mouthfuls of lime sorbet and it is some time before I realise he isn't nodding or shaking his head or saying 'Really?' and 'Oh dear, what a pity' in appropriate places.

'Don't you like my brother?'

'Like him?' He shrugs. 'He's a decent enough bloke. At arm's length.'

'Has Matthew done something to annoy you, apart from being a decent enough bloke at arm's length?'

'Don't get mad at me, Ruth. You did ask me if I liked him.'

'He can be a bit irritating at times, I know, but underneath he has a good . . .' I'm not sure my brother does have a good heart. Sometimes I wonder if he has any heart at all. 'He means well.'

'I don't know what that old cliché means.'

Neither do I. Mother uses it a lot, it's her standard excuse for people who behave badly.

'Do you think your play will have a long run?'

Safe subject number three.

'It depends what you mean by long. I'd be quite happy if it played to full houses for a couple of months but,' he shrugs 'an unknown playwright plus unknown actors doesn't usually make for commercial success.'

'Have you always wanted to be in the theatre?'

'I don't think I ever made a conscious decision. I got involved in school plays and when I left I joined a touring company and from then on . . .' We've both becoming mellow now, drifting into that lovely state where inhibitions begin to fall away and we talk about hopes and dreams. His not mine. Mine are all under lock and key. They'll never see the light of day.

His gentle voice is hypnotic. If I listen to him much longer and stare at these flickering candles I shall go into a trance. I lean back in my chair, shoes off, utterly relaxed. I haven't felt this good in ages.

'You look lovely this evening, Ruth.'

Is he making fun of me? Is he putting on an act? 'Pause with glass half-way to lips, lean back,

145

narrow eyes, look at her adoringly, murmur something flattering, bring wine glass to lips, gaze at
her over the rim . . .'

In the bathroom I take a long look at myself in
the full-length mirror. I'm still a bit pale, despite
Clarin's, and I could lose a few more pounds but
he's right, I *am* looking good. To hell with Sister
Anne! All the grey has been rinsed out of my hair
and replaced with highlights. Mother looked
surprised but said nothing. Kitty was ecstatic. I
primped and fussed and fretted with it, missing
my permed curls, but I do like it – now that Ian
likes it.

By the time I come out of the bathroom I can't
make up my mind if I'm a reincarnated Cleopatra
or Mata Hari – I'm so enticing, so seductive. I'm
also drunk.

'Over here.'

He is on stage, on the raised dais, sitting on one
of the sofas, long legs sprawled out. The lights
have been turned down very low and there's sweet
music coming from somewhere. No doubt the
record player's hidden too. It's Schubert, I
think . . . Oh dear, I'm much too old for this. I sit
on the edge of my seat, glance at my watch.
'Oughtn't we to be going?'

'Come here.' He pats the place next to him.

This is ridiculous. I'm forty-four and he's
only . . . He laughs at my expression. 'What do
you think I'm going to do? Rip off your knickers
and have my way with you?'

Put like that it does sound rather stupid. Obviously I've been flattering myself, the wine has gone to my head and given me delusions. I sit next to him and he puts his arm around my shoulders and grins. 'Well, I am.'

He kisses me quickly, lightly, on the cheek, on the neck. Teasing kisses, questions. Shall I do it again? Shall I stop?

He kisses me the way Anthony did after we'd been going out for a few weeks, my first kiss.

CHAPTER 16

I was in love with Anthony and I desperately wanted to make love with him but I was a paid-up member of St Mary Magdalene's in those days. I was 'saving myself for marriage'. We all were.

Poor Anthony, I'd let him get so far and then get all protective about my honour. Heavy petting, they called it then. A prick tease they say today. It was as hard on me as it was on him. I'd lie in bed afterwards, not knowing what to do to relieve the tension in my body. Masturbation was an even greater sin than fornication.

After Anthony left the years sped by and though I dreaded being a spinster, untouched, untouchable, I never found anyone else I wanted to marry. Not that I met many men. I wasn't a 'joiner', Matthew's friends were all too young, and there's not much chance of romantic encounters on the 7.32 to Waterloo when everyone's half asleep.

Several men at The Trust asked me out and some of them were very persistent but I couldn't work up any enthusiasm for those earnest young accountants and actuaries. Anyway, The Trust frowned on what they called 'romantic liaisons' between staff and I agreed with them. It must be horribly embarrassing to take dictation from a man you've loved and lost.

So I set out to find myself a lover – not a life partner, I think that's up to fate – but someone who would relieve me of my virginity. He had to be a man I didn't know, a man I could make use of and return to anonymity when the affair was over. I don't say that I actually thought in quite such callous terms but it is what I wanted and what I finally found.

He was married. We used to meet in the evenings whenever he could get away. Mother thought I was at art class, his wife thought he was working late – why do women keep falling for that old story? We never talked, I don't know how many children he had, what his interests were, and he knew nothing about me. All we wanted of each other was sex.

We used to drive a long way from Guildford and park in country lanes. It was late autumn, too cold for frolics in the long grass. We had no choice but to do it in the back of his car. I don't recommend it to any but the most ardent or desperate. Somebody's leg is always in the way, an elbow in the eye, a knee in the groin, a cramp at the wrong moment. It becomes more of a comedy turn than a grand passion.

It ended quickly. It was too tacky for both of us. He went back to his wife, his little fling over, but I had woken a part of me that screamed to be satisfied. I wanted a man, I wanted to love and be loved, I wanted, I wanted . . .

I packed up what Mother coyly calls 'the sensual side of our nature' in a little box and put it with all my other dreams in a bottom drawer. There it has lain over the years, quietly rotting. But with skilled fingers and gentle mouth Ian Trevelyan has prised open that box and let it all come tumbling out.

He leads me, unresisting, into the bedroom, undresses me slowly, covering my face and neck with kisses, caressing my breasts, running his tongue around my navel, opening my thighs, licking, probing, until I am panting. When he enters me I groan and cling to him. He moves slowly at first, very gentle but insistent until, my back arched, my mouth open in a silent scream of ecstasy, I erupt.

We lie for a long time afterwards. I think he's fallen asleep, he's so heavy. How sweet it is, his heavy, sweaty body on mine. He stirs, lifts himself onto his elbows, looks down at me. 'Ruth. Ruth, my darling, my love, would you like some more coffee?'

What I'd like is a cigarette but I'll settle for coffee. He pads off to the kitchen, not bothering with a dressing gown to cover his nudity. I can imagine him walking down Oxford Street stark naked, completely self-assured, unconcerned by the stares and giggles. Now that I see him without clothes I realise he's not the half-starved beanpole I thought. He's light boned but well muscled.

I lie back on the bed, nestling under the soft,

plump duvet. I'm glad he likes a little comfort at least. There's not much to look at in this room except a wicked cactus and a blank canvas. It's a room to sleep in or make love in. Maybe that's the point. Nothing distracts from the purpose at hand.

I think Ian Trevelyan is a man who gets on with life, not bothering to stop and look at the view. And yet there's something of the dreamer in him. He gave that away over dinner.

I want him to make love to me again. I want to lie here all night in this starkly simple room with him next to me, in me.

'Sugar?' he calls from the kitchen.

'No thanks.'

I sit up and drape the sheet around me, a stupid thing to do since he has already kissed and caressed every inch of my body but when you're making love it's different. I'm sitting demurely on the edge of the bed covered from neck to ankle when he comes back carrying two mugs. Mugs? Finest crystal for pre-seduction wine, ordinary mugs for post-coital coffee.

'Are you feeling cold?' He grins, amused by my sudden display of modesty.

'No . . . er . . . well, yes, a bit.'

He puts the mugs on the floor, no bedside table with peach silk lampshade here, opens the wardrobe, how silently the doors slide back, everything in this place runs on well-oiled casters, and brings me a dressing gown, a towelling bathrobe actually. Is it hers?

He wraps it round me – is there perfume on it, talcum powder, something, anything that tells me about Tasha? – and bends to kiss me.

'You're beautiful.'

He looks down at me, still naked, smiling that enigmatic smile. Without thinking – should I, shouldn't I, is it a thing a nice girl would do? – I lean forward and kiss the tip of his penis.

'Well, don't stop there.'

I shall never see this man again. Nobody will ever know about this night. I shall go home and pretend there's no such person as Ian Trevelyan. But not now. I'm not Ruth Webster any more. I don't know where she's gone. Just for this moment I'm free of her.

I run my tongue around, round and round, very slowly. He groans and opens his legs, straddling me. I stroke him, moving very delicately, the lightest touch. I've never thought of myself as a courtesan but I think I'd be quite good at it. This could be my new career.

'Oh Christ,' he murmurs.

I use my tongue, my lips, moving back and forth gently, as he moved in me, going a little further every time, pressing a little harder. He pushes me back onto the bed, enters me roughly, thrusting hard, his fingers digging into my bottom . . . It's ten o'clock before I remember we should be at the play.

'I'll take you another night,' he says, then bursts out laughing as he realises the double entendre.

'But shouldn't you be there?'

'What for? To hover over them like a mother superior?' Oh, I wish he hadn't said that. If Mother Teresa were hovering over me now . . . 'They're quite capable of getting drunk and wrecking the set without me.'

I'm flattered he's chosen to spend the evening with me instead of his actors. He's the kind of man I've longed for, a man I can laugh and cry with, a man . . . I must stop thinking like that. Stop right now.

'Thank you.'

'For what?' He's puzzled.

'For everything.' For making love to me, for making me feel I'm worth making love to, even though I'm only a bedwarmer between one lover and the next.

'Don't talk crap!' He sits up abruptly, glowering at the non-painting on the wall. It's just a mirror, I realise, you can see whatever you want in it. Right now I see an angry young man. 'You've done one hell of a job on yourself, haven't you?'

'I don't have any delusions, Ian.'

'And what does that mean?'

'I'm the wrong side of forty. All right, I know it's a cliché but –' I have more to say, much more, but his mouth stops me and his arms tighten around me and I'm falling, falling away from this world. We're just two naked bodies, ageless, timeless, floating in space.

'Stay,' he says.

'No, I must get back. I've got to,' I'm not going to tell him the truth, 'I've got to go to Guildford first thing tomorrow.'

Mother's in bed when I get home. She has switched on my electric blanket and put a thermos of hot milk and a plate of arrowroot biscuits on my bedside table.

I undress very slowly, stripping in front of the mirror, watching myself, running my hands over my body, remembering his touch. There is a knock at the door.

'Just a minute.' I put on my dressing gown.

'Are you all right, dear?'

'Just a minute, Mother.' Safely covered I open the door. I have never seen my mother's body, save for a brief glimpse of one breast, and she hasn't seen mine since I decided at twelve I was grown up. 'Thanks for switching on my blanket. Oh, and the hot milk. I shall sleep like a top tonight.'

I don't want her to come in. I want to get into bed and lie there thinking, reliving the evening over and over again.

'Did you have a nice time?'

'Yes, very, thanks.'

'How was the play?'

'Not bad.'

Mother rarely reads theatre reviews. She leaves me to decide what we should go and see. But 'not bad' is safe – just in case. We stand and look at each other, I with my hand on the doorknob, she waiting to be invited in.

'Good night, Mother.'

She turns to go, disappointed. She wanted to sit on the edge of my bed, hear what we did, what we said. It's not like me to be such a clam.

'Did you have a nice evening, dear?' I don't want her to go away looking like that.

'Matthew came and we all played cards.' He must have been in a very obliging mood. Matthew loathes cards. I wonder how much he touched Mother for this time? Enough to tide him over Christmas, at least. 'He cheered Kitty up. He made her laugh a lot. She was her old self again by the time he left.' Kitty adores him. She has aided and abetted Mother in spoiling him but she hasn't had to live with the result. Mother pauses at the foot of the stairs. 'I told Matthew where you'd gone.'

And what did Matthew say when you told him, Mother? Did he say Ian Trevelyan had a reputation for taking women back to his flat and seducing them? Did he jeer about us, his middle-aged sister and her gigolo, the old maid and her young lover? Is that what made Kitty laugh so much?

'Good night, Ruthy.'

'Good night, Mother.'

I was going to sleep in the nude tonight, feel the sheets against my body, revel in their touch, but I put on my nightdress, the brushed nylon with long sleeves and lace yolk. I'm Ruth Webster again.

Welcome home.

CHAPTER 17

I feel a fool in the harsh light of this December morning. I burn with shame at the things I did last night and . . . Oh God, I hope I'm not pregnant. No, I can't be, I've just had a period. But I must be more careful in the future. What future? I'm never going to see this man again . . . I must see him again, even if I have to drive to Hampstead and sit outside the house, staring at his window, waiting for a glimpse of him. It hurts just to think of him. This is ridiculous.

'Ruthy.' Mother holds out the phone to me. I was going to take Rob for a long walk. I need to keep moving I'm so jittery. It's the maddest, loveliest, damnedest feeling in the world. 'It's for you, dear.'

'Hello, love.'

'Hello.' I wrap my fingers round the receiver, nestling it into my neck. Mother's gone into her sitting room and Kitty isn't up yet so there's no one to see the daft expression on my face and hear my tremulous voice.

'Am I going to see you today? I've still got the car. I could come over and pick you up.'

'No, don't do that . . .'

'Ruth, please.'

'I could be there by four.'

Kitty's door opens and she comes down the stairs, tying up her satin dressing gown. She's fascinated by the telephone, convinced that every time it rings it's for her. She hovers around me, smiling.

'Can't you come earlier? Come to lunch. Come right now. We could spend the whole day together.'

'All right, I'll be there at one o'clock.'

'I'll meet you at the station. Bye, love.'

'Bye.' I hang up.

'Are you going out with your boyfriend again?'

'Oh, Kitty, I keep telling you he isn't my boyfriend, he's just an acquaintance. And he's a young man. He's only a year older than Matthew.'

'But lots of women marry younger men, darling.'

'For goodness sake, Kitty,' my laugh sounds strained, 'don't be so silly.'

The door to Mother's sitting room is ajar. It's her private domain. We've always had our own little cubby-holes in this house, Mother's sitting room, Daddy's study, Matthew's den.

Mother's room is decorated in green, walls, curtains, carpet, although the walls are almost hidden by paintings and photographs, dozens of them, landscapes, seascapes – gentle seas, no storms allowed in here – rustic scenes, wild animals of the less ferocious variety, badgers and moles. Matthew and I are on these walls, of course, and so is Daddy – Daddy with the Lord Mayor of London, Daddy in his freemasonry regalia, Daddy with his senior managers. He was a fine looking man, not handsome, but he had an air about him.

'Mother, Ian's having a few friends over, some of the people in his play, and he thought I might like to meet them, since I didn't last night.' I'm becoming quite an accomplished liar. 'I won't be late though. I don't want two late nights in a row.' God knows why, I've nothing to do all day but sleep.

'But Ruthy,' she looks up from her sewing, it's another cushion, another gift for one of the ladies of the village, 'have you forgotten we're going to Bill Fordham's this evening?'

Oh hell, the silly season's started, cocktails with Major Fordham, dinner with the Willoughbys, a party at Mrs Lloyd-Molyneux, same old clique, same old snobs.

'I'm sure he won't mind if I don't go. He'll never notice I'm not there . . .' Not with thirty or forty people milling around, calling greetings to each other across the room, assessing who's there and, more importantly, who's been left out, the little snubs that will keep them happy for weeks.

'Of course he will. He's very fond of you.' He's very fond of Mother actually. 'I think you should put off your friend, dear, since you already have a previous engagement.'

'I'd much rather spend an evening with Ian's friends than –'

'Mine?'

'Ours.'

'Please yourself.' Said with a sigh. 'You do what-ever you think best . . .' Do what you think best, not what you want to do. Never that.

'You must bring your boyfriend here,' says Kitty, blissfully unaware that she's making the situation ten times worse. 'I'd like to see him. Is he very handsome?'

I put on another of my new outfits, a dress in burnt orange bouclé with a fitted jacket. 'It goes perfectly with your colouring,' said my fashion guru. What a peacock I'm becoming. The skirt's a bit shorter than I'm used to wearing but these high heels make my legs look good. A gold pendant and matching earrings – and I'm ready for the catwalk.

'Well, I'm off.'

Kitty, sitting cross-legged in front of the fire reading the newspaper, looks up eagerly. 'Have a lovely time, Ruthy.'

'Goodbye, Mother.'

'Goodbye, dear.' She keeps her eyes firmly on her sewing.

I hover in the doorway, wishing she'd say some-thing, give me her blessing.

'Bye, Kitty.'

My aunt holds up her face for a kiss like a little child.

I turn at the door and look at the two of them, two old women. They seem so helpless . . . Oh, that's nonsense. They're both healthy, they both have more than enough money to keep them in comfort. By the general standards of this country they're privileged. They have a good life, a full social life, Mother has anyway and Kitty will soon fit into it. It's obvious she's a permanent fixture now. So why do I feel so guilty about leaving them? I have a right to my own life. I'm not their keeper, am I?

'If anything should happen to me you'll look after your mother, won't you, Ruth?' How often those words have come back to haunt me.

'Of course I will, Daddy.'

I was too young to understand what I was promising. I would have promised him anything, but how could he ask such a thing of a child?

I can barely sit still on the train. It seems to be moving so slowly. Go fast. For the love of God, go faster! I'm longing for him, longing. It's disgusting, it's delightful to want someone so much.

He's standing by the ticket office at the top of the stairs, hands in pockets. Something about him says he's been waiting for a long time. He looks tense, not at all like the easy-going fellow I know. Has he been going through the same torture as I?

'I thought you'd changed your mind. I was going to wait another ten minutes and then come out and get you.'

'I'm sorry. The trains are terrible on Sunday. They always seem to be working on the line.'

I never go anywhere on Sunday. It's my stay

home day, do a bit of painting, write letters, get my clothes ready for the week. A comfortable day at home with Mother. If we go out in the evening it's only for a walk or drinks with friends.

We drive in silence to his house, not bothering with fill-in chatter, glancing at each other now and then, thin smiles. He grabs my hand and we run for the door, laughing. It's too funny, this desperate urgency. We run up the stairs? Run? Only yesterday I could barely walk up them.

'Ah, so there's the lady.'

An elderly man appears in the hall and smiles up at us. We stop dead, like two children caught in the act.

'Ruth, this is my uncle, Graham Ashworth. Graham, Ruth Webster.'

He's not what I expected. What did I expect anyway, a cross between Oscar Wilde and the Marquis de Sade? Graham's a rather frail old man with fine white hair, pale blue eyes set in a sea of wrinkles and a puckish expression. He's half the size of Ian. There's no family resemblance whatsoever.

'You're not rushing her away, are you? Come in for a minute. Let's have a drink.'

Oh no. No!

I turn obediently and walk back down the stairs but Ian grabs me by the arm and hauls me back up. 'Another time, thanks, Graham. You'll be seeing a lot of her.'

'I hope so.' He beams, giving me a long, appraising look. 'Enjoy yourselves.'

I resist the temptation to giggle. Is it that obvious?

Like kids going to a party we run into the bedroom and throw off our clothes. Why did I primp in front of the mirror for ages, trying on scarves and jewellery, when the first thing I do when I get here is take everything off?

I want him in me again and again, in me, in the very centre of me, in my heart, my soul, my being. We make love and sleep wake and love again. It's dark too soon.

'Stay,' he says.

'No, I can't, I've . . .'

'Got to do something terribly important in Guildford tomorrow morning.' He smiles. It isn't a knowing smile or a leer. He understands.

'I'd better go soon, Ian. It'll take ages to get home.'

'Don't be daft, I'll drive you. Are you hungry?'

We prepare a feast, laughing, stopping every few minutes to kiss. He makes a Spanish omelette while I toss the salad and put garlic bread in the oven, great chunks of it dripping with butter. I don't care, nothing can kill me now.

'"A book of verses underneath the bough, a jug of Mosel, a loaf of garlic bread and thou beside me singing in the wilderness . . ." Sing, woman!'

'I can't.'

'Sing or you won't get any supper.'

I'm no performer, I leave that to Matthew. I feel very foolish, raising my voice in a wobbly soprano and singing,

'Under the greenwood tree
Who loves to lie with me
And turn his merry note . . .'
'Unto the sweet bird's throat.'

Ian's voice is as bad as mine. 'Not exactly top of the pops, is it?'

'We used to sing that in music class.'

Sister Augusta. The gentlest and most unworldly of the nuns. I remember Sonia, who loved to stir it up, asking her if 'who loves to lie with me' meant 'lie' in the biblical sense. Poor Sister Augusta. She blushed so hard I thought she'd burst a blood vessel. We never sang that song again.

We curl up on the sofa, hugging each other. It's not easy eating with my left hand but I'm not about to let him go.

Ian glances at the window. 'Blast, it's started snowing.'

I should have worn boots. These pretty shoes were a mistake. The car is cold but he's brought a blanket to wrap round me.

'The roads look very slippery.'

'Stop worrying, I'm a good driver. I've only had six accidents this year and none of them serious, unless you call running over the odd arm or leg serious.'

It's snowing hard now and this draughty little car was obviously made for fine weather. It stalls at every light.

'This is going to be a long journey,' Ian mutters, fumbling with knobs on the dashboard. One windscreen wiper has gone on strike and the other is thinking of coming out in sympathy. This car must belong to one of his impoverished actor friends, it should have been humanely put down years ago.

'Darling, I wish you'd just drive me to the station.'

'And I wish you'd just shut up. Where the fuck is the choke?'

The car stutters and coughs for a few miles and finally sighs to a halt.

'Shit! Now what?'

He leaps out, opens the bonnet and peers inside. He's such a tall man and this car is so low he's practically bent double. I suddenly get a fit of the giggles. He reminds me of that French actor, what was his name, the one in all those Monsieur Hulot movies? There's a hilarious scene where he's bending down, peering at an engine, utterly perplexed. I can see the same expression on Ian's face. You can tell from people's expressions if they know what they're looking for under a bonnet . . . 'Ah, dirty fuel in the carburettor, a leak in the brake cylinder.' Ian is frowning and rubbing his chin, looking very earnest. A sure sign of ignorance.

He gets back in, hair wet with snow.

'Bloody thing's only fit for the scrap heap.' He slams the steering wheel angrily. I'm surprised it doesn't drop off. 'We'll just have to leave it here. I'll come back for it in the morning.'

'Where are we?'

'God alone knows. Norbury, I think.' This is not

the moment to tell him we've been going in the wrong direction but it was my fault too, I should've been looking at traffic signs instead of at him. 'We've got fuck-all chance of finding a taxi.'

'I think I can get a train from –'

'Don't talk wet, there are no trains at this time of night.'

'I think there are.' I scrabble in my purse for a timetable. I have nothing but the return half of my ticket, two five pound notes, a compact and a lipstick. It's the purse of a woman who's used to having a man look after her.

'So now you'll have to stay the night.'

'Oh, Ian, I –'

'Well, you've got a choice, either you stay or I come back with you.'

I don't want all the fuss of putting him up at our house, Mother pouting, Kitty giggling. 'No, Ian, I –'

'Oh for God's sake, Ruth!'

'I can't. It's just . . .' I feel so stupid. How can I explain to him that a forty-four year old woman doesn't want her mother to know she's sleeping with a man. But he's understood.

'Look, tell your mother it's my uncle's house and he suggested you stay for the night. If you like we'll put him on the phone, make him do his quavery old fart in his dotage act, too old to get it up let alone put it in. After all, I wouldn't want her to think her daughter's virginity is in danger . . . Hey, there's a taxi. Come on!'

He gets out, waving his arms.

We abandon the car, bundle into the taxi and huddle together for warmth. I'm shivering. Cold or fear? Am I that afraid of Mother's disapproval? Does she think I'm still a virgin? Does it matter what she thinks? It's pathetic at my age. Girls who work for me, seventeen years old, sleep with their boyfriends, live with them, have babies by them – so why do I feel so ashamed? I'm not a whore, I don't give myself to any man who happens along, only to this man because . . .

'Feeling better now?' He hugs me, kisses my forehead. 'Warmer?'

I pull him down, kiss his mouth. It was meant to be a light kiss but if it wasn't for the taxi driver leering at us in his mirror I swear I'd be flat on my back on this cold leather seat . . . I love you, Ian, I love you. I don't care what anyone thinks. I don't give a damn if they approve or not. I love you.

CHAPTER 18

Graham is delighted we're back. This time he insists we join him for a drink.

The living room is huge, it stretches from one side of the house to the other, and it's comfortably furnished, not starkly modern like Ian's, not chintzy like ours. This one has soft leather chairs, magnificent Persian rugs, their colours glowing in the warm light, lots of oriental pieces, exquisite coffee tables inlaid with mother of pearl, fiercely proud lions and Tang horses, porcelain jars and bowls, a whole wall of books, no paperbacks, a log fire burning in the grate. Graham has surrounded himself with beauty and comfort. I wonder what he thinks of his nephew's austere taste?

I dial our number while the two men roast their behinds and sip Scotch. 'Hello, Mother.'

'Ruthy? Where are you?'

'I'm . . .' Say it. Go on, say it! 'I'm at Ian's. His uncle's, actually,' Coward. 'They're both here.' Please speak up, Graham, so Marmy can hear you and know her little girl's safe. 'The weather's absolutely awful. Ian was driving me home but the car broke down and we had to come back here.' There's a room full of people, honestly, Marmy, crowds of them, I'm not alone with Ian if that's what you're thinking.

'Why didn't you get the train back?'

'I've only got these light shoes on.'

'I could have asked Peter to meet you at the station.' She never liked me staying overnight with school friends either. I always had to be back at the appointed hour, safe in my own bed.

'It wouldn't be very kind to ask him to come out in this weather.' Peter's our very obliging neighbour. 'It's snowing.' I have a mental picture of Peter ploughing through knee-high drifts looking for a lost lamb.

'I know that, dear.'

'I'll be back in the morning then. I'll get the first train . . . Well, not the first but I'll be home as soon as I can.'

They're both listening, Ian and Graham, as I stumble and stammer. A sixteen-year-old would have handled it with more aplomb A sixteen-year-old wouldn't have bothered to phone at all.

'Well now, come over here by the fire, my dear.' Graham hands me a drink. 'When you've warmed up I'll show you my collection.'

Nude boys?

Ian groans. 'Oh no, the price you have to pay just to get a Scotch in this house.'

Now that I'm back in the warm I feel exhausted. My back aches and my head is ringing. I think I

168

could actually fall asleep standing up, like a horse. I'm trying to make intelligent conversation with Graham but I know I sound moronic.

Ian takes the glass from my hand. 'I think I'd better get her upstairs before she drops.'

Graham squeezes my arm. 'I'll show you my collection in the morning.'

'Yes, I'd love to see it.' I'll be gone before he gets up. I couldn't cope with pornographic statues and paintings.

I'm almost too tired to climb the stairs, three flights, I'll never make it. I'll just curl up here on the bottom step, thanks.

'Do you want the rest of this Scotch?'

I shake my head and Ian downs it in one gulp. 'Come on then.'

He helps me undress and get into bed. I'm sleeping naked for the first time in my life, an odd feeling, vaguely immoral. Some time later I wake briefly as he gets in beside me, curls himself round my back, cups my breast in his hand, rests his head in the nape of my neck.

'We should sleep like this for ever,' he murmurs.

Amen to that. Amen and amen and amen.

In the morning he has gone. There's a note on the pillow. 'Gone to sort out the car. Back for breakfast.'

I'm glad he's not here to see me. I was too tired to wash last night so my face is a mess. I shower, shampoo my hair, the new hairstyle is so easy, a quick fluff with the towel, a brush, and it's done.

169

Half past eight. I should be on my way, I promised Mother. But I can't just walk out . . . I phone home, feeling stronger now, more in control, it's amazing how different you feel in the morning, and Kitty answers. 'Just tell Mother I'll be back in time for lunch.' I cut her off before she can start asking questions about my 'boyfriend'.

I riffle through his wardrobe. I'm pretending I'm only looking for something to wear but, of course, I'm looking for evidence of Tasha, a jacket, a pair of shoes, a scarf. I want to feel them, sniff them, find out what kind of person she is. She's becoming an obsession.

I put on one of Ian's sweaters and a pair of jeans. The jeans fit me round the hips but the length . . . I turn them up and up and up. Same with the sleeves of the sweater. I look comic but I feel comfortable. I can pad around, get his breakfast when he comes back, play the little wife . . . I must stop thinking like that. This is just a fun affair, a brief encounter. That film always annoyed me. I thought they should have run away together. Why on earth did she go back to her dreary husband when she could have had Trevor Howard? But then other people's problems are so easily solved, aren't they? And it was only a story.

I make a cup of coffee, ascend the stage front left and take up my position on one of the sofas. Lights, curtain up . . . No, I couldn't live in a place like this. I can't understand how he does either. There must be a side to him I haven't seen yet.

Don't be a clown, there are many sides to him you haven't seen. Just because you've slept with him doesn't mean you know him through and through.

I used to think that when you gave yourself to a man – now there's a coy, old-fashioned expression – you were his and he was yours and you automatically knew all there was to know about each other. Nonsense. Total strangers meet, mate and move on. The body doesn't reveal the secrets of the mind. Not through your genitals, anyway.

What I want now, more than anything, is a cigarette. A cup of coffee and a cigarette, the perfect start to the day. Will I ever get over this wretched craving?

He comes in, his face red with cold, cursing. 'That's the last time I borrow anybody's car.'

'Did you find a garage?'

Withering look. 'I walked miles. They were all busy. Every fucking car in London broke down last night.'

'So where is it now?'

'Where we left it.'

I try not to look shocked. Other people's property is sacrosanct. Whatever is borrowed must be returned in immaculate condition. I hardly ever borrow. And certainly not a car.

'So what are you going to do?'

'I was given the number of an outfit that'll tow it. It's going to cost a bomb to get it fixed.'

'I'll pay.'

'Okay.'

I was quite sure he'd refuse. In my world men pay. But I'm not in my world any more.

'I'll get breakfast. Eggs and bacon?'

'You won't find any bacon.'

'You don't like it?' I thought everyone loved bacon. Just the smell of it in the frying pan, sizzling . . .

'I probably would. I just don't eat it.'

'Oh . . .' The penny drops. 'Are you vegetarian?'

'Right.'

'But you ate chicken and ham pie at our house.'

'It was bad enough being an unexpected guest, Ruth, I didn't want to add to it by being an awkward one who wouldn't eat your mother's food.'

We eat cross-legged on the rug, poached eggs, mushrooms, tomatoes and piles of toast for him, cereal and fruit for me. I overdid it last night, I'd better be sensible today. He never remarks on what I eat, never asks how I'm feeling, never tells me to take it easy. I've almost forgotten about my heart. The palpitations and odd little pains have gone.

After his third cup of coffee he takes his jeans and sweater off me and we lie back and make love. I don't recognise myself any more, this woman sighing and groaning on a rug. I must have left Ruth Webster at home, painting thimbles, going for walks with Rob and Kitty, sipping cocktails at the Willoughbys.

He props himself up on his elbow. 'Yes, I know,

I know, you've got to go. But you must see Graham's collection first. You promised.'

'Oh, Ian, I'm not very clever at art. I mean I can't tell a Cezanne from a seesaw.'

'There are no Cezannes, it's not that kind of collection.' He winks. 'Look, don't panic, they're not that bad really. Well, some of them *are* a bit raunchy, to be honest. They're based on the Kama Sutra – you know, two hundred ways of doing it. The thing is not to blush. If he thinks it's embarrassing you he'll get out some of the really hot numbers and even I feel they're a bit over the top.'

I can't cope. I simply wouldn't know what to do, what to say . . . Ian is on his back, convulsed with laughter, clutching his belly like the laughing Buddha. 'Your face!' he gasps. 'You should see your face.'

'Shut up. Shut up, Ian, it isn't funny.'

'They're bonsai.'

'What?'

'Graham's collection. Little trees, bonsai. He's got dozens of them.' He ducks, narrowly avoiding a well-aimed cushion. 'For God's sake admire them, even if you think they're a travesty.'

'But I think they're beautiful.' I've often looked at bonsai in the florist's. 'I've always wanted one.'

'If he takes a shine to you he'll give you one, but he must be quite sure it's going to a good home. He may even come out and vet your place first, right light, right degree of heat, congenial atmosphere, that kind of thing.'

'They're very expensive.'

'Depends on their age. Most of Graham's are of ancient vintage so they must be worth a few hundred each, maybe more. Not that money is a problem for my uncle. He made his pile in stocks and shares. Shrewd fellow. You'd never think it to look at him, would you? Innocent as an angel, pure as a snowflake. The total opposite of my mother. She tries to act tough but she's a jelly baby underneath.'

'Do they get on well?'

He pulls a face. 'There was an earthquake in the family about forty years ago and we're still suffering from the fallout. Mum hardly ever sees her brother now.'

'Why?'

'She married downmarket and everyone was gutted – well, everyone on her side of the railway lines. My father's a doctor, no aspirations to being a brain surgeon, just a good old quack.'

'I don't call that downmarket.' I can just imagine telling Simpson he was just a good old quack. He'd have pulled out my life support.

'Well the Ashworths did.'

'So what kind of jobs do they do?'

'I have two brothers, one's in the Foreign Office – currently in Bombay or Bangkok, I can never keep up – the other's a silk. I'm the odd one out, need I say?'

'They don't approve of what you're doing?'

'They gave up on me years ago.'

'And your uncle?'

He gives a sardonic shrug. 'Graham's only helping me to give my father one in the eye. Oh, I don't mean he's not a generous bloke, it's just that he loathes Dad.'

'Because he's a doctor?'

'Because he's an upstart.'

'For daring to marry your mother?'

'Graham thinks he took advantage of Mum's naïvete, made her run away with him – elope, as they used to say. It's been Montague and Capulet between them ever since. I sometimes wonder if it was all worth it.'

'Don't you care for your father?'

'He's a good man.'

'That doesn't answer my question.'

Enigmatic smile. 'We're totally different people, we have nothing in common.'

'I think it was cruel.'

'What?'

'The way your mother's family behaved. They sound like . . .' I hesitate.

'Snobs? Of course they are.'

'Has Graham ever been married?'

'Once, centuries ago. There are two kids some-where. They'll no doubt come out of their burrows when the will is read, not to mention a host of other little Grahams from the wrong side of the blanket.'

'I think you're just making him out to be a devil.'

'Let me give you one word of advice, my

love – don't for God's sake bend over to pick anything up when he's around or he'll have you in the family way before you can say ouch!'

'He seems a sweet, harmless old gentleman. He's certainly been very generous to you, letting you have this place for nothing and buying all the furniture.' I wonder why I have to come over as a tut-tutting maiden aunt all the time. It's probably years of practice with Matthew.

'Look, I'm not criticising him, I love the old bastard. And you're right, I'd be living in a grotty bedsit in Catford if it weren't for him.'

'I gather artistic directors don't make much money.'

'I'm what those politically correct nerds call "economically challenged",' he grins.

'So why do it? It's a bit thankless, isn't it, working for nothing?' The banker's daughter talking. Find yourself a sensible job, young man, a position with a future, a pension.

'Have you ever loved something so much that you'd do it for the joy of it?' Yes, I have, Ian, but I didn't have the courage. I went down the correct path, the appropriate path for an unmarried woman in the nineteen-fifties. I realise now, too late, it was a dead end.

He misunderstands my expression. I can tell he pities me – poor old Ruth, her feet are so firmly on the ground she can't look up and see the stars, she doesn't even know they're there.

'What about television?'

'What about it?'

'Well, I'd have thought it was easier.'

'You must be joking. Anyway, I happen to be in love with the live stage. I'd go barefoot and wear rags as long as I can keep working in it.'

He'd go barefoot and wear rags if it weren't for dear old Uncle Graham.

'Are you staying here for Christmas?'

'No, I'll be in Bath for a few days. I like to catch up with my folks once a year just to remind them what I look like, but I'll stay if you want me to. I'll come over to your place.'

Mother on edge, Matthew sneering, Kitty in a twitter.

He reads my mind. 'So come here. We'll spend Christmas together, just the two of us.'

Sounds like paradise.

'I couldn't, Ian.' Absenting myself from the family hearth at Christmas? And talking of family hearths . . . 'I must go home. It's almost eleven.' So much for getting back early.

'One for the road?' He pushes me back on the rug.

'Oh Ian, no.'

'Oh Ruthy, yes.'

CHAPTER 19

I stop on the way out to say goodbye to Graham and take a quick look at his bonsai. They're in the conservatory, a beautiful place decorated in his favourite oriental style, precious pieces, jade, amber, interspersed among the delicate little trees. Huge sloping windows stretch from floor to ceiling letting in the brilliant winter sunshine. But it's so cold.

'I keep them at about three or four degrees all year round,' he explains. 'They're very happy in this temperature.'

'May I touch them?' I nearly said stroke. I want to feel those tiny leaves, the perfect little cones.

'Of course. They love it.'

'Are they very old?'

'This one,' he takes my arm and leads me to a chestnut set apart from the others like a king with his courtiers, 'was born in 1878. It belonged to one of my uncles. He was the one who started me on this hobby.'

'They must be terribly difficult to rear.' I meant grow. I can see Ian smirking out of the corner of my eye.

'You get the knack of it after a while. They need plenty of light, water, fresh air, no draughts, no frost. Pruning and nipping is the real art.'

'I think I'd be too frightened to touch them, they look so fragile.'

'Ah, that's what everyone thinks but you mustn't be deceived by their appearance.' He's passionate about them. That's what he and his nephew have in common, passion. He explains that the Japanese found the inspiration for bonsai in nature. Normal trees growing on the sides of bleak mountains, putting down roots in rocky crevices, buffeted by wind and rain, become stunted.

'Everything is against them but they hang on. They never give up. They put up a braver fight against adversity than many of their bigger brothers growing in gentle, sheltered places.'

'It seems an odd thing to do though, I mean to deliberately grow a tiny tree.'

'You don't find them beautiful?'

'Oh, I do, yes. I think they're wonderful. It's just that everybody seems mad on growing things bigger and bigger today.'

'Bigger and better, at least that's what they think,' he shakes his head. 'I saw a monstrous freak in Waitrose the other day. It looked like a cross between a lemon and a pumpkin. God knows what it tasted like.'

There must be thirty or forty trees here, a forest of mighty midgets with fierce dragons and golden lions sheltering beneath their tiny branches. I wish

I had time to stay and enjoy them but I'm fidgety. I shan't be home till four or five at this rate.

We take a taxi to the station. 'Graham's got a fleet of cars but he won't let anyone touch them,' says Ian wryly. 'They're like his bonsai, something to be admired, not used. I can't understand that.'

'Won't he let you drive them?'

'Not a hope. Well, I suppose he would if it were a matter of life or death.'

'When are you going to Bath?'

'Is there some connection between Bath and death?' he grins.

'It was just a straightforward question.'

'Christmas Eve.'

'Only three more days.' Mother has a fine collection of invitations on her mantelpiece. I still feel guilty about missing Major Fordham's party. 'How long will you be there?'

'I try to duck out early but I'm usually nailed to the spot for a week by my mother. Fair enough,' he shrugs, 'I don't see her the rest of the year.'

A whole week, a whole week without seeing him . . . I buy my ticket, go through the barrier and down the stairs.

'Ruth!' He shouts something at me. I can't hear what he's saying. There are hordes of people coming down, blocking him from my view. I go back up a few steps.

'What?'

'I said I love you.'

The whole station must have heard that time.

People turn and stare. A man laughs and winks at me. 'Lucky girl,' he says.

Lucky girl.

Mother's in the kitchen washing up when I get home. We used to have live-in housekeepers, a couple, the husband did odd jobs. Mother got rid of them when Daddy died. We have a cleaning woman now who comes in twice a week.

'Hello, how are you?' I give Mother a peck on the cheek. Nothing in return. 'Where's Kitty?'

Kitty's always hovering somewhere near her like a little satellite.

'She fell down the stairs last night and sprained her ankle. I think she must have been sleepwalking. I had an awful job getting her up to bed.'

'Has she seen Simpson?'

'He was too busy to come out. Apparently there's a lot of flu around. He said he'd see Kitty if I could get her to the surgery. It's such a pity I don't drive, I feel so helpless when something like this happens and there's nothing I can do.'

I am not going to feel guilty. Why do I have to be here all the time to hold Mother's hand, carry Kitty up and down stairs, drive them to the doctor?

'Why didn't you ask Peter to take you?'

'He's away on business. And I could hardly ask Judith to help, not with her bad back.'

'Well, why didn't you get a taxi?' Oh, forget it. She's not going to let me win this one whatever I say. 'I think I'll go and lie down for a bit.'

'Very well.'

No offer of tea? No sympathy? She hasn't even asked me how I am.

'Ruth.'

'Yes, Mother.'

'I'd be grateful if you could spare me some of your time tomorrow. I have to go into Guildford to do some shopping.'

'But I thought you'd bought all your presents?'

'I was referring to food, dear. We shall be five on Christmas and Boxing Day.' She's already filled the larder to overflowing. There's enough in there to keep us going till Easter. 'Of course, if it's inconvenient . . .'

'Not at all, Mother. When would you like to go, morning or afternoon?'

'Whichever suits you. I don't want to upset your timetable.'

Why doesn't she just come right out with it and tell me what she thinks of me for staying the night with Ian? Have I got to put up with this all over the holidays? 'I'll check my diary, dear. I might just be able to squeeze you into my hectic schedule.' Two can play at that game.

Kitty gets up after dinner. It seems the ankle isn't so bad after all and she and I decorate the living room with holly wreaths and silver cones. We put on a record and sing along with the King's College boys. Mother thaws in the atmosphere of peace on earth, goodwill to women, and brings in a plate of hot mince pies and a dish of thick cream. Has she forgotten I'm not allowed such wickedness?

The Christmas tree is smaller this year, I couldn't cope with our usual eight-footer. We smother it with coloured balls and tinsel, pile presents underneath then sit in front of the fire, watching the sparks paint fairytales on the backplate, sipping hot punch. I can't remember when I've felt happier at Christmas, not even that one twenty-three years ago when Daddy shook Anthony's hand and said, 'Take good care of her. She's very precious.' I was too young to know what happiness or sadness really was. I know now what life can be. My heart attack came just in time.

'Are you coming to the carol service, Ruthy?'

Mother asks the same question every year. And gets the same answer. She goes to church, always has, always will. I envy her her certainty.

'You won't change your mind?'

'No, Mother.'

I don't think I should go to His birthday party in His house when I haven't given Him a second thought all year.

CHAPTER 20

The bridge club afternoon coincides with Christmas Eve this year and there's to be a party during the tea break. There are crackers on the green baize tables and a gift at every place, cushions for the ladies, as usual, and Mother has bought decorative jars of Patum Peperium for the men.

The game is played with the usual intensity but at half time battle lines are broken and troops from both sides rush forward to greet the enemy with hugs and seasonal greetings. Kitty and I, who have been lurking in Mother's sitting room watching a Cary Grant film, go in and add our noisy goodwill. We put on silly hats, pull crackers, blow squeakers in each other's face, ping balloons back and forth and laugh at schoolboy jokes.

Clive Henshaw is in great form, braying his head off. I think he's singing *Silent Night* but I couldn't swear to it. Mrs Pryce is reminiscing about Christmas Past with Mrs Henshaw, who readily agrees that things just aren't the same any more. Mrs Fussel's had too much to drink and wants to dance. She's showing Jane, or is it Jean, how to do a Viennese waltz. Now she's trying to persuade Wolf to dance with the other twin but at fifty-four he's still a shy virgin and needs much coaxing.

There will be noisy arguments during the second half of the game, all the irritations of the year erupting under the influence of Mother's potent punch. They will all huffily change partners, only to slink back to the old ones again in the New Year. Rob and I will escape for our afternoon walk. I don't think Kitty will be joining us. She appears to be incapacitated at both ends, too much alcohol on the knees and the brain. At the height of the fun, if that's the word for it, she touches my elbow. 'I think that was the doorbell, Ruthy. Shall I go?'

'No, I will.' It's probably more carol singers. I'm still wearing my paper hat, a dunce's cap in bright red with streamers sprouting from the point.

'Very becoming,' he grins. 'You always manage to find clothes that match your eyes.'

I was flushed when I opened the door but all the blood drains from my face. I'm still staring at him, my mouth opening and closing like something in an aquarium, when Mother comes out.

'Who is it, dear? Oh, Mr Trevelyan. Do come in.' She is more composed than I am.

They all stop talking and stare at him, glassy-eyed.

'This is Ian Trevelyan,' says Mother, 'a friend of Matthew's.'

'Don't let me interrupt,' he says.

'We're having a party.' Mrs Fussel totters up to him. 'It's our Christmas bridge party.'

'Ah, a game I don't play, I'm afraid.'

He's quite at ease, not at all discomfited by the inquisitive eyes sizing him up.

'I could teach you.'

'Silly old fool,' mutters Henshaw but fortunately Mrs Fussel's a bit hard of hearing. Anyway she's too busy plucking at Ian's sleeve and gazing up at him with a wicked gleam in her ancient eye.

'Will you have a glass of punch, Mr Trevelyan?' I do wish Mother would stop calling him that. 'A mince pie? A piece of Christmas cake?'

'The cake looks delicious. Did you make it?' He knows perfectly well she did.

'I always make my own.'

'Then I couldn't possibly refuse.'

The soft soap has started. Despite herself I can tell that Mother's going to fall for it again.

'That's for you, by the way,' he says in an aside to me, pointing to a box he's left in the hall. 'It's from Graham. You must've made a fantastic impression on him.'

While Mother cuts another slice of cake for Ian and refills his glass – I do hope he hasn't borrowed his friend's car again – I take the box into the kitchen and open it very carefully, terrified that in pulling out the wads of tissue paper I might also tear off a fragile leaf.

It's a tiny bush with a trunk no thicker than my thumb – Rhododendron Simsii Satsuki. Graham has written three pages of instructions for me on how to look after this precious gift – 'always keep the soil moist. Prune the roots every winter. In summer trim the side shoots and pinch out the growing point to maintain a good shape . . .' It's like adopting a child.

The party's under way again. I can hear Ian talking, getting along famously with everyone. They've discovered he's in the theatre so they're telling him about the shows they've seen, the actors they like or dislike. Mother's piling food into him. That's the third time she's said, 'Are you sure you won't have another slice of stöllen?' She's obviously forgotten that he's supposed to be diabetic and so has he.

Kitty hobbles in, wobbles actually, her eyes shining.

'Is that your young man, Ruthy? He's awfully nice. He's . . . Oh Ruthy,' she catches sight of my tiny rhododendron bush, 'isn't that beautiful. How lucky you are. I've always wanted a bonsai.' But they were too big to fit in her pocket. 'Where will you put it, in the greenhouse?'

'No, it's a mess, dear. And some of the windows are broken. The poor little thing would freeze in there.'

'What about in here then?'

'Much too hot. I know, I'll put it in the hall, that's a more even temperature. Oh no, that's no good, what about when we open the front door.'

'Why don't you put it in the bathroom? Plants always grow well in bathrooms, it's all the moisture, and there's a big window.'

'Yes, that's a good idea, Kitty.'

'It's like a baby, isn't it?' She encircles it with her arms. 'Something small and weak to be looked after.'

I'm about to explain to her why bonsai aren't at all weak but a hush from the living room indicates that hostilities have resumed and Ian comes into the kitchen. Kitty stays, chirruping over the bonsai. Ian makes a sign behind her back that I should get rid of her. I'll leave the botany lesson for another time.

'Kitty, dear, would you go and see if anybody wants tea now? I'll put the kettle on.'

She hobbles away, pleased to be of help.

'You should just see the lovely present Ruthy's got,' she cries as she goes into the living room and is greeted with stony silence.

I'm in his arms the minute she's gone. 'I had to see you before I left.'

'I'm so glad you came.'

'I've got something for you.'

'Oh Ian, you shouldn't have.' Such a stupid expression. Why shouldn't he? Why didn't I buy something for him?

'Open it when I've gone.'

'But I've nothing for you.'

'I'll accept a kiss in lieu of.'

I put all my love, all that I feel for him in that kiss. This is the closest to heaven I shall get on this earth, his arms around me, his lips . . .

'Excuse me.'

We spring apart – or, rather, I spring away from him. Mother carries in a tray of dirty plates and glasses. She didn't have to bring them in now. Normally she leaves the washing up until everyone's gone. She bangs the tray down on the counter and turns on both taps full blast.

'Well, I'd better be on my way,' says Ian, pulling a face at me. 'I've got to get to Bath this evening. Goodbye, Mrs Webster.'

'Goodbye, Mr Trevelyan.' She doesn't turn round.

'I hope you'll have a very happy Christmas.'

'Thank you. I hope you will too.'

I can hardly hear her over the rushing water, the clatter of plates. She'll break all her precious bone china if she goes on like that.

I go to the door with him. 'How did you get here? Did you take a taxi from the station?' Stupid of me, he doesn't have the money for taxis. He must have walked. 'I'll drive you back.'

We drive in silence and park the car.

'Ian, I'm sorry about that. Mother . . .'

'Let's not talk about it.' He puts his arms around me. 'We can talk later. We'll have all the time in the world to talk later.'

What does he mean 'all the time in the world'?

The car park's deserted but somebody might come along at any moment, a neighbour, one of the professional gossips . . . 'And there they were, the two of them, wrapped round each other, I would never have believed it of Ruth Webster. And at her age!'

'I want you. God, I want you so much.'

'Not long now, my darling. Just a few days.'

'I'm like a schoolkid. I can't even sleep at night.'

'I love you, I love you.'

Too soon the train takes him away. The winter sky is cold and grey, the trees bare. Why didn't I ask him to stay? Why didn't I go with him?

I suddenly remember his gift. I have it with me, thrust in my pocket. It's some little bauble, of course. After all he can't afford much. But it's the thought that . . . Now I sound like my mother. It's quite heavy, a paperweight perhaps? I take off the wrapping. A little face beams up at me, its belly twitching with laughter.

He's given me his jade Buddha.

CHAPTER 21

Uncle Frank always arrives at nine o'clock on Christmas morning. He sets out in the middle of the night in his old banger 'to avoid all those cars and coaches tearing down the motorway. You'd think it was Le Mans the way some of them drive.' I can't remember a Christmas when I haven't run to open the door to his cheery face. He puts his boxes under the tree with the rest of the presents. We'll open them later when Matthew arrives.

Neighbours come in for a drink, Mrs Greer, the Turners, the McLaughlins. 'Drop in about eleven if you can spare a minute or two,' says Mother every year, and every year they arrive on the dot, decked out in their best. They'll leave just as promptly at twelve as if someone had shouted, 'Time, gentlefolk, please!'

I wear another of my new outfits, a trouser suit in shades of lavender, and am much admired.

'Ruth, you look wonderful.'

'You're so slim.'

'That colour really suits you.'

I shrug and mumble something mildly disparaging about myself, lapping up their flattery.

'I thought you were supposed to be sickly,' says Uncle Frank, looking at me with obvious admiration. 'Heart or something, your Mother said.'

'Oh, I'm fine now.'

'I think you're a fraud. You just wanted a long holiday,' says Peter Turner.

'I only wish I could wear my hair like that,' says his wife. 'It's taken years off you.'

'I think old Simpson's giving her monkey glands.'

'Come on, Ruth, tell us where you've found the elixir of life. We could all do with a couple of gallons.'

I give them the kind of smile that made the Mona Lisa famous. I'll bet she had a lover too.

'When are you going back to work, Ruth?'

'I'm not.'

'Ruthy's left her job at The Trust,' says Mother.

'I was pushed out actually.'

This causes a minor commotion, cries of 'That's disgusting' and 'How unfair after all these years.'

'You were offered another job,' insists Mother.

'Chief Bottlewasher.' I can laugh about it now. 'Grade Five.'

The Trust did me a favour. I feel like writing old Bridgey a thank you note with copies to Valerie Pierce and whatever his name was, the genius who dismantled my department. In a couple of years another genius will come along and put it back together again. How pathetic, how unimportant they all seem now. 'As a matter of fact I'm going on a cruise, the Caribbean.'

Cries of approval this time. Mother goes out to baste the turkey. Kitty limps after her. I don't know why I said it. I don't want to go. Two weeks away from Ian . . . I'll cancel it. I'll lose my deposit but that doesn't matter.

Matthew arrives just after three, true to form. Pity the pubs open on Christmas morning, they must ruin many a Christmas dinner. He makes his entrance stage right, bellowing a carol. He's brought a girl with him, another of his adoring little dollies, I can hear him introducing her to Mother and Kitty. There's no suggestion of an apology. It doesn't even occur to him that he should have phoned first to check that it was all right to bring a stranger on such a family occasion.

'And this is my big sister Ruthy.'

'Ruth, actually. Hello.'

I hope I don't look as surprised as I feel. She's quite different from the usual run of girls Matthew picks up. She has blonde hair cut so skilfully that whichever way she turns it falls back into place, and hazel eyes with long, long lashes. They must be false, surely? She is very small and perfectly proportioned like a Dresden doll but I know, even before I take her beautifully manicured hand in mine, that this lady is not made of fragile porcelain.

She's dressed in a kimono, black with a dragon picked out in red and gold beads on the bodice, its tail stretching around her waist and down the back of the skirt. You have to be very confident to wear something like that.

'Hello, Ruth,' she smiles. 'I'm Tasha. Tasha Page.' She has a beautiful voice too, very low, smoky. Men must love it.

I'm aware of Matthew watching me closely. He must be enjoying every moment of this.

'Hello, Tasha.' I shake her hand warmly. 'I'm delighted to meet you.' Her smile sparkles. Mine positively dazzles.

'Christ, Ruthy, what've you been doing to your-self, you're all tarted up? And the hair. Where's the permed mop we all know and love? You look like Britain's answer to Liza Minelli.'

'Thank you for the compliment . . .' which, of course, it wasn't.

'Painted away the grey too, I see.' He stands on tiptoe, making a great show of peering at the top of my head. 'They've done a nice job.'

Poor Matthew, he was hoping I'd have an attack of the vapours, run out of the room in a storm of tears when he introduced me to Ian's beautiful young girlfriend. I've disappointed him.

'You've got boils on your neck again, I see.' He was plagued with an erupting skin all through his adolescence. 'Still, I'm sure they'll go when you grow up.' I sweep past him into the living room and pour myself a drink. My hands are shaking.

I have a spiteful tongue, as spiteful as his when needs be.

'Oh, we've found a bit of bite, have we?' he shouts after me. 'Now I wonder where we got that from, eh?'

I suppose I shall have to put up with the hints and taunts all through Christmas. But it's only a bit of fun, he'll protest when challenged, lost your sense of humour, have you? Sticking in the knife under the guise of mirth and jollity – it's such an old trick.

Now I know why Ian loathes my brother. Did Matthew poach his girlfriend or did she go willingly? I keep imagining her with Ian in that flat. She probably wanders around as he does, naked. She must be exquisite, no bulbous breasts, sagging thighs, stretch marks where the fat has disappeared. They meet, smile, touch, two beautiful, strong young bodies, he draws her close, kisses her, pulls her down onto the rug . . .

'Kitty, darling, what have you done to your ankle, you silly girl?' 'Uncle Frank, still smoking that filthy pipe? You must have half the farmyard in there.' 'Marmy, what a feast!' My brother fills the house with noise. He's always on stage – look at me everybody, listen to me, me, me or I'll throw a tantrum.

We open our presents. I get a bedjacket from mother – very appropriate, a silver penholder from Kitty – wonder if I should take it back to Fortnum's and leave it on the counter when

195

nobody's looking with a note saying sorry? There's a cigarette case from Uncle Frank – poor dear, he didn't realise. Thank God there are no cigarettes in it or I'd really be in trouble. Nothing from Matthew. He hasn't brought any presents, not even for Mother.

'Just couldn't afford it this year.' He pulls the linings out of his pockets. 'Empty,' he grins. 'Sorry.'

Don't you worry, baby boy, Marmy will fill them for you.

Dinner is a difficult time for me. Uncle Frank can't understand why I keep refusing roast potatoes, chestnut stuffing, bread sauce . . . 'No Christmas pudding, Ruthy? How about some trifle then? Oh come on, a little can't hurt you, you're thin as a rake.'

It wouldn't be so bad if I didn't long for all these delicious things. I have such a sweet tooth and Mother always surpasses herself at Christmas. All I can offer my drooling taste buds is a banana and yoghurt. Plain, low-fat, skimmed milk yoghurt.

Uncle Frank smothers his pudding in cream. Matthew and Tasha have seconds of everything. Mother is delighted to have such hearty appetites at her table again.

Kitty's enchanted with Tasha. She can't stop looking at her, touching her. 'Aren't they lovely, Ann?' she keeps saying to Mother, admiring Tasha's jet earrings, her bangles, her rings. 'I've never seen anything so pretty,' she says, running her fingers over the tiny beads on Tasha's kimono. 'Where did you buy it, dear?'

Kitty will be decked out in kimonos for the rest of the year. I can see it will be the new craze.

'I didn't buy it, I made it.'

'Made it?' Kitty squeals. 'How clever of you.'

'Well, it's my job. I design costumes for the theatre.'

'Oh, so you're in the theatre too.' Kitty gazes at her like a little girl, stars in her eyes. Tasha is the fairy on the top of the Christmas tree. 'You must meet a lot of famous actors and actresses.'

Tasha nods and smiles.

'What are they like?' Kitty leans towards her, eager to hear all about these exotic creatures.

'Oh, ordinary, really. A lot of them are quite empty people, they only seem to come alive when they act.'

Kitty's disappointed. Matthew doesn't look very pleased either. Ordinary? Empty? He sees himself and his fellow thespians as supermen, giants bestriding the world, not earthbound nonentities like bankers. He's always having a dig at them, although it's a banker's money that supports him and probably will for the rest of his life. When Mother dies Daddy's estate will come to Matthew and me. I don't know how much it is, Mother has never said, but Daddy was a very shrewd investor. Matthew will blow his share and prowl around me for handouts.

'Now, you all go away and leave me to do the

washing up.' Uncle Frank says the same thing every year and gets the same reaction.

'Good heavens no, Frank. You go and relax.' He needs to, poor fellow, after an exhausting morning sitting in the armchair reading the paper and drinking cups of coffee followed by glasses of sherry brought to him by Mother and Kitty.

At Christmas our dishwasher is suddenly pressed into active service. It must be a terrible shock to its system after lying idle all year. Tasha begins to rinse and stack the plates.

'There's no need to do that, dear.' Mother shoos her out of the kitchen. Apparently Tasha is another person in dire need of relaxation. Matthew is already stretched out on the sofa. I long ago gave up the battle to make him do something in the house. And Mother never even tried.

'Isn't Tasha lovely?' says Kitty dreamily.

Mother nods agreement. 'I'm glad Matt's found a nice girl at last. I only hope he holds on to her.'

'So do I.' I didn't mean to say it so forcefully. They both turn and look at me, surprised. They don't know who Tasha is, of course, and I'm not about to tell them.

'Are there any more glasses in the living room, Ruthy? Go and see, dear, will you?'

Uncle Frank's snoring contentedly in the armchair, Matthew and Tasha are lying on the sofa, their mouths glued together, his hand kneading her breast. I collect the glasses, clinking them together noisily. Matthew unwinds himself, glares at me, takes Tasha's hand and leads her up the stairs.

'Which room are we in, Marmy?' he yells.

'The same as last time, dear.'

They stumble up the stairs, pausing to kiss again half-way.

The washing up done, the kitchen and dining room tidied, the fire made up, the rest of us sink into lethargy until tea time. Kitty falls asleep on the sofa, Mother in the armchair facing Uncle Frank. Even Rob is too full of turkey to move.

I go to my room. I'm too keyed up to sleep – how could my brother bring Ian's girlfriend here? – but if I take a pill I shall be out for hours. I'll read for a bit.

As I flip through the pages, only half concentrating, I suddenly become aware of a noise, a rhythmic creaking coming from the room above . . . Oh no! That's all I needed.

Damn Matthew. Damn him!

CHAPTER 22

Kitty wakes me at seven to say that supper is ready. I'm not hungry and I don't feel like facing them, especially Matthew and Tasha, but I can't let the side down, not on Christmas Day. It'll be over soon, anyway. Only four more days and Ian will be back.

Mother has laid out a buffet in the living room, the remains of lunch plus as many sausage rolls, mince pies, cakes and biscuits as the table can hold.

'What a spread,' cries Uncle Frank, rubbing his hands gleefully as if he hadn't eaten for weeks. Tasha comes in, smiling, followed by Matthew, scowling. I've lived with my brother long enough to recognise all his moods immediately. The boisterous bonhomie has gone. He'll be sullen for the rest of the evening.

'Shit!' He slaps a hand over his mouth when he sees the table. He doesn't give a thought to how hard Mother has worked, the hours of baking she's done. She's put so much into it, looked forward to this day, but Matthew will spoil it. Again.

'It all looks absolutely delicious, Mrs Webster,'

says Tasha. She seems to have the knack of ignoring Matthew's boorishness but then she hasn't had to put up with it for years and probably won't, despite Mother's and my fervent wish. 'All home made? How clever you are. I wish I could cook.'

I suppose Ian does the cooking. Soufflés, Spanish omelettes, ratatouille, eggplant parmigiana – he pretends he's just an amateur, throwing a few ingredients together and hoping for the best, but everything he makes tastes wonderful. And there's no fuss, no performance of the kind that surrounds Mother when she's in the kitchen. But then cooking is Mother's whole existence, to Ian it is a thing apart.

Tasha looks wonderful after an afternoon of making love, soft and glowing, the way Mills and Boon think a woman should look. I wonder if Graham's taken a shine to her? What man wouldn't? My eyes are puffy from too much sleep and I've made them look even worse with make-up.

Uncle Frank loads his plate with cold turkey, ham, sausages. Tasha shakes her head, she's had enough meat – how did she get along with her vegetarian lover, I wonder? – but she'd adore one of those exquisite meringues, they look so divine, what a marvel Mother is. Kitty takes a meringue too, gazing at her idol as she eats, matching her mouthful for mouthful. Matthew's offended that he should even be offered anything.

'Don't keep stuffing it down my throat,' he snarls at Mother. 'I'm not a bloody goose.'

'Ruthy?' she turns to me, her face impassive. If he hurts her – of course he hurts her – she never shows it.

'I'll have a small slice of Christmas cake please, dear. It's so good.' I don't want it, I shouldn't have it, but I'll eat it if it kills me.

'Let's play games after supper,' says Kitty brightly.

'Oh Christ!' Matthew groans.

Kitty looks dashed. 'I meant charades, that kind of thing. Charades would be fun, wouldn't it?'

'Oh sure, a laugh a minute. And afterwards we could listen to some of Marmy's 78s,' he sniggers. 'Glen Miller's my favourite. What about you, Tash? Or would you rather foxtrot to Victor Sylvester?' He pulls her to him and tries to whirl her around the room.

'Oh, Matt!' She pushes him away, laughing.

'I'd like to play Monopoly.'

'Yes, yes, Monopoly.' Kitty claps her hands excitedly.

'Uncle Frank will play, won't you? It's easy, you'll enjoy it,' I say as he starts to protest. 'Tasha?'

'Of course,' she says, not looking at Matthew.

'Mother?'

'Oh, come on, Ann,' says Kitty. 'There are six of us so we can divide into . . .'

Matthew switches on the television. 'Good,' he says, standing in front of it, arms crossed, legs astride, 'the movie's just starting.'

'We're going to play Monopoly, Matthew.'

'I'm not stopping you.'

'We can't play with the television on.'

'So go in another room. This isn't the only bloody room in the house.'

I'm trying very hard to stay calm. I don't want to spoil Christmas for everyone.

'It's *The Day of the Jackal*,' says Kitty, her eyes already glued to the screen. 'Have you seen it, Frank?'

'What?'

'*The Day of the Jackal*.'

'We've all seen it, Kitty. About a hundred times,' I snap.

'Turn it up a bit, Matthew darling,' she says. 'I can't hear.'

I get up and leave them all watching the film. If I go into my bedroom I shall just get into bed and fall asleep. The perfect escape. I'd like to sleep right through until Monday. Mother won't mind if I use her sitting room. I haven't done any painting for a while . . . No, damn it, I will not spend Christmas evening painting thimbles. I wonder what Ian's doing?

'Mind if I come in?' Tasha peers round the door.

'Of course not.'

'I've seen enough television.'

'Me too. Would you like to go for a walk?'

'Great idea. I could do with some fresh air.'

I look doubtfully at her floor-length kimono. She laughs. 'Have you got something you could lend me, an old pair of jeans, a sweater?'

I've never possessed jeans but I do have an assortment of trousers, all of which will be far too big for her. But even a sack would look Gucci on her.

We take Rob. I warn Tasha about him but 'he's so sweet, he's got such lovely sad eyes' and she insists on holding the leash even though he's pulling her shoulder out of its socket.

We walk in silence for a while, glad to be out, breathing the cold night air. There's no one about, the lane is in darkness save for the lighted windows glowing at the end of long, dark driveways. The Willoughbys have put a huge Christmas tree in their garden. The Turners have gone one better and covered their copper beeches with twinkling lights. Suddenly I feel much better. I could walk and walk – all the way to Bath.

Tasha's wearing a light coat, belted loosely, but she doesn't seem to be cold. There are so many things I'd like to say to this girl, so many things I want to ask her. Instead we shall chatter amicably about her job, my job, her interests, my hobbies . . .

'I hear you're seeing Ian Trevelyan.'

Well, she's gutsier than I am.

'I'm . . . er . . . Yes, I have seen him once or twice.'

'He's a nice guy.'

'Yes. Yes, he seems very nice.'

'We lived together for three years, you know.'

My heart is fluttering madly. Is she telling me he's

her property? Is she warning me off? 'Are you interested in the theatre?'

'Yes, very, but I don't know much about it . . .' apart from reading our local library's copy of *The Stage* from cover to cover every week. I wouldn't dare have it delivered to the house.

She laughs. 'By the time Ian's finished with you you'll know everything about it.'

By the time Ian's finished with you . . . In the last scene of *Carmen* the orchestra plays three or four bars that sound like a death knell warning her of her doom. I can hear them now. By the time Ian's finished with you . . .

I shudder, drawing my collar closer around my face. 'So cold,' I murmur.

'Would you rather go back?'

'Of course not.' I move out of reach of her helping hand. 'Don't you enjoy the theatre then?'

'Oh, I adore it. Absolutely. But I like to get away from it too. When I get home I just want to flake out, talk about something else.'

I know what she means, Ian does go on and on about it. But that's one of the things I love about him, his enthusiasm. I must ask her, but I don't know how to put it, so I might just as well come right out and say, 'Did you and Ian have a row?'

'Yes. Of the blazing variety.' Little smile. 'We were always bitching at each other about something, you know what it's like when you've lived with a man for a long time . . .' I don't but I'd love to. 'But this time it was different because I'd fallen in love with Matt.'

'I suppose Ian was very upset.' I try to sound indifferent. I want to know all about it, every word that passed between them, but I mustn't let her think I'm pumping her.

'It's difficult to know with him. He yells and screams but it's all over in a minute and he goes back to his own world again. It's only the theatre that really matters to him. He's determined to be a great director and he won't let up until he's reached the National or Stratford. He wants to see his name in lights, the critics raving, the world at his feet.'

It sounds more like Matthew than the Ian Trevelyan I know. Is she right or is she just being acid? Lovers who've recently split up are not famed for their honeyed words.

'I hadn't thought of him that way, craving for fame, I mean.'

'No, no, don't get me wrong, he doesn't want fame. He wants recognition as a first-rate director, which he is, and he'll move heaven and earth to get it. It's the only way to be. If you're not you might as well get out of the theatre. But he's a lovely man and I still love him very much in my own way. It's just that Matt has . . .' she hesitates, looking for words to describe what my baby brother has done to make her give up a man like Ian, 'he's kind of bowled me over.'

I suppose it's difficult for any woman to imagine

her brother bowling another woman over. There are too many memories of him in nappies, then his knees covered in cuts and bruises, then his face covered in spots . . . Matthew's good-looking, not in a conventional way, but he has boyish charm, oh yes, he has that in abundance. And he must be sexually attractive, he's had enough girl friends.

'I find him very exciting,' Tasha laughs.

Even in the darkness I can see her eyes shining. So it's Matt's performance in bed that's hooked her. And when the thrill of whatever happens between the sheets has worn off? When she's fallen out of lust with him – and knowing my brother's ability to destroy relationships I don't think that's too far off – what then?

'Do you live in London, the centre I mean?' Anywhere near Hampstead is what I really mean.

'I've found a flat in Putney. Do you live here or do you have a place in town?'

I've lived in this house, in this road, in this village most of my life, Tasha, but I'd rather not admit it, not to you.

'I'm looking for something in Camden Town.' Really? That's news to me.

'That's fabulous.' Tasha is impressed. 'I have loads of friends there. Which part?'

'Oh, I'm looking at a house . . .' A huge Victorian with Fay Weldon on one side and Alec Guinness on the other, we glitterati like to stay together. 'What are you working on at the moment?' I'd better shut up about Camden Town before she discovers I hardly know it.

'I've got a play starting at the Lyric in January. Lots of fabulous costumes, very 1920-ish, but it's becoming an absolute nightmare. My director, a total maniac, keeps adding bits or taking them out. This is the first day I've had off in months – can you believe it? And just when I thought everything was done that wretched man called me in the middle of the night and said he wanted . . .'

She tells me all about that wretched man, whom she obviously worships, their quarrels, their laughter. I can't help smiling to myself, watching her lively face, the eagerness in her voice, she's as much in love with the theatre as Ian is. They must get along famously when they're not 'bitching' at each other about something, the way people do when they've been together for a long time.

Matthew is waiting in the driveway when we get back, hacking at the gravel with the heel of his shoe. He's in such a pout it's funny.

'You've been long enough,' he snarls at Tasha.

'It's such a beautiful night, Matt, so clear. Just look at all the stars.' She must be really infatuated with him not to lose her cool. Or does she enjoy being kicked around? Maybe it's a novel experience, maybe that's the attraction. 'We walked and walked and talked and talked, didn't we, Ruth?'

'Let's go.'

'But –'

'Come on.' He takes Rob's leash from her hand, puts it in mine, and pulls her towards the car. 'I've loaded our gear.'

'At least let me say goodbye to everyone, Matt.' She tries to wriggle out of his grasp. 'I can't go without thanking your mother and –'

'I've done all that. Come on, Chrissake, get in.'

'But what's happened?'

'What d'you mean what's happened? Why should anything have happened?'

'Matthew!' He stops short, turns to look at me, eyebrows raised. 'You can't go yet.'

'I'll go when I bloody well like.'

'You will not go when you bloody well like, you ungrateful little sod.' Mother expected him to stay until Boxing Day. He always does. She'll be heart-broken if he leaves now. 'It's about time you grew up and stopped being so selfish.'

For one moment he looks taken aback, then he clutches his ribs – the ham actor all the way – throws back his head and bellows with phoney laughter.

'Shut up!' I loathe his laughter more than his sullenness. Whenever I lost my temper with him as a child he always laughed, taunting me. 'I said shut up, d'you hear? Shut your mouth or I'll shut it for you.' I take a swing at him but he's too quick. He grabs my wrist and pushes me to one side. I stumble over Rob, who's frightened by this paroxysm of rage and barking furiously.

'Whatever's happening? All this shouting. Come inside, for goodness sake, all of you.'

'It's all right, Marmy, we're going.' Matthew looks at me with mock pity. 'But you'd better take Ruthy indoors before the poor old thing goes completely bananas.'

'You bastard!'

'Ruthy, please, it's Christmas.' Mother takes my arm.

'Christ almighty, I've never seen her so lively,' Matthew jeers. 'Nothing like a good screw to buck you up, eh Ruthy Wuthy?' My heart starts to pound. 'You watch out for him, old girl, he'll lay you and leave you, mark my words.' Tasha frowns, starts to say something to him but he shouts her down. 'You know what they say, Ruthy, there's no fool like an old fool and I suppose you've got to get it where you can at your age.'

I'm going to kill him. I'm going to put my hands round his throat and . . .

'Come along, dear.' Mother, afraid that we're about to become another 'domestic' statistic, grabs my arm and holds on tenaciously. Matthew roars out of the driveway, gravel flying, and waves gaily to us as he turns into the lane. Tasha looks straight ahead, her mouth set in a tight line. Somehow I don't think that relationship will last the night.

'Come along, dear, come along. Frank!'

My uncle lumbers out and puts his arm around me. Between them he and Mother almost carry me into my bedroom. I'm aware of Kitty fluttering around making little whimpering noises. 'Poor Ruthy,' she keeps saying. 'Poor Ruthy.'

'Pills, Frank. On the dressing table. Kitty, get some water. Breathe deeply, dear, just keep breathing deeply. Kitty, go and get the water. Now! You're all right, dear, you're all right.'

Mother holds my head while I swallow the pills and gulp down some water. Frank and Kitty hover, their faces swimming in and out of my vision.

'I'll sit with her for a while.' Mother waves them out of the room. When they've gone I turn my head and sob into the pillow, tears of shame, humiliation. I'm aware of her stroking my hand the way she did when I was in hospital.

The sedatives are beginning to work. Drowsily I watch her pull the curtains and turn out the lights. She stoops over me, kisses my forehead. As she opens the door I see Frank and Kitty in the hall, silhouetted against the light from the living room.

'How is she?' whispers Frank anxiously.

'Poor Ruthy,' whimpers Kitty. 'Poor little Ruthy.'

CHAPTER 23

T hank God I'm excused all the parties on account of what Mother calls, I've heard her say it so many times, 'a slight setback in Ruth's health.' She refuses to go herself. I've tried to persuade her but it's useless, she will not leave my side. I'm allowed up provided I venture no further than the living room and once there I'm swathed in rugs, my every wish attended to. I no longer care.

I wish . . . I don't know what I wish any more.

'There's no fool like an old fool.' The words haunt me. I see Matthew jeering, his mouth wide open, back arched, roaring with laughter.

I've put the laughing Buddha in a drawer out of sight. I must give it back to Ian. No, I'll send it, I don't want to see him any more, I can't. The whole affair's so shabby. 'Nothing like a good screw to buck you up.' Matthew's right, that's all it is. And how did Matthew know about it? Did Ian tell him? Has he told everyone he's found this sad old woman in need of a good screw? God, I feel such a fool.

Ian has phoned every day. I know it's him

because Mother's voice becomes cold and clipped as if she's getting rid of a persistent salesman. She tells him I'm sleeping and can't be disturbed.

Sunday. He comes back from Bath tomorrow.

'I think I'll go away for a bit, Mother, just a few days. I'd like some sea air. I'll go down to Mildred's.'

'Yes, she'd like that, dear.'

'I'll drive down in the morning, make an early start.' Six, seven o'clock, before he's awake, before he phones me again.

'Take plenty of warm clothes with you, Ruthy, you know how cold it can be on the coast at this time of year.' Colder still in my aunt's house, a dark, dreary place overlooking a leaden sea. It will suit my mood admirably.

Mother packs for me, duvet, electric blanket, hot water bottle – just in case the socket in my room doesn't work. I'm too lethargic to argue. I'd take the bed too if she could get it in the boot.

'Kitty, would you like the bonsai?'

'Of course I'll look after it for you, dear.'

'I meant would you like it for yourself, as a present?' I cut short her protests, offer no explanations. 'Here are the instructions for looking after it.'

'I'll take good care of it, Ruthy. Promise.' Leaving it with Kitty is as good as throwing it in the dustbin, she'll drown it for a few days then forget about it. Graham would grieve if he knew what was about to happen to his beautiful little rhododendron but I can hardly send it back to him.

It's snowing when I leave. I'd like to take Rob for company but Aunt Mildred has three yappy, snappy Yorkshire terriers that wouldn't take kindly to an intruder.

'Drive carefully, dear. Stay on the motorway. They say the roads are treacherous.'

The countryside's magnificent and I have it all to myself. I drive along minor roads, I'm in no hurry to get there. I'm just glad to get out of that house. I can't stand the coddling any more, the sympathy, the looks Mother and Kitty exchange behind my back. And I jump every time the phone rings. I can't talk to him. What can I say? Go away, leave me alone, can't you see how degrading it is, a middle-aged woman getting a cheap thrill from a younger man? Have I become as desperate as that?

Mildred is like Daddy, a nervous, wiry person. She's lived alone for years and loves it. She's seventy-six but spryer than someone half her age. She has no time for sickness or malingering. There's nothing a brisk walk along the front can't cure.

She's put me in a room overlooking the sea. The windows are wide open and the cold is biting. I wanted to suffer, to scourge myself for my sins, but not this much. Summoning every ounce of courage I close the windows.

'You keep that house of yours too hot.' She

speaks in a high-pitched staccato, punctuating every sentence with a nod of the head. 'You're like a couple of tropical plants, you and Ann.'

'Kitty lives with us now.' I tell her about the shoplifting, the depression.

'I'm not at all surprised. She's a fool of a woman, won't face up to life, never would. Thank God she didn't have children, she'd have made an appalling mother. And how are you? I must say you're looking better than I expected. A strict diet, I suppose, plenty of exercise? Good. You've got your mother's frame, unfortunately, but a few more pounds off the hips and you'll be trim enough.' But never a dry old twig like you, I hope. 'I'm an early riser, I'm usually up and about by six. I'll bring you a cup of tea, if you like, though of course I never touch it myself.'

She drinks cold water all year round. It's difficult to believe she and Daddy came out of the same womb. He loved Mother's cooking, a Scotch or two before dinner, Turkish coffee and a cigar afterwards.

'I'm glad you arrived early. You can come to Sainsbury's and give me a hand with the shopping.'

Oh goody, Aunt Mildred, that's just what I want after a long drive.

I intended to go for walks by the sea on my own. I want time to think, to grieve, to try and get things into perspective, but whenever I appear with my coat on my aunt drops whatever she's doing, pulls on anorak and wellies and insists on joining me. Has Mother told her to keep a constant vigil? What does she think I'm going to do, throw myself off Beachy Head?

'Glad to see you're so fond of walking, Ruth. Not like your brother. He came down once.' And only once. 'I couldn't get him out of the house. Lazy little wretch stayed in bed half the day. What's he doing now? Still that theatre nonsense?'

I wonder where Matt and I get our love of the theatre from? Not Daddy's side of the family, that's for sure, but Kitty loves anything to do with putting on a show, playing charades, dressing up. I'll bet she'd have loved to go on the stage but, like me, never dared say it. They'd have drawn and quartered her, too.

Mildred strides along, forcing the pace, and we engage in brisk discussions about the decline of moral values, the unions – 'quite disgusting how they're holding the country to ransom. I'd shoot the lot of them' – the rise in the crime rate, the curse of the unemployed . . . She inherited a size-able sum from her father and married a wealthy old man who obligingly died a few years later, swelling her coffers. There's no sight of the money, however. She certainly doesn't spend it on herself, nor does she give it to her family. Her presents to us have always been in the soap and socks range. I'd rather hoped she might be a secret philan-thropist, distributing alms to the poor but . . .

'I agree with Mrs Thatcher, people today are

always looking for hand-outs. They should learn to stand on their own two feet.' She's lucky that her two feet are so well shod – and not because of anything she's done either.

She's heavily involved with volunteer work. Old people are her speciality. 'You should come with me on my home visits, Ruth.'

Yes, that would really set me up, Aunt Mildred. An afternoon with some sad old woman living in one room with nothing but memories to keep her warm. I'd put my arms around her and we'd weep our hearts out. Mildred, on the other hand, must do a splendid job – 'Stop whinging. Pull yourself together!' It must be a great comfort to them.

We're up at dawn and early to bed. There's no television and if I dare to tune to any station other than Radio Three I'm frowned back into my seat. I didn't bring any of my light romances, I've had my fill of that particular sedative, but there are plenty of edifying books in my aunt's library – Macaulay, Trollope, Thackeray, the complete works of Dickens. I make a start on *The Old Curiosity Shop*.

By the third day I've had about all I can take of boiled fish and parsley sauce, hot water that passes for tea, the laziness of young people today, the yapping Yorkies and the cloying sweetness of Little Nell. But I must hold on, just a little longer. I'm safe here, hidden. He'll never find me . . . But what if he isn't looking? What if he doesn't give a damn anyway?

New Year's Eve passes without celebration in bleak house. Aunt Mildred doesn't believe in it. 'It's just an excuse for people to get drunk and make fools of themselves.' Some of us can do that without getting drunk.

This chill sea air has certainly put colour in my cheeks and the spartan life has stiffened my spine . . . Oh God, I'm beginning to sound like her. If I stay here much longer I shall start looking like her as well. I thank her kindly for her hospitality, give her a farewell gift, a pot plant the florist assured me would survive in Arctic conditions, kiss her leathery cheek and go.

Mother gives me a very warm welcome and Rob runs round in circles, barking himself hoarse.

'Oh, we did miss you, darling, we did,' cries Kitty, hugging me with tears in her eyes.

It's good to be home.

CHAPTER 24

I wake the following morning with a dry throat and throbbing head. The change from Mildred's morgue to this hothouse has been too abrupt for my system.

'You'd better stay in bed, dear. I'll bring you some lemon and honey.'

Damn! Just when I was on my feet again.

I stagger out of bed and look at myself in the mirror, bleary eyes, runny nose . . . Happy New Year, Ruthy. 1979's off to a brilliant start.

Kitty comes in with two letters for me. One is from a friend who went to Australia for a holiday after she left school and never came back. She's had two husbands and three daughters, or it might be the other way round, and is about to embark on a career as a model – promoting fashions for the fuller figure, if the photographs enclosed are anything to go by.

Mother brings in hot lemon, aspirins and Vick's Vapour Rub – perfect gifts for the woman who has everything. I hand her the letter, she likes to know what my old school friends are doing.

'Paula was always empty headed,' she says.

I rip open the second envelope. There's a sheet of paper folded once, handwriting I don't recognise, a very bold, rather jagged script that fills the page – 'Darling,' My heart lurches. 'I've dialled your number so often my finger's worn out. Your mother gives me the brush off. To put it bluntly, and she does, she thinks it would be much better if I pissed off. Apparently I'm only making you unhappy??? Please phone – at least let's talk about it. I love you.'

Mother and Kitty are watching me, waiting to share the letter. I want to leap out of bed, do a mad dance around the room. To hell with Matthew, to hell with Tasha. To hell with the lot of them . . .

'It's from Ian. I must give him a call.'

'Ruthy.' Mother puts out a hand to stop me. 'Ruthy, don't you think . . . ?'

'Pass me my dressing gown, will you, Kitty love?' Her ankle is better, I notice. She flits around, getting my dressing gown, my slippers, twittering on about my boyfriend.

Mother leaves the room, her face a thundercloud. I know she's worried that I'll be hurt. I know she's only trying to protect me. But I'm forty-four for God's sake. She had no right to tell him to stay away. And as for making me unhappy . . . I dial his number, clutching the phone with a sweaty hand.

'Hello, it's me.' I can't say much. Kitty's standing right next to me. She has no tact, poor love, and

I'm sure Mother's straining to catch every word though she's pretending to work in the kitchen. 'I've been staying with an aunt for a few days.'

'Why did you go? You didn't tell me you were going.'

'I'll tell you about it later.' I'll never tell him. It was just another stupid shouting match with Matthew. When he's in one of his moods he says the first thing that comes into his head.

'Look, Graham's having a bash here tonight. Come over.'

I feel rotten, my head's full of wet sponge, it's my first day home and Mother's given up a dinner party tonight to look after me.

'Oh, Ian, I can't.'

'Please, love.'

'It's so difficult.'

'Please. I must see you. I'll come out and get you.'

'No. Meet me at the station as usual.' As usual. Old friends, old lovers, our routine well established. 'What time shall I come?'

'Right now. This very minute.'

'Seriously.'

'I am serious. It's been so long since I saw you.'

'I'll be there after lunch, about three o'clock.'

'Are you going to see your boyfriend?' says Kitty when I hang up.

'Darling, he isn't . . .' Oh give up. Anyway he is. 'I'm going to a party his uncle's giving.'

'Oh lovely. What will you wear?'

I hadn't thought of that. Graham's party – that means a lot of smart, sophisticated people. I can't turn up in green taffeta or looking like a Grecian urn. One of my new outfits? But they're not right for a party. Oh to hell with it, I shall just have to buy something. Back to my friend in Guildford.

'We had quite a rush for New Year's Eve,' she says, 'but I think we can find something you'll like. You've lost more weight, haven't you? You must be the only person who's lost weight over the holidays,' she laughs. 'I think this would suit you.'

She shows me a dress in brilliant flame with the lowest neckline I've ever seen, even on Liz Taylor. I love it but I haven't the confidence to wear it. I'd spend the whole evening with a wine glass stuck in my cleavage. I send her back to look again.

'May I ask what kind of party it is?' Cocktails with a dowager duchess, she means, a fund-raising dinner for the Guildford Tories, or a rave-up with the local jet set?

'It's a friend who lives in Hampstead. I imagine the people he's invited will be –' little nude boys and girls '– mainly young people, theatrical types.'

'So it's a bit trendy?' Trendy? Me, going to a trendy party?

'Of course, ethnic is still very fashionable.' The earth mother look. No thanks. 'Then how about this?'

Black trousers, very full, a low-cut matching bodice, a gold-sequined over-blouse. I pay another ransom note and leave. Mother is nowhere to be seen when I get home.

'She's lying down,' says Kitty, perplexed by her sister's behaviour. 'She says she's got a headache.' Not very original. Mother and I have never been protagonists though. I wish she'd be happy for me.

I show Kitty my new outfit and she is enchanted. She wants me to put it on but I'm feeling too tired. All this excitement plus my wretched cold are sapping what little energy I have. I must stop off at the chemist on my way to the station and buy something stronger than aspirins. I don't want anything to spoil this evening . . . Oh no, if I take drugs I won't be able to drink.

'May I try it on, Ruthy?' Kitty says.

'Of course, dear. Only do be careful, won't you, I think the bodice could rip quite easily.' I meant the overblouse but obviously bodice-ripping is on my mind.

While I wash my hair Kitty in a state of great excitement takes off her dressing gown, she's hardly out of it these days, and puts on the trousers and top and swirls in front of the mirror, squealing with delight. 'It's so glamorous! It's so –'

'Ssh! Be quiet, Kitty, you know Mother's got a headache.'

It's no use, she's off in fairyland dancing with a handsome prince and I can't bring her down to earth. Why should I try? She doesn't have much pleasure any more. Poor little Kitty, it's a dull house for her.

'Are you going to put it on now, Ruthy?'

'No, put it back in the box, will you, dear? Use lots of tissue paper.'

There's no answer when I knock on Mother's door. The room is in darkness, the curtains pulled tightly shut. She's lying on the bed with pads over her eyes.

'Mother . . . Mother . . .'

She's pretending to be asleep but her eyes are watchful behind that cotton wool blindfold. I creep out and close the door softly behind me. I would have liked to kiss her goodbye. I would have liked it if she'd said enjoy yourself, Ruthy, make the most of your life while you can, you're only middle-aged once.

Kitty hugs me at the front door and starts to sob, burying her face in my shoulder.

'Darling, what's wrong?' I stroke her hair, trying to soothe her. How can I leave her like this? I phone Ian, I'll be a little late. He's suspicious. 'I am coming, darling. I promise. It's just that there's a little problem here.'

'Your mother . . . ?'

'No, no, I'll tell you later.' I seem to have so much to tell him later.

I make tea for Kitty and sit with her on the sofa. She's trembling, the cup clattering against the saucer.

'What's wrong, dear? Why are you so upset?'

It's the New Year, full of memories, places she used to go with her husband, parties, dances, all gone now. 'I keep thinking about him in that cold ground, Ruthy. He's all alone.'

She starts sobbing again and I cry with her. Am I crying for her or for myself? All the misery and frustration of these past few days comes flooding out.

'Oh Ruthy, I'm so sorry upsetting you like this.'

'Kitty, love, I must go, I've got to get the train.'

'Of course. Have a lovely time, darling.'

And what about you, Kitty, alone here with my angry, sulky mother? What kind of a time will you have? I feel afraid for her. She's so confused by the hostile silences, frightened by the outbursts of temper. I ought to stay with her. I could tell Ian I'll see him tomorrow or . . . No! I won't keep putting off my life.

'Tomorrow and tomorrow and tomorrow creeps in this petty pace from day to day . . .' I was in *Macbeth* at school. Funny that fragment should come back to me after so many years. 'And all our yesterdays have lighted fools the way to dusty death.' I was one of the witches. Type casting, Matthew said.

'I'll be all right, darling,' says Kitty. She gives me a reassuring smile, a bit wobbly but brave, and pushes me to the door. 'Have a lovely, lovely time with your boyfriend.'

I don't agree with Mildred, I think Kitty would have been a wonderful mother. She's so loving, so forgiving. And if she'd had children I'm sure she wouldn't be so childish herself.

I repair the damage to my face in the train. My new outfit's in the box, my dressing gown and toilet bag too. Stupid of me but I don't want to turn up on his doorstep with an overnight bag. In case the neighbours see? Do Hampstead neighbours give a damn who sleeps where and with whom? Does anyone any more?

I'm strung half-way between the suffocating cosiness of the house in Surrey and the exhilarating freedom of the flat in Hampstead. Which way shall I go, forward or back? Or shall I stay in limbo for ever?

CHAPTER 25

He's waiting at the top of the stairs, pacing up and down.

'Very nice.' I admire the long red scarf he's wearing. 'A present from Santa?'

He wraps it round my neck, uses it to pull me towards him, kisses me, not a hello peck but a kiss full of the frustration of ten tedious, wasted days. 'Why didn't you tell me you were buggering off like that?'

Before I can answer he kisses me again. Everyone must be looking at us.

'Let's go and I'll tell you.'

'I've got Simon's car.'

'I thought you said you'd never use it again?'

'After all I've paid out in repairs?' After all I've paid out, but let's not split hairs. 'I practically have half shares in the damned thing. Get in.'

On the way I tell him about my stay with Mildred, making up an excuse for going, a tiff with Mother about something inconsequential.

'Why didn't you wait till I got back? You could've stayed with me, silly cow . . .' He stops, shakes his head. 'No, of course you couldn't. That's what the fight was about, wasn't it? She hates my guts.' I open my mouth to protest but what's the point. 'She sees you as her little cub to be protected from big bad wolves like me, doesn't she. No wonder she stopped you marrying that other bloke.'

'Anthony? Oh no, it wasn't like that. She was practically out of her mind with grief about Daddy. She didn't know what she was doing.'

'Don't keep making lame excuses for her, Ruth.'

I've never thought of Mother as possessive. But there were signs, now that I look back, even before Daddy died, the little criticisms of Anthony, the suggestion that I should wait till I was older, I was too young to know my own mind . . . She only had my best interests at heart, of course, better to break it off now than regret it later. But what Mother said never had much effect on me in those days. It was Daddy who mattered.

'And when he died you took his place.'

'It was my fault not hers. I should've married Anthony and kept an eye on her from a distance. It's just that I felt so . . . so responsible for her.'

'Guilty is the word, Ruth. Guilt. It's their stock in trade.'

'I couldn't leave her on her own, not after Daddy . . .'

'She didn't give you much choice from the sound of it. I hate clichés, Ruth, but the one about aprons and strings does rather spring to mind. And she's made sure the knots are tied pretty tight.'

'She only wants me to be happy.'

'Oh, sure. As long as being happy means spending the rest of your life with her.'

'I could leave if I wanted to.'

'Come on, Ruth,' he scoffs, 'you couldn't leave her then and you can't leave her now. Look at you, you're all in knots because she's giving you a bad time over me. D'you really think you could look her in the eye and say "Mother I'm leaving you" – without floundering around in a sea of guilt, I mean?'

She has Kitty now. Kitty will never go back to living on her own again, she can't, she'll stay with Mother till the end of her days. Mother doesn't need me any more.

'Of course I could.'

'Good.' He pulls up in front of Graham's ginger-bread house, switches off the ignition, pockets the key and sits for some time, staring ahead. Then he turns to me and puts his hand over mine. 'Do you love me, Ruth?'

'You know I do.'

'How much?'

'More than I thought I could ever love anyone.'

'And I feel the same about you. Come and live with me.'

'Oh no, I couldn't.' I pull my hand away.

'But you just said . . .'

'No, I . . . I love you, I do, but I . . .'

'Oh, I see.' His face breaks into a grin. 'You couldn't live in sin, you mean?' It's a huge joke.

'Ian, I'm forty-four. I'm a bit old for that kind of thing.'

'Here we go again.' He gets out of the car, thrusts his hands in his pockets and glowers at me.

'It's all right for kids, Ian, but –'

'It's all right for big boys and girls too, *Ruthy*.'

'Just listen to me for a minute, will you? I come from a very straight, middle-class family . . . All right, so it's hilariously funny, we're pathetic old fossils –'

'Not you, Ruth. You've just allowed yourself to be sucked into –'

'But I am, I am like that. I can't help it. It's the way I was brought up.'

'Hats, stockings, gloves, home by ten o'clock or Daddy will scold, a chaste kiss on the doorstep . . . All right,' he holds up his hand to stop my protests, 'so what are these very straight, middle-class values you live by?' We're in the house now. I do hope Graham can't hear us. 'Well?'

A convent education for a start. Then a lifetime with Mother, her values, her morality, her sense of duty . . . It's so easy for him. There are no walls around his world, no rules, no catechism.

'Well?'

'Oh, Ian, I . . .'

'Let me spell it out for you – marriage, a *naice* house,' he mocks, 'with four bedrooms, three kids, two dogs and one car . . . OK, if that's what you want, I'll buy it.'

'What do you mean?'

'Let's get married.'

'Don't be so silly.' I shouldn't have said that. He's angry. 'I'm sorry. It's just that . . .' I shake my head, mumble something incoherent.

'Do you love me?'

'I've just told you . . .'

'If I were say, forty-nine instead of twenty-nine, would you marry me?'

'But you're not forty-nine.'

'Just answer the question, Ruth.'

'But if you were forty-nine you wouldn't be the same person.'

'That's a load of balls and you know it.'

I wish he wouldn't shout. What if Graham's listening?

He pushes me into the conservatory and closes the door.

'Look, it's quite simple. If I were forty-nine, would you marry me? Look at me.' He takes my face between his hands. 'An honest answer, for Christ's sake. Would you?'

'I don't know.'

'You do know.'

'Well, all right, yes, I agree if you were forty-nine I probably would, but –'

'Good, that's settled then.' He gives me a hug that nearly crushes all the breath out of me and opens the conservatory door. I reach out and grab his arm.

'It isn't settled, Ian. Just stop and think a minute,

darling. The difference in our ages may not matter to you now but –'

'You're absolutely right.' He shakes me off.

'When I'm older –'

'I'll be older too.'

'But you deserve better.'

'Better?'

'I mean, you should have a normal marriage.'

'What the hell are you talking about?'

'Well,' I'll play my ace now, 'children.'

Apparently fertility in women plummets after about thirty-five. Of course there's always a chance of getting pregnant in your forties but it's one in . . . Oh, I don't know. A lot.

'Ruth, you may not have noticed, out in very straight, middle-class Surrey, but some people – in fact, a hell of a lot of people – don't want children. And as far as I'm concerned there are too many people on this bloody planet as it is – so we'll be doing the world a favour.'

Trumped! I've no other cards up my sleeve. 'Ian, I don't know . . .'

'Well, I'll leave you here for a bit until you do. The cool air should clear your brain.'

Before I can stop him he closes the door of the conservatory and locks it, grinning at me from the other side.

'Ian, please!'

He presses his nose against the glass, flattening it, and crosses his eyes. This is ridiculous. He mouths something at me.

'What?'

'Marry me!' he bellows.

'Don't be so . . .'

'If you call me silly again . . .' He clenches his fist and waves it at me. 'Say you'll marry me or I won't let you out.'

'It's freezing in here.'

'Of course it is. You'll probably die of pneumonia.' He turns and walks away.

'Ian!' Now I'm yelling.

'What?'

'Please let me out. This isn't funny.'

'Say you'll marry me.'

'Ian, please . . . !'

'Say you'll marry me.' He stands there, hands in his pockets, a smug smile on his face. He'll never give in, it isn't his style.

'Well?'

Oh God what am I going to do?

'Well?'

'All right.'

He strides back and puts his ear against the glass. 'All right what?'

'I will.'

'You will what?'

'I will marry you.' What am I saying? The criticism, the jeers, the gossip I'm letting myself in for. I shall keep the village tongues clacking for years.

'Remember,' he points to the forest of little bonsai behind me, 'you said that in front of all those witnesses.'

I'm shaking so much I can hardly stand. 'It's this wretched cold.' It's shock. 'I've got a fever.'

'Come on.' He helps me up the stairs. 'Bed's the place for you.'

I can't believe it. I've agreed to marry him. I'm going to be Mrs Trevelyan.

CHAPTER 26

It's past eleven when I wake up, sweating heavily. I can hear voices, laughter. The party is well under way.

'How're you feeling?'

'Grim.' I'm boiling hot, my throat is swollen and when I try to get out of bed I feel sick. 'You go, Ian.'

'Not without you.'

'But I can't.'

'Then we'll stay here.'

'Oh darling, please.'

'I said we'll stay . . .'

'Oh, all right, I'll get up . . .' There's a tremendous shout from downstairs, people cheering. 'What on earth's happening? Are they playing a game?'

He glances at his watch. 'Midnight. It's Graham's birthday. They're bringing it in in style.'

'His birthday? Why didn't you tell me? I haven't got him anything.'

'Just give him a big kiss, he'll love that. I'll go and get some champagne.'

I must go down, if only for a few minutes. Graham has been so kind to me. I feel very ashamed about his bonsai . . . Oh Lord, he's sure to ask me about it and I'm such a bad liar. I drag myself out of bed, shower, drench myself in Vent Vert, comb my hair and flop into a chair exhausted. I'm dizzy with fever and my mind is in turmoil . . . I'm going to be married. Married! It doesn't matter how many times I say it I still can't believe it.

Without thinking I pick up the phone. It's a long time before Mother answers.

'Hello, dear, it's me.'

'Ruthy, what's wrong?' I've frightened her. In our house the phone only rings after midnight with bad news. 'Where are you?'

'Nothing's wrong, dear. I'm at Graham's.'

'Who?'

'Graham, Ian's uncle. He's having a party, I told you.'

Silence.

'It's his birthday.'

Silence.

'Mother, I've got some marvellous news. Ian and I are going to get mar –'

'I'm very tired, Ruth, I'd like to get back to bed. Good night.'

There's something so insulting about the buzzing of a dead line, like a long raspberry. Ian comes back with a bottle of champagne, three glasses and Graham.

'What's wrong?' he bends down, looks into my face.

'Nothing, it's this wretched cold. My nose won't

stop running. Happy Birthday, Graham. I won't kiss you, you don't want my germs.'

I don't think germs or anything else would bother him at the moment. His eyes have a glazed look and he's swaying slightly in the breeze.

'You'll never believe it but I brought in ten crates of Bollingers, ten, and those drunken yobs have almost guzzled the lot. I've managed to keep some for you though, my dear. Here,' he fills a glass to the brim and weaves towards me, 'take this with you while you get dressed. And hurry up, everyone's longing to meet you.'

I go into the bathroom sipping champagne, deliriously happy one moment – I'm going to be Mrs Trevelyan! – terrified the next. I think I've become schizoid, Guildford Ruthy and Hampstead Ruth are battling it out inside my head. Another sip of this champagne and . . . Ah yes, Hampstead Ruth is taking over. Long may she reign!

I struggle into my trousers and top. Just getting dressed is exhausting me but I'm determined to go to the party, Cinderella will go to the ball . . . No, not Cinderella any more, those days are over.

'Magnificent!' cries Graham throwing his arms around me and kissing me despite my health warnings. He takes my arm, I think he needs to hold on, and escorts me down the stairs. There seem to be hundreds of people milling around and I'm so plugged up the noise they're making rebounds in my head, like swimming underwater. He introduces me but I can barely hear a word anyone's saying so I just keep nodding and smiling and making the occasional bland comment like the Queen on a walkabout.

Leather in various shades of black seems to be all the rage in Hampstead this winter. And miniskirts, most of them worn by women whose legs would look more at home on a Jacobean table. I'm sure she knitted that dress herself, it looks like a big string bag . . . He's definitely wearing make-up, I can see where the foundation ends . . . That's a nightie, I know because Kitty has one just like it . . . Imagine dying your hair that colour . . . I can see right through her top and, Good Lord, I can see right through the skirt too and she hasn't got a stitch on underneath . . . That's my outfit over there. Damn!

'And this is a dear friend of mine,' says Graham, introducing me to a very strange creature. I don't know if it's male or female. 'Natalya.' Ah, thanks for the hint, Graham. 'Madame is a sculptor,' he says, kissing my hand and disappearing into the crowd.

Madame gives me a searching look that goes on and on. I don't think she's admiring my bones. At this rate we shall stand here looking at each other all night. I must think of something to say, something witty, sophisticated, but all I can think of is . . .

'Do you sculpt?'

Well, I'm glad she kicked off, anyway.

'No, I'm afraid I don't.' It's the standard response of the British middle classes. We say it without thinking. Sorry. Excuse me. I'm afraid. Why should I be afraid? I don't want to sculpt, never have, never will.

'But do you enjoy sculpture?' She sounds like Garbo, the same accent. I'm so stuffed up I sound like Donald Duck. 'Does it excite you?'

'Yes.' No. And I certainly don't like all the modern stuff, reclining figures with holes where their stomach should be.

'What, specifically?'

What does she mean, the sculptor, the style, the period?

'Rodin.' Good choice. 'I particularly enjoy Rodin's work.'

'Which piece?'

'*The Burghers of Calais.*' It's the only one I can dredge up on the spur of the moment. Didn't he do *The Thinker* too, or is that someone else?

'Why?'

It's so noisy in here. 'I'm sorry I can't hear you very well.'

'Why do you particularly enjoy *The Burghers of Calais*?'

If I'd known there was going to be an exam I'd have swotted up. 'Because it's . . . I think it's superb.'

That didn't score me any points.

'It isn't his best work.'

'Isn't it?'

She gives me another long, searching look, sighs deeply and walks away.

'Madame is a right pain in the arse, isn't she?' says someone standing behind me. 'That's the trouble with sculptors, they all think they're mini-Michelangelos – and come to think of it, he was a right pain in the arse too.'

He's a young man, half my age – why do I keep thinking like this? – long hair, a bit scruffy, not dressed for a party, not this one anyway.

'She's certainly intimidating.'

'Yeah, she tried it on with me. I told her I used to chip away at blocks of limestone but then I grew up.'

'Do you really feel that way about sculpture?' Have I found a soul mate?

'Course not, I think it's brilliant but I was no good at it. That's why I'm a scenic designer. It's the only thing I can do.'

'A scenic designer, how interesting.'

I sound like someone making small talk for the sake of it, which is precisely what I'm doing. I know nothing about sculpture or scenic design. I'm completely out of my depth here. Where the hell is Ian?

'It's okay, we can talk about the weather if you like.'

Oh God, am I that transparent? 'I'm sorry, I'm not a very arty person.'

'Arty?' he laughs. 'No, neither am I.'

'I mean I don't do anything . . . well, apart from . . .' Shut up. He does not want to hear about the ancient and noble art of thimble decoration.

'Apart from?'

'I paint. A bit.'

'A bit of what?'

Oh well, here goes. 'Thimbles.' All right, have a good laugh and get it over with.

'Really?' He actually looks interested.

'Oh, it's nothing, it's just something I enjoy doing, it passes the time.'

'It must be challenging trying to express something on such a tiny surface.'

'It is. That's what's so fascinating about it. I could never work on a huge area, the way you do.'

'Couldn't you? Take a look at this room. Imagine it's a stage. What would you do with it?'

'I don't know what you mean. It's a party, I'd . . . I'd just . . .'

'Sure it's a party, everybody enjoying themselves – or are they? The couple over there had a right ruck before they came, you can tell from the body language. This bloke on our right with the bald head and pony tail fancies that bloke's wife. The tart with the tits is a transvestite, only the bloke chatting her up doesn't know it yet. So, would you still leave the scenery as it is?'

And I always thought I was so perceptive.

'No, I'd make it express the underlying tension. I'd . . . er . . . I'd use colour. Not these lovely rich colours, I'd use something jarring like black, white, scarlet . . . Yes, yes, black and white with scarlet spots, blotches – Oh, what's the word?'

'Bloodstains. You obviously see this party

becoming violent. I'd better leave before the action.'

'And I'd have a piece of – Oh, I don't know, furniture, something completely out of character like a – I know, a piece of modern sculpture, all holes and jagged edges, something that makes you feel uneasy because you can't understand it.'

'Not bad,' he nods. 'That's not bad.'

I'm about to mumble something self deprecating when he says, 'I'm working on *A Doll's House* at the moment. What would you do with that?'

'Oh well, a gilded –'

'No. No cages. They've been done to death.'

And obviously not a doll's house either, unless . . . 'I'd paint the set just like the inside of a doll's house.' He's about to stop me again but I've got the bit between my teeth now. We scenic designers don't like being interrupted. 'I'd make it really sugary sweet, all pink and frilly,' and lots of embroidered silk cushions,' but I'd make the dolls bizarre. I'd give them broken bodies and confused, frightened little faces.'

'That's not a bad start for someone who isn't arty,' he laughs. 'Maybe you should come and work with me.'

'Where do you work?'

'Everywhere. I'm a freelance. I've just finished a set for the slavedriver.'

'The . . . ?'

'Ian, our host's nephew. D'you know him? He's . . . What?'

A woman shouts at him from the other side of the room, points at her watch. 'Oh shit, we've got to go, babysitters. Look, here's my card. What's your name?'

'Ruth Webster.'

'Give me a call some time, Ruth, I'd like to have a chat with you – and I mean a chat not a chat up, not with a wife, a mortgage and ten-month old twins.' He pulls a face. 'Cheers.'

I hate being alone at parties. I stand there, in a sea of chattering, laughing people, all of whom seem to know each other, trying not to look like a baby that's been left in a railway station in a handbag. I paste an inane smile on my face. Oh no, Madam Natalya's coming back. She wants to chisel another lump out of my morale. But there's Ian . . . I beckon frantically to him.

'Where've you been?'

'Where have *you* been?'

'Oh Christ, we're into the old married routine already,' he grins. 'Come on, let's dance.' In the sitting room a dozen couples are wrapped around each other in the semi-darkness swaying to the music of the Beatles. 'Sorry about this,' he says. 'It's one of Graham's little failings. He's stuck in a boring time warp.'

'But I love the Beatles.'

'Oh shit!' He pushes me away from him, a look of disgust on his face. 'Have I made a terrible mistake?'

I close my eyes, nestle in his arms and we sway

along with the rest. He murmurs the words of the song – '"Why she went away I don't know, she wouldn't say. I said something wrong . . ." Did I?' He pushes me away again, looking at me searchingly.

'Did you what?'

'Why did you go away, Ruth? It wasn't just a row with your mother, was it?'

'It was Matthew.' I have to tell him, I don't want there to be any secrets between us. 'He was very spiteful.'

'About me?'

'He said you were just using me, that you would . . .' The words stick in my throat, 'that you would lay me and leave me. That's exactly what he said.'

'He's a lovely bloke, your brother.' His hands tighten around me for a moment, an involuntary spasm. So he'd like to strangle Matthew, too. 'Pity he wasn't left out on a barren hillside in the blazing sun at a very tender age.'

'You didn't tell me about him and Tasha.'

He shrugs. 'I didn't care about Tasha going but I was hacked off when I heard she was shagging a creep like Matt.'

'So why did you stay friends with him?'

'If I started bearing grudges in this business, Ruth, I'd end up not talking to anyone.'

'Did you tell Matthew that we were . . . ?' Shagging each other. I can't quite get my tongue around that one.

'No.' He grins. 'I'm not a fuck-and-tell man. But even Matt can put two and two together and come up with something approaching four.'

'She's very attractive, Tasha.'

'How do you know?'

'Matthew brought her home for Christmas.'

'What?'

'Mother was delighted he'd found such a nice girl at last but I can't understand why she –'

'Look, there must be something more interesting we can talk about than your brother and my ex-girlfriend.'

I can understand how he feels. It must be hard to live with a woman for three years and then she goes off with someone else, even though you're no longer in love with her.

'Ian, I think I'm going to be sick.'

The lavatories on both floors are in use. There's nothing for it but a dash back to the flat, my hand over my mouth. He holds my head while I retch into the basin, undresses me quickly, helps me into bed, then goes off to get me a hot drink and aspirins . . .

I'm on that train again, that long, empty train. I'm so frightened I can't breathe. I know what's going to happen. The tunnel's up ahead. I must get out of this compartment. I fumble with the door handle but it won't budge. I hurl myself at the window, banging, punching with clenched fists, but I can't break it. I can't –

'Help me! Help me!'

'All right, Ruth. All right, you're here, you're here with me. It's all right, love.'

I cling to him for a long time, my heart pounding. 'Just a stupid nightmare. I have it all the time.'

He brings in water and a towel and washes it away. 'Want to talk about it?'

'No.' I don't even want to think about it. It's part of the old Ruth, the old life. I want to bury it. 'What time is it?'

'Almost one.'

'Is that all?'

He laughs and rolls up the blinds. Sunlight pours in. I've been lying in this dark room dreaming of death when outside the world is ablaze with life.

'What can I get you?'

'Tea. Lots of it, please.'

'Coming right up, lady.'

Will it be like this in years to come? Will he wait on me when I'm old? He comes back with a pot of tea, two mugs and a pile of toast.

'Oh, Ian, I couldn't . . .'

'Fine, because it's for me.' He stretches out on the bed. I sip the tea but I can't taste it, my mouth is so foul. 'Feeling rotten?'

I nod and wish I hadn't.

He gets off the bed. 'I'll let you sleep. Do you want me to close the blinds?'

'No.' No more darkness. 'What are you going to do now?' I mean don't leave me and he knows it.

'I'm going to sit by the window and read. If you

need me I'll be right here.' He kisses my forehead, strokes my cheek. 'Don't make such a big deal of it, love. It's your nightmare, remember, your plot, your script. Why don't you rewrite it? Give it a happy ending.'

I doze on and off all afternoon. Every time I swim back to the surface he's sitting in the same place by the window.

'What are you reading?'

'Scripts.'

'For something you're going to put on?'

He shrugs. 'I like to see what new writers are doing.'

The next time I wake the room is in darkness save for a small reading lamp by his head. I watch him for a long time until he feels my eyes on him and looks up, puts down the sheaf of papers and crosses to the bed. 'More tea?'

'Something cold, please. My throat's so dry.'

'Graham's been up a couple of times to see how you are. He's very taken with you. I'm afraid when my back's turned he's going to make a play for you.'

'Oh shut up. And all that nonsense about him and little boys. You're such a liar.'

'No, no, I just find the truth boring. But apart from that one tiny flaw I'm perfect.'

'And you're a clown.'

'Could you learn to love a clown?'

'I already do – No, Ian, don't. Don't be a fool. You'll get my cold. Ian!'

CHAPTER 27

I dream of Kitty, Kitty falling through space, twirling round and round like a top. I keep trying to grab her but she slips through my hands. Ian is up and dressed when I wake.

'What time is it?'

'It's eight of the clock and all's well. Except for Ruth.'

'No, I'm feeling a bit better. Are you going out?'

'Yes, a meeting.'

'Sounds very businesslike.'

'We're thinking of starting a new group. It's not much more than a pipe dream at the moment, probably nothing will come of it, but talk's cheap. Look, I must go.' He gives me a very husbandly kiss on the cheek. 'I'll tell you more about it when I get back. I've instructed Graham to come up every hour on the hour to check you're still alive. Don't look like that, only joking. Anyway if you need him just shout. He's a good bloke, he'll come when called or stay discreetly in the background.'

'When will you be back?'

'A couple of hours, I imagine.'

'You'll be back for lunch then?'

'Sure.'

I fall into a sweaty sleep when he goes, floating to the surface, sinking down again. A discreet but persistent series of little knocks wakes me up.

'Only me.' Graham's cherubic face appears around the corner. 'Sorry, there's no door to knock on. My nephew doesn't approve of such old-fashioned things. Shall I go away?'

'Oh no, please.' I run my fingers through my hair. It feels like greasy seaweed. I'm beginning to smell revolting too.

'Can I get you something to drink?'

I point to the jug of lemonade Ian has left by the bed.

'Oh, I thought that was a sample for the doctor. Well, it's good to see you laugh, Ruth, you must be on the mend. Perhaps I could get you something to eat. I'm a passable cook, not as good as Ian, but usually what I produce is edible.'

'Ian said he'd be back for lunch.'

'I was referring to tea, what my grandmother used to call high tea, since it's almost five o'clock. Don't look so distraught, my dear. Illness is very disorienting, you lose track of time. Ian's gone to the theatre, I suppose?'

'A meeting . . .'

'Ah, a meeting.' He sits on the end of my bed. 'My nephew has been known to go to a meeting and not return for days. His record was just over a week.'

'But he said he'd phone if he was going to be late.'

'He never phones, believe me. Ian is full of good intentions but once he gets involved in anything to do with the theatre the rest of the world just slips away. I hope you're a patient woman, you'll need to be. What kind of a meeting was it, do you know? A new play?'

'No, he's getting together with some people to –'

'– form a new group. Yet another one.' He shakes his head. 'He'll come back all afire about it but by the end of the week the whole thing will have fizzled out like a Catherine Wheel in the rain – I know, I know what you're thinking, what a cynical old tit this man is, he's lost all his zest for life, but frankly, Ruth, there's no room for another of those fringe groups. And I'm not saying anything to you that I haven't said to Ian. There are dozens of them, all over the place, and all starving. Nobody wants to go and see that slice of life stuff any more. And it's always the nastiest slice, have you noticed, the bit that's covered with mould.'

I mustn't laugh. It would be disloyal.

'Have you seen any of his productions, Ruth?'

'No, I was supposed to but . . .' We stayed here and made love instead.

'They're very good, I don't deny it. But not enjoyable. I go to the theatre to be entertained and if there's a little medicine in with the sugar I don't mind as long as I can't taste it. But my nephew has no time for that. Everything has to be deeply meaningful . . . Oh dear, why did I use that ghastly Americanism?'

'Ian seems very dedicated.'

'Dedicated? He's obsessed. But I'm tiring you, I do apologise.' He gets up. 'Are you sure you won't let me bring you something to eat, a sandwich, a scone? Very well. If you should need me,' he produces a tiny silver bell from his pocket, 'just ring this. It's small but piercing. I shall hear it wherever I am and come running. Your devoted slave, Ma'am.' He salaams and leaves.

Sleep again, a disturbed sleep, troubled thoughts whirling around my brain. Ian hasn't phoned and he promised he would. What if he does stay away for days, weeks at a time? Could I stand the uncertainty of a life like that? Daddy was always so punctual, phoning to let us know even if he was going to be ten minutes late.

I force myself out of bed and have a shower. A liberal dusting with talcum powder, a drenching with Vent Vert and I smell if not feel much better.

He comes in just before midnight. 'Oh love, I'm so sorry. We didn't even stop to eat, people just kept bringing in Danish and coffee.'

'I'll go and get you –'

'No, I'm not hungry,' he pulls me back. 'Christ, Ruth, I think we've really got something going this time.' He's so excited he paces up and down, slamming his fist into his hand as if he's punching all obstacles out of the way. Apparently they've

251

rounded up some of the best people in London. With so many theatres black and others foundering there's a lot of talent going begging.

'I believe in the star system, Ruth. Audiences want to see their favourite faces and those faces want to be seen because if they're out of the spotlight too long they're history. People have very short memories.'

'But could you afford to pay the kind of money they want?'

'So my idea is to put old established actors together with new writers.' He didn't even hear me. 'There are some brilliant playwrights around but nobody's got the guts to use their work. The big guns, the National and their ilk, only back those who are already half up the ladder – and then they have the nerve to pat themselves on the back for "discovering and encouraging brand new talent". Bollocks!'

'But will the top actors want to appear in plays written by unknowns? And will they work in the fringe theatre for a pittance?'

From the expression on his face it's obvious he considers me a blanket of the wettest consistency.

'Look, how many times have you said whatever happened to old so and so, I haven't seen him for ages? The answer is old so and so is resting, which is a polite way of saying he's hanging around, chewing his fingernails to the elbow and wondering when the bloody phone's going to ring . . . Oh yes, believe me, even the greats have their bad patches. D'you know, only fifteen per cent of actors are employed at any one time? Don't you think the other eighty-five would jump at the chance of being seen in something worthwhile, even if the dosh wasn't up to West End standards?'

'But they can work in rep. There are a lot of good provincial theatres like Chichester and –'

'But that's the point, love, they're provincial. I'm talking about a theatre close to the centre of London at provincial prices. The West End puts a hell of a lot of money into a production and then they've got to charge the earth for seats just to break even. We could stage things on a shoe-string and offer the public cheap seats. In other words, West End quality for fringe prices.

'We'd start performances much earlier too, maybe seven o'clock, so people can come straight from work and get home at a decent time or have a meal afterwards. The present system's stupid when you think about it. There isn't time to eat before the performance, especially if you live or work outside London, and everything's closed down afterwards, except for a few supper clubs that rip you off. We might even consider putting on two performances, one starting at, say, six thirty, the second at ten, if the actors can stand the pace.'

'And do you think it will work?' I'm trying hard to keep the doubt out of my voice.

'Yes, definitely. And so does everyone else.'

'Is Tasha part of the group?'

A mistake. The incandescent smile turns to a scowl. 'Why d'you keep banging on about Tasha?'

'I'm not. I just wondered, that's all.'

'No, she isn't but she may come in later. After all she just happens to be one of the best costume designers in London and we'd be bloody lucky to get her.'

'Well, I hope you do.'

Obviously I didn't sound convincing enough. 'Look, it's over between us, okay? She did mean a great deal to me but she doesn't any more.' He swallows a mouthful of coffee, chokes, swears.

'There's no need to be so angry, darling.'

'You keep dragging her in. You keep –'

'But I only asked.'

'And if it isn't Tasha it's your age or your heart or your mother or . . . It's one fucking thing after another.' He jabs a finger at me, not at all the calm, easy-going man I know. 'Sometimes I feel I'm running along a road chasing you, Ruth, only you keep throwing stuff in my way, tintacks and bits of glass.'

'I'm sorry, darling, I promise I will never mention Tasha or my age or my heart ever again. Cross my heart and hope to –' No, I won't say that.

He stops prowling and frowns at me, lips pursed. Then he laughs. 'Silly cow!' He leaps onto the bed, nearly bouncing me off. 'I love you. I want to marry you. Is that so difficult to understand?'

With his arms around me and his mouth

covering me with kisses it's getting easier to understand all the time.

'Tell me more about the new group. Have you found a theatre yet?'

'Of course we have. There's a place in Streatham going for a song.'

'Streatham?' I wish I hadn't sounded quite so gobsmacked.

'Okay, so it's not the most salubrious place in the world but it wouldn't cost much to convert the building, a bit of carpentry, a coat of paint. It would hold about two hundred, I wouldn't want more anyway.' He springs to his feet again. 'I'm not worried about getting the actors, they'll come. As for writers . . .' He points to the pile of scripts he left on the table by the window. 'We'll get the place, we'll get the talent, all we need now,' he presses his palms together and looks beseechingly towards heaven,' are angels. And I think, touch wood, I think we've found one, a fellow who's made a pot of money out of building cardboard houses and now wants to come up in the world and sees "the arts" as a way of doing it. We're having lunch with him tomorrow. We'll turn his head with thoughts of meeting all those luscious young actresses, cocktails in the green room, clandestine suppers after the show. Before he knows what he's doing the poor sod will be begging us to accept a cheque for half a mill and we'll be on our way.'

'Half a million?'

'That's just for starters.'

I pull a face.

'Oh come on, that's nothing to these cowboys. They pay more than that for a yacht.'

'What's his name, this wealthy little angel?'

'Ned Nurgles.'

'You're joking.' I can't stop laughing. 'Ned Nurgles? I don't believe it.'

'Who cares what he's called, Ned Nurgles, Mickey Mouse . . . ? Ruth, Ruth my love, my sweeting,' he gets onto the bed again and snuggles up to me, 'do you know what this means? I'll have my own theatre at last, my own theatre run my way. Does that make me sound like a megalomaniac?'

'It certainly does. But a nice one.'

'I'm sorry about just now, blasting off at you like that. How are you feeling? I should have asked before but I'm so wound up I don't know my arse from my elbow at the moment.'

'I envy you. It must be wonderful to want something so much it hurts.'

'I want you so much it hurts,' his arms tighten around me, 'but I don't think you feel that way about me.'

'Well, to be honest I would rather have Ned Nurgles. Mrs Ned Nurgles . . . just think of it.'

'His name may be ugly but his wallet's beautiful.'

'But surely you could get money from the Arts Council?'

'Blood from a stone. Christ, I'm so tired.' He

stretches, yawns. 'It doesn't hit you till you stop. I need some sleep.' He pulls back the covers and gets into bed, fully dressed.

'Aren't you going to take your clothes off?'

'No, I'm not.'

'And what about washing?'

'What about it?'

'How disgusting.'

'So I'm a dirty, disgusting megalomaniac. Have you been talking to your mother?'

'I phoned her last night while you were downstairs getting the champagne.'

'Ah, now I understand the tears. Bitchy, was she?'

'Very abrupt. I told her I had a cold – well, she knew that anyway, and that I wouldn't be home for a while. I didn't say how long.'

'For ever.' He puts his arms around me. 'Tell her for ever.'

CHAPTER 28

He's nervous, cuts himself shaving, spills coffee on his sweater, can't find anything. 'Break a leg, darling.'

'If Nouvy Nurgles doesn't come across,' he jokes, 'I'll break his.'

When he's gone I get up, enough of this illness nonsense. I feel dreadful but I won't stay in this wretched bed a minute longer. I shower and rest, pull on clothes and rest, put on make-up and rest. Wonder how Ian's getting on? He'll be meeting the little angel now. I feel sick with worry, like a mother thinking about her child on his first day of school . . . Please let it be all right. Please don't let him get hurt.

'Graham?'

No answer.

I can't bring myself to ring the little silver bell. It's insulting to summon the owner of the house as if he were a butler.

'Graham?'

I go downstairs feeling like a burglar. The place is so silent, like a museum full of beautiful things but no visitors.

'Graham?'

'In here, my dear. In the conservatory looking after my little ones. How are you?'

'Fed up with staying in bed.'

'Of course you are, dreadful bore. Stay here and talk to me. I'll just finish watering this juniper. How is your little fellow, by the way?'

'Oh, he's fine.' Change the subject. 'I was going to clean the flat but I can't find anything. Do you know where Ian keeps the dusters and things?'

'Bless you, we have a sweet young woman who comes in three times a week to "do" us. Is it Wednesday?' He glances at his watch. 'Pity. That means she won't be here till tomorrow. You'll have to wallow in filth till then, I'm afraid.'

'I just wanted something to do instead of mooning around all day.'

'Do you play chess?'

'I meant work.'

'Good heavens, nobody here works. I certainly don't. Ian dabbles at it. Even the charlady takes it very easy, she shifts dirt from one place to another, interspersing each activity with a cup of coffee and a fag . . . I take it chess is not your game?'

'No. I play bridge – well, I used to.'

'Will you join me for lunch then? There are a number of pleasant little restaurants in the neigh-bourhood.'

'I couldn't eat anything, I'm sorry. And I don't think I could walk far, I feel very shaky.'

'But, my dear, I'm not asking you to walk

anywhere. It's simply a matter of slipping on a coat and getting into a car. And I'm quite prepared to carry you over the threshold if it will help, although it's some years since I went through that ridiculous performance.'

It seems churlish to keep saying no. I could always pick at a salad, I suppose. 'All right. Thank you.'

It's quite a mild day. Even so Graham insists on wrapping a rug round my legs and turning the heat full on. 'This is an old car,' he says, 'full of draughts.'

'It's beautiful.' A Daimler, lovingly preserved. It must date back to the 1930s. Major Fordham has one like it, only his is not as well cared for as this and he never takes it out of the garage. I think he's just waiting for the right price to come along.

'Are you interested in cars? I have a Bugatti and a Morgan. You could take a look at them when we get back if you feel up to it.'

'I don't know much about cars really.'

'Oh, my dear, neither do I. But I do love cars for their own sake. Not the modern tin boxes, of course. They have no character, no style. I'm referring to earlier models, built with an eye for luxury. If I lived in the country I'd be a second Montagu of Beaulieu.'

'Would you like to live in the country?'

'Absolutely not. I've lived in this house for thirty years and been very happy here but we all have our little dream of a cottage in the country, don't we? I hope to God mine never comes true. I'm sure I'd go mad in the wilderness. Now what would you like to eat? Italian? No, not quite the thing for a delicate stomach. A slice or two of uncomplicated roast lamb – or are you a vegetarian like my nephew?'

Not yet. Mother couldn't cope. But when I'm married . . . Married. I still can't quite believe it. I'm going to get married.

Graham is well known to the maitre d' and we are led to a quiet table in the corner. 'Well,' he says after we have ordered drinks and starters, 'what news of the meeting? Is our boy flying high or in the depths of despair because someone has pricked his balloon yet again?'

I wish he wouldn't speak like that about Ian. It's so easy to be cynical.

'Oh dear,' he pretends to look contrite, 'I've said the wrong thing, haven't I? But you must remember, Ruth, I've known him a lot longer than you and I've had to live through any number of these wild schemes. He's always going to revolutionise the theatre. And that's all very fine provided you have the reputation, the experience and the resources to achieve it. At the moment Ian has none. He's only been directing for a few years and as for money I for one would not back such a dubious runner. I've been a gambler all my life and always studied form very carefully and my opinion is that this horse will either win by ten lengths or fall flat at the first fence.

'I've told him he's got to do a lot of spadework first, get himself recognised by the people who matter before I'll consider putting any of my money into his projects. And they must be sane projects, I won't support pie in the sky. Of course he thinks I'm a – what's the expression? – a tightarse,' he laughs. 'Ah, here's your starter, my dear. Now just eat as little as you want, don't push yourself just to please me. I know you've no appetite but I do appreciate your keeping me company like this. And I wanted to have a chat with you.'

Is this going to be an avuncular chat, I wonder? Am I going to be warned off? What little appetite I had has disappeared.

'Ian wants to marry me. I suppose you know.' We might as well get straight to the point.

'Yes, he told me. I think you'll be very good for him.'

I hadn't expected that. 'I'm afraid I'm too old.'

'Nonsense, you're afraid other people will think you're too old.'

'I have so little to offer him.'

'You have yourself, what else is there to offer? You seem to be full of doubts, Ruth, don't you love him?'

'Oh yes, yes. It's just that . . . well, I had a heart attack in September, quite a severe one, and it's left me feeling very, I don't know, very helpless. I'm not the strong person I thought I was.'

'Physically strong, you mean? We're all subject to disease, Ruth, even the Samsons.'

'It shattered me.'

'Don't worry, my nephew is strong. He's a bit woolly at the moment but he'll grow out of it. I think you'll find he has a certain rock-like quality under the froth of youth. I speak disparagingly of his ideas but not of him. I've always liked and respected Ian.'

'I wonder what his family will think.'

'Ian has never cared what his family or anyone else thinks. I suspect you are referring to your own family.'

'My mother doesn't approve.'

'Mothers rarely do.'

'I feel so stupid. I'm forty-four and I'm upset because my mother's angry with me.'

'Ah, but you're not forty-four in your mother's eyes, Ruth, nor in your own eyes when you're with her. When it comes to our parents we're all frozen at some vulnerable age, anywhere between zero and five, which is why they have such a hold over us. It's a pity we're not more like animals. After a certain age the cubs no longer recognise their parents and their parents so far forget their roles as to mate with their own offspring. Which is why I've always insisted that incest is a perfectly natural, acceptable phenomenon. And, of course, it's a sensible way of keeping money in the family . . . You have such a lovely laugh, my dear. You know you remind me of an actress, I remember her in Upstairs Downstairs. What the devil is her name?'

So many people have said that.

'I'm the poor man's Nicola Pagett.'

'Nicola Pagett, of course. Such a beautiful woman. I wonder what she's doing at the moment.'

Enjoying life, I hope. Squeezing every drop of happiness out of every minute, which is what I'm going to do. I suddenly feel so elated I tuck into the roast lamb with a gusto I wouldn't have believed possible an hour earlier. Without much persuasion Graham starts telling me about his travels in the Far East. He seems to have been a loner all his life and yet I don't sense loneliness in him. I must ask Ian about the missing wife. Did they divorce? Is she dead?

'Well, I've heard quite enough of my voice for one day,' he says, summoning the maitre d'. 'Next time I want to hear about you.'

'There's not much to hear. I've led a very dull life by comparison with yours.'

'Then don't compare it with mine. You're too modest, my dear. The meek are only blessed in the Bible.'

We drive home through the darkening streets. I haven't felt this contented for ages. I'm quite sure now that marrying Ian is the right thing to do. I thank Graham for the lunch, give him a hug and stumble upstairs, feeling very sleepy and a bit queasy too. It was foolish to eat so much on an empty stomach but it was fun, good for my soul if not my body. I'll take a couple of aspirins and lie down for a while before Ian comes home.

He's slumped on the sofa, staring into space, the picture of misery.

'What happened?'

'I even had to pay for my own lunch.'

'Oh, darling . . .' He meant it to be funny but neither of us can laugh. 'Wasn't he at all interested?'

'Yes, very interested. In making money. He doesn't give a fuck about actors, plays. Do you know what he wants? Some "lively" shows, by which he means tits and bums . . . Where have you been anyway?'

'Having lunch with Graham.'

'Oh yes,' he looks at me with a sour expression, 'I wish I had half the money he's wasted on lunches and dinners.'

'He speaks very highly of you.'

'Words are cheap.'

'Darling, I've got some money.'

'Yes, you told me. You've got eighty-five grand in the bank. I don't think we could get a pro- scenium arch for that, but thanks all the same.'

'I could ask Mother to let me have my share of Daddy's estate.'

'You will not.'

'But why – ?'

'Promise me you'll never ask her for money.' His fingers dig into my shoulders, hurting me. 'Promise!'

'But –'

'No.'

'Ian –'

'Just leave it at that, okay? I don't want any of *mummy and daddy's* money. If you want to help out with your money when we're married, that's fine.'

'Of course. We'll put all we've got into one pot and take out what we need.'

He gives a short, humourless laugh. 'I've nothing to put in, Ruth. I never had. I think of money as something you use to do things with, to make things happen. I'm not a very promising prospect, am I? As a husband, I mean.'

'We'll get by, don't worry. I'll work. I could probably get a job with The Trust.'

'Surely to God you wouldn't go back there?'

'If it would help us, darling. And they pay well.'

I've had a couple of chats with Deirdre . . . No, not chats, we're not friends any more. I can't forgive her for not warning me what was happening while I was away but she says I'm missed. And Bridgey might forgive if I were to grovel a bit.

Ian puts his arms around me, looks at me for a long time, running his fingers over my face, sketching my eyes, my mouth. 'I don't deserve you, Ruth,' he says. 'I don't deserve you but I'm bloody well going to hold on to you.'

I've been here a week. I've phoned Guildford several times but it's always Kitty who answers, Mother is conveniently out. I must go home now and make my peace with her. 'Anyway, what's the point of staying here?' I tease Ian. 'You're never around.'

'Don't leave, Ruth. Please don't. Once you go you'll never come back.' There's an urgency about him, a vehemence that frightens me. 'She'll find a way of splitting us up. She'll talk you out of it.'

266

'Darling, I've promised to marry you, I've given you my word and nothing will make me break it.'

'Will I see you soon?'

'I'll come straight back.'

'When will you marry me?'

'As soon as you want.'

'Do you mean that?'

'Of course I do.'

'I wish I could believe you.'

'Darling, it's very late and you're supposed to be meeting those people at nine.' Someone in the group has found another potential backer. There is to be no lunch this time, just a meeting in an office in Clerkenwell in the morning. This one sounds like what Ian calls 'another bums and bonk man'. It's a waste of time and he knows it but he has to go through with it, just in case. Surely there's someone who can help him? If only Graham . . . If only I . . . When I think of all Daddy's money in stocks and shares, mounting up, hundreds of thousands. And for what? My old age?

Our cleaning lady's vacuuming the dining room when I get home. She's a bit deaf so I have to tap her on the shoulder.

'Where's my mother, Mrs Humphreys?'

There's no sign of Kitty or Rob so I suppose they've all gone for a walk.

'She gave me these before she left.' She takes the front door keys out of her apron pocket and puts them on the table.

'Left?'

'She and Mrs Barber went yesterday morning.'
'Went where?'
She shrugs.
'Did my mother say when they'd be back?'
Another shrug. Mrs Humphreys is one of those who mind their own business and get on with the job, women who come and go with no more than a good morning and a goodbye. A taciturn treasure.

Perhaps there's a note in my room or Mother's sitting room. I rush from one to the next like a little girl on an Easter egg hunt. How cluttered this house is, bulging with coffee tables and love seats and fat cushions and embroidered footstools and shirred satin lampshades and silk flowers. I have come to appreciate the austere elegance of Ian's flat, there's room to move around in it. At one o'clock Mrs Humphreys knocks on my door to say she's leaving. I give her back the keys.

'You'd better keep them. I'm not staying.'

Why should I hang around waiting for mother? I won't go yet though. Maybe she and Kitty just went for the night. Went where? Mother doesn't like leaving her home. Everybody has to come to her.

I might as well have a quick nap. The cold's almost gone but I still feel draggy. I wonder how much longer I'll be sleeping in this bed?

CHAPTER 29

I wake an hour or two later feeling uneasy. I must find out where Mother's gone. I phone Mildred to thank her for her hospitality. Guildford Ruth would have done it days ago.

'Your mother? Good Lord no, I've never managed to prise Ann out of her shell, Ruth, you know that.'

I dial Mrs Luke's number to wish her a happy new year.

'I haven't seen you and your mother in ages, dear. We must get together.'

She's not at the Rushtons either. And I'm sure she wouldn't go to Uncle Frank. Why didn't Kitty tell me they were going away? I've called every day and she didn't mention a word about it.

It's eight o'clock. I dial Ian's number. No answer. I wander from room to room, looking out of windows, listening for the telephone, the crunch of tyres on the gravel. This is ridiculous. I make supper, an omelette and salad, and tip it in the bin. I wish I could have a cigarette, just one. I'll go out and get a packet, I need something to calm my nerves and I can't keep taking Valium. No, it's too late, everything's closed around here. But there's a cigarette machine in The Rat & Parrot . . . Stop it! Stop it!

I don't know how many times I've dialled Ian's number. If Mother and Kitty aren't back by ten I'm going. Why should I stay in this empty house when I could be with him? There's nothing worth watching on television and I've read the same page of this novel over and over and still can't remember what it says . . .

It's midnight, they won't be back now, I might as well go to bed. I'll take a couple of sleeping pills. If I don't I shall lie here staring at the ceiling all night. How silent the house is. Where is Ian? Surely he can't still be with his angel. Is he celebrating? Is he depressed? Does he think I've let him down? I should have been there when he got back. I feel like a child again, Mother's left me, Ian's angry with me. Thank God the sedatives are beginning to work.

I'm still in a deep sleep when I hear the key in the door, voices. It's almost midday, I've practically slept the clock round. It takes me a while to work out where I am. I pull on a dressing gown and open my bedroom door. Kitty's standing in the hall holding a suitcase, Mother's outside paying the taxi.

'Where on earth have you been?'

'Oh Ruthy, how lovely to see you.'

'Where have you been?'

'We went to Chichester. It was such a lovely

place but terribly expensive, Ann treated me. We've had a marvellous time . . . Look, I'm as fat as a pig.'

Stupid of me, I should have remembered that hotel, it's Mother's favourite. She and Daddy used to go there to celebrate anniversaries.

'You might have let me know you were going away, Mother.'

'You can't expect me to stay here waiting for you to come home, Ruth. I have a life of my own, you know.' I've never seen her like this. 'This house isn't a hotel, I don't run it just for your convenience.'

'Well you won't have to run it just for my convenience any more, Mother, because I'm getting married.'

For one moment we're all frozen, like a game of statues, Mother bending down to pick up her suitcase, Kitty half-way up the stairs, I with my arms crossed, defiant.

'Ruthy!' Kitty rushes down, almost falling in her excitement. 'Ruthy, darling, congratulations – Oh no, I shouldn't be congratulating you, should I, it's the bridegroom. Oh, I don't care I'm so happy for you.' She smothers me with kisses. 'When? When?'

'We don't know yet.' I watch Mother's face over Kitty's shoulder. 'As soon as we can.'

'Oh Ruthy, it's so exciting. Will you have a big wedding? Will you – ?'

'Kitty, go and make a cup of tea for us, please,' says Mother.

'I'll do it.'

'No, Kitty will.' It's a command.

Kitty goes into the kitchen, looking back at us, bewildered, wondering what she's done wrong.

'I'd like to have a word with you, Ruth.' Mother goes into her sitting room and I follow. 'Close the door, please.' She sits down and folds her hands in her lap. She looks very composed. She reminds me of the nuns at Our Lady of Ransom. I envied them their serenity, their sureness that they had got it all right and the rest of us had got it all wrong.

'How much do you know about Mr Trevelyan?'

'Ian, Mother. His name's Ian.'

'How much do you know about this man?'

'Everything that matters.'

She tilts her head sideways and raises her eyebrows in a sardonic question.

'All right, I know what you're getting at, he doesn't have much money . . .' he doesn't have any but I'm not about to tell her that, 'but he's very talented, he'll get to the top, everyone says so.'

A wry smile. 'Do they?'

'People who know.'

'I see.' She dismisses them in two words. People who know, people who matter don't work in the theatre, they work in banks.

She smooths her skirt over her knees. Her hands, beginning to buckle now with arthritis, run back and forth, ironing out imaginary creases. 'What do you know of his background?'

'His father's a doctor, they've always lived in Bath, Ian left school when he was sixteen to join a touring company, he came to London when he was . . . Look, what's the point of all this?'

'Did you know his uncle supports him?'

'He lives in Graham's house rent free if that's what you mean. His uncle happens to believe in him, he thinks Ian will –'

'Did you know he lived with Tasha for three years?'

'Yes, what of it? He's probably lived with lots of –'

'And that she paid all the bills?'

I didn't know but it doesn't surprise me and I'm not in the least concerned. I'll be quite happy to pay all the bills too. 'Why not, if she was earning a good salary and he wasn't? What does it matter who pays?'

'Did you know that he asks everyone for money?'

'Mother, he's trying to get a new theatre group going. He's not asking people to give *him* money, he's asking them to give it to – to a project. I know it's hard for you to understand but he's mad about the theatre.' An unfortunate expression. 'He loves it, it's his whole life.'

'Did you know – ?'

Did you know? Did you know? I'm getting sick of this interrogation. 'Oh, for God's sake!'

'Did you know,' she ignores my outburst, 'that he's married and has a child.'

It's like a punch in the mouth. I sit down, drawing my dressing gown around me, tightening the belt. I'm not dressed for battle. 'Who told you that?' My voice comes out as a croak. 'Oh, dear Matthew, of course. It's just the kind of rubbish he would –'

'He's telling the truth.'

'Matthew? The truth?'

'You don't believe it because you don't want to.'

'Mother, don't be ridiculous, it's just Matthew being spiteful. Ian isn't married.'

'Oh, he probably isn't now, I imagine he's separated or divorced but it's strange he didn't tell you, isn't it? It's unfortunate you had to hear it from me.'

Tasha. Of course. Tasha told Matthew, Matthew told Mother . . . Ian has a wife and a child, he probably has to support them, that explains why he's always short of money. Why didn't he tell me, why, why? Mother looks so smug. Does my unhappiness please her that much?

'Well, thanks for all the exciting gossip, dear.' I get up and go to the door, feigning indifference. 'Oh, and do thank Matthew as well. And tell him not to bother to come to my wedding. In fact, I hope I never see the bastard again.'

'Don't be a simpleton, Ruth, can't you see what this man's like? He shirks his responsibilities, lives off everyone, he can't have any pride to live off a woman. Surely it's obvious why he wants to marry you. He came here, saw this big house, realised you would inherit –'

'It isn't my money he wants, I know because

274

I offered him everything I'd got.' My turn to be smug. 'I even said I'd ask you for my share of Daddy's estate and he wouldn't let me, he made me promise I wouldn't.'

'You what? Are you that desperate that you must buy a man?'

'I'm not buying him. I –'

'You stupid little fool!' The composure has gone, her face is contorted with anger. 'You told him how much you expect to inherit when I die, is that it? Well, let me tell you, Ruth, if you marry that man you will not inherit one penny of my money.'

'It isn't your money, it's Daddy's. And anyway –'

'It most certainly is my money, he left it to me, everything.'

'Well, I don't want it.' I'm losing control of my voice, tears are choking me. 'I don't want any of it, neither does Ian.'

'Neither does Ian? I doubt that,' she sneers. 'I'm very disappointed in you, Ruth, I thought you had more sense than to let a man lead you by the nose, a man so much younger than you.'

'But what does it matter if he's – ?'

'Fifteen years younger. That's too much, Ruth. You're a mature woman and he's . . . well, from the way he behaves he clearly hasn't grown up.'

'That's a horribly insulting thing to say, Mother. Just because he doesn't live the way you think everyone should, just because he doesn't put on a grey suit and go to some dull job in the City every day . . .' My voice is trembling, gurgling in my throat, but I can't stop now, there are things that have to be said. 'Probably everyone will despise me for marrying him but I don't care. Ian loves me.' She turns away, pretending to laugh, a hateful sound. 'And even if he doesn't, even if he only wants me for my money, could my life with him be any worse than it is now? What have I got? Tell me, Mother, what have I got to look forward to? I'm an old maid . . . Yes, yes, I'll say what everyone thinks, I'm on the shelf. So I'll spend the rest of my days in this house with you and Kitty. Doing what? Playing the piano, painting thimbles, taking Rob for walks, waiting to grow old, waiting to die. Even if Ian leaves me in a few years, even if he takes every penny I've got, I'll have something in return, some love, some memories, something more than this empty existence. Oh Mother, I've been happier in these past few weeks than I've been in my whole life. I wouldn't have believed it possible . . .' Tears stop me from going on.

There's a long silence, broken finally by Mother's voice.

'I'm sorry it's been so terrible for you living here all these years. I had no idea. I certainly did my best to make you happy.'

'Mother, I didn't mean . . .' I try to put my arms around her but she turns away.

'How stupid I've been. I should have made a life of my own, I should have remarried . . . Oh, I had offers but I turned them down. I didn't want to upset you and Matthew by bringing a new man into the home. I thought only of you two.'

'Mother, I *am* grateful, I –'

'Grateful?' I don't recognise her any more. The soft, gentle woman has been replaced by one filled with bitterness and resentment. 'Oh yes, you've just told me how grateful you are for your empty existence.'

'You don't understand –'

'No, I certainly do not.'

My heart's fluttering and I have a pain in my chest but I manage to speak fairly calmly. 'I'm sorry we have to part like this.' It's all over between us now, the ties broken, the bonds of a lifetime. But if I don't go now I shall be buried here for ever. 'Thank you for all you've done, Mother. I know you did what you thought was for the best.' She's standing by the window, her back towards me. 'Goodbye then.'

'Ruth.'

'Yes?' I turn back eagerly, hoping that her love for me has overcome her resentment, that she's going to wish me well. I don't want to leave her like this.

'Kitty has to be in court tomorrow morning.' Damn, I'd forgotten about that. 'That's why I took her away, I wanted to take her mind off it. She's been very distressed.'

And I have been too selfish to even think of poor Kitty. 'What time is her case coming up?'

'She has to be there at ten.'

'Marylebone, isn't it?' That means we shall have to leave here by eight. I'll go to Ian's afterwards. 'I'll stay here tonight and go with you.' Only a few more hours, less than a day, and I'll be with Ian again. All this will be a bad memory, a nightmare he'll help me erase.

Kitty comes in with tea on a tray.

'Let's take ours to your room, dear. I'll help you unpack.'

'Is everything all right, Ruthy?' she whispers as we go upstairs.

'Of course it is.' There's no point telling her about my miseries, she has enough of her own. She hasn't said anything about tomorrow, never mentioned the shoplifting or the court case in all the time she's been here. I'm not exactly relishing tomorrow myself. I don't know what I'll do if they sentence her, hurl myself at the magistrate begging for mercy? Making a scene would be a good idea, it would get me in the papers, I could draw attention to these poor little souls who can't help themselves. But I'm too British. My upper lip is cemented in place.

Surely they won't put her in prison, not for a first offence? They can see she's not a criminal. They'll just give her a good talking to, won't they? But what if they decide to make an example of her? Oh please God no, don't let them do that to Kitty . . .

'Ann doesn't want you to marry that man, does she?' Kitty whispers, closing her bedroom door.

'Mother's a bit upset, that's all. Mothers are

always upset when their daughters leave home, even when their daughters are as ancient as me, but she'll get over it. After all, she has you now.' I give her a hug. 'Now tell me about Chichester. Did you have a good time?'

It was all carefully planned, it seems. When Kitty told Mother I was coming home Mother wanted me to find the house empty. I feel ashamed for her. Kitty, who neither perceives nor understands people's evil intentions, chats on about her 'holiday'. She has a talent for detail. She even noticed the pattern on the hotel china, the colour of the waitress's lipstick, the music the pianist was playing. 'It was from *Brigadoon*, Ruthy. It reminded me of the first time I went out with Julian. We went to a little restaurant in Soho –'

I wonder what Ian's doing? He hasn't phoned. Somehow I feel more upset about that than anything else that's happened today. Why didn't he tell me about his wife? I'll be the second Mrs Trevelyan, the second-hand Mrs Trevelyan. And he has a child. I wish it hadn't been Mother who told me, anyone but her. And Matthew, how he must have revelled in it, pouring all that poison in her ear.

'– and he gave me his address.' Kitty's holding out a slip of paper. 'He said he'd like to see me again.'

'Who?'

'Mr Dawson.'

'Who's Mr Dawson?'

'The man I've been telling you about.'

'Oh. Oh yes . . . Did he? How nice.' I look at the address. It's written in the shaky hand of an old man. 'So you made a conquest on your holiday.'

She blushes and laughs delightedly. For one brief moment behind that lined, dried-up face I see a young girl. How pretty she was.

'It's so exciting, Ruthy, about you getting married, I mean. I honestly never thought –' She stops abruptly, aware she's about to put her foot firmly in her mouth. Even Kitty isn't that tactless.

'No, neither did I, darling, but miracles do happen. Just think, this time next year I shall be Mrs Trevelyan and you might be Mrs Dawson.'

'Ruthy, no! Oh, you're so naughty.' She gets up and does a little jig around the room. 'Not me,' she says wistfully, catching sight of her reflection in the mirror, 'I'm too old.'

Too old. I'm tired of hearing it. Why are we both too old to love, too old to be happy?

'Shall we take Rob for a walk?' I want to get out of this house. I want to run away. Oh God, please make the morning come soon.

It's a lovely day, crisp cold air, blue sky, sunshine. Every day in the New Year has been brilliantly sunny so far, a good augury.

'Ann didn't say goodbye to us.'

'She's sulking.'

'I wish she wouldn't. It makes me feel . . .' She shivers.

'Me too.'

280

'Take no notice of her, Ruthy, you do what you want.' She takes my arm and snuggles against me. 'You only live once.'

When I get to a phone box I ask her to wait outside for a moment with Rob. I tell her I'm going to phone my boyfriend, silly word for someone my age but she loves it, overjoyed to be in on the intrigue.

I was simply going to tell him that Kitty's case comes up tomorrow morning and I must stay and help her through it. I was going to keep it light, no mention of the row with Mother, but before I can stop myself I'm pouring coins in the slot, telling him every word that passed between us.

'Why didn't you tell me you were married?'

There's a long pause.

'I thought it would frighten you away, Ruth. You latch on to any excuse to run. I was going to tell you later, when you'd learned to trust me.'

'And you have a . . . Mother says you have a child.'

'I got married at eighteen, I was a father at nineteen. Quite ridiculous, babies having babies. If my parents hadn't come down so hard on us, if they hadn't been so bloody determined to stop us from marrying we probably wouldn't have done it. I know I'm shifting the blame but kids at that age don't think sensibly, especially boys, and I was going through my teenage rebel stage. It's not something I'm proud of.'

'Do you ever see your wife?'

'She isn't my wife any more and what's the point of seeing her? We have nothing in common, we never did.'

'But what about the child?'

'Daniel was barely a year old when we split. I tried to see him, I got a court order, but it was such a hassle, he was like a bit of rope with us tugging each end. It wasn't fair on him, so I gave up.'

Daniel. It's strange how when you give someone a name they become real. He was just the child before, now he's a little boy, Daniel.

I suddenly remember Kitty waiting patiently outside. She's stamping her feet and banging her hands together to keep warm. 'Oh, darling, I'm sorry.'

'It's all right, Ruthy.' She's so forgiving. If she were frozen into a block of ice she'd still crack it with a forgiving smile. 'How's your boyfriend?'

'He's fine. He's . . .' Oh no, I forgot to ask him how the meeting went with the new angel.

CHAPTER 30

Dinner's a restrained meal. Kitty and I keep up a barrage of chit-chat, Mother responds in monosyllables. I'm surprised she's come to the table at all, I thought she might have had another of her convenient headaches.

Thank God for Kitty, I don't know what I'd do if she weren't here. But then if she weren't I wouldn't be either. I'd be away now, safe with Ian. We'd be curled on the sofa together, our arms around each other . . . I can't eat this food, it's choking me. Kitty isn't eating either, she hasn't touched her plate.

Afterwards Mother goes into the kitchen, icily refusing any offers of help with the washing up, and Kitty and I flop into armchairs in front of the television, relieved that the ordeal's over.

'What do you want to watch, Ruthy?'

'Anything. I don't mind.'

'There's a James Bond film starting at half past eleven.'

She loves all that glamorous nonsense and I'd love to escape for a few hours but . . . 'We can't stay up to watch that, dear. We have to be in court at ten tomorrow morning. That means we've got to leave about eight.'

'Oh yes,' she says airily. 'Oh yes, I forgot that.' Forgot? It hasn't been out of her mind for one second. I can see it in her eyes, haunting her. 'There's something on Saint Lucia,' she says. 'It looks quite interesting.'

Anything. Anything that will make the time pass so I can get through this night. If only I could wake up and find it was all over, Kitty acquitted, Mother restored to her usual good humour, and me . . . I only want to be with Ian. I don't care about his marriage, his child. Who am I to sit in judgement on him? I was going to marry at twenty. I might have had a . . .

'What?'

'I said shall we watch the programme on St Lucia?'

'Yes, yes, that's fine by me.'

We sit for a while gazing at the screen, white beach, blue water, scorched tourists. I think St Lucia's one of the places we stop at on the cruise – Oh hell, I'd forgotten about that. I must cancel it. I'll phone the travel agent tomorrow.

Or maybe we could go to St Lucia for our honeymoon.

Kitty changes the channel to some vacuous American sitcom. A few minutes later she switches it to a panel game, then a documentary about wildlife in Australia.

'Kitty, for goodness sake, you're making me giddy.'

'Sorry, Ruthy. Shall I turn it off?'

'No.' I might as well watch kangaroos mating. It passes the time. 'I'd like to see this.'

She picks up a magazine, flips through it, puts it down, picks up another one, flips through it. I don't want to keep chiding her, I know she's on edge about tomorrow but . . . 'Darling, do you think you could try to relax?' Try to relax – what a ridiculous thing to say. Stupidly I've run out of sleeping pills. She'll probably prowl round the house all night keeping us awake.

'Sorry, Ruthy. I'm sorry.' She's so contrite I feel guilty. Poor wretch, I can imagine what she's going through.

'Kitty.' I get up and put my arms around her. 'Kitty, love, it's going to be all right tomorrow, you'll see. Simon Fairfax says there's absolutely nothing to worry about. He'll be there and he'll explain to the magistrate that you've been under a lot of strain because of –'

'Oh I know, I know, I'm not worried, Ruthy.' She picks up another magazine. 'Have you seen the clothes in here? Look, isn't this a pretty sweater? The colour would suit you.'

I've tried so often to make her talk about the court case but she always flutters away, twittering hysterically about something quite irrelevant. It's like trying to net a butterfly. And I was never any good at that either. I go back to my chair and watch the documentary, what's left of it. Kitty gets a pack of cards out of the bureau.

'Ruthy, would you like to – ?'

'No, dear, I'm trying to watch this.'

'Sorry.'

It's boring. Once you've seen a hundred kangaroos hop across the screen the novelty wears off . . . My eyes feel so heavy. It's been a long, worrying day and I'm quite exhausted.

I wake to the sound of Mother's voice. She's banging on a door, shouting, 'Kitty! Kitty!'

I run up the stairs. Mother is outside the bathroom. She turns to me, a look of terror in her eyes. 'Kitty won't answer.'

'Has she been in there long?'

'I heard the water running ages ago . . . Kitty! Kitty, let me in. Please!'

I push her aside. 'Kitty, it's Ruthy. Come on, darling, open the door.'

There's no sound. Mother and I look at each other, too frightened to say what we're both thinking.

'We must force the lock –'

'– break the door.'

'Get Peter. Quick!'

While Mother's away I keep trying to make Kitty open the door but even as I'm pounding on it and shouting I know the truth. I won't admit it though. If I don't say the words there's still hope.

Peter Turner runs up the stairs with a wrench in his hand. 'I'll have to break the door. Sorry.'

I don't care if he smashes it to smithereens as long as we can get to Kitty before . . . before . . .

He puts the wrench under the handle and heaves. There's a splintering sound and the door swings open. He stands back, doesn't want to offend Kitty by barging in. I notice out of the corner of my eye that Mother takes a step back too. I push past both of them.

My first thought when I look in the bath and see all that bright red water is that my silly, dithery aunt has overdone the bath salts. She's lying, half submerged, her eyes open, staring at the ceiling.

Mother screams, startling me. It had all been so unreal until then, as if we were in a film, watching ourselves in some disembodied way. Now she's shattered it and the reality comes crashing in.

'Oh no,' groans Peter Turner. He takes my arm and tries to pull me away but I shake him off.

Mother's screams are getting on my nerves. 'Take her out,' I say to him very calmly.

'Ruth –'

'I'm all right. Take Mother downstairs, please.'

When they've gone I kneel by the bath and stare at my aunt's frail body. How could such a tiny thing hold so much blood? The knife is on the floor, it's the small one Mother uses to chop vegetables with, razor sharp. I can't see Kitty's wrists. I wonder if she made a clean cut or did she make a mess of it? What does it matter now? She's free. They can't humiliate her tomorrow. Nobody will ever hurt her again.

I close her eyes, kiss her forehead. I want to take her in my arms but it's too late. The time for loving Kitty, the time for comforting her is gone.

Mother is in her sitting room with Peter, her head buried in her hands.

'I wonder if you'd mind calling the police, Peter?'

'I already have. Is there anything else I can do?'

'No. Thank you very much for your help.'

I put my arms around Mother and together we weep for the pathetic little woman lying in the bath upstairs. There will be one less for the magistrates to pass judgement on tomorrow, one less bewildered, frightened face staring at them from the dock.

CHAPTER 31

When the police come they want to talk to each of us separately. Mother goes in first while Peter and I wait in the hall, avoiding each other's eyes. The doctor arrives. Simpson's on holiday this week so it's the relief doctor, a much older man. He gives us a brief nod and goes up to the bathroom.

'What was she talking about just before she died?' the police ask me. 'What was the last thing she said to you, Miss Webster?'

'Sorry. She said she was sorry.'

'For what?'

'For everything.' She was always saying she was sorry, for talking too much, for laughing too loudly, for singing out of tune, for being a nuisance. Sorry.

'Miss Webster . . .' They want a more precise answer.

'I was watching television and I asked her to be quiet.'

'Was there any indication that she intended to take her life?'

I'm just popping upstairs to slash my wrists, Ruthy. Sorry.

'No.'

'Very well, Miss Webster, thank you. Perhaps we could have a word with Mr Turner now.'

I take Mother up to her room and put her to bed. Her body contracts in spasms, she can't stop sobbing. I've run out of sleeping pills. Damn! I was going to get some more tomorrow. A car draws up outside. There are footsteps on the stairs, voices.

'Don't leave me, Ruthy.'

'Just for a moment, dear.'

The undertakers are in the bathroom. 'There's no need to come in, Miss Webster. Just wait outside, if you would.'

'But I want to be with her.' It's not right to leave her alone with these strange men.

One of the policemen stands in the doorway, blocking my way. 'It'll only distress you, Miss.' He puts an arm around my shoulders and leads me down the stairs. Strange how such a small act of kindness can move one to tears.

They're bringing Kitty down now.

'These are her personal belongings, Miss Webster.' They put her rings on the table, bid me goodnight and leave. The house is silent once more.

This is her wedding ring, a thick gold band, much too cumbersome for Kitty's tiny finger, what was Julian thinking of to buy her such a big ring? There's an inscription on the inside, so worn I can hardly make it out. '– for ever and for ever and –' I must give it to the undertaker to put back on her finger.

I make some hot milk for Mother. She wanders round the room, wringing her hands. 'It's my fault. I let her down.'

'Of course you didn't, dear. You took her into your home, you did everything you could for her. Kitty . . .' I can't say Kitty wanted to die even though it's the truth. 'Kitty couldn't cope.'

'It's my fault. It's my fault she died. I let her down.'

'I'm going to call the doctor.' I should have asked him for a sedative when he was here.

She clutches at me, panic in her eyes. 'Why? What's wrong? Are you ill?'

'I'm all right, dear, I'm all right.' I make her lie down on the bed. 'There's nothing wrong with me, Mother, I'm just going to ask him to give you something that will make you sleep.'

'Sleep, sleep,' she sobs like a sick child.

I phone the relief doctor, apologise for disturbing him again. What a dreadful job they have, called from their beds in the middle of the night to cope with women who've slit their wrists and in the morning their waiting rooms full of sniffles and moans. No wonder Simpson looks sour.

The Turners knock at the door. They huddle together, wanting to help, not wanting to interfere. 'Why don't you both come and stay with us for a while till this is all over?' They mean till the funeral, of course. This will never be all over for Mother and me.

I thank them and send them away.

The doctor arrives, gives Mother a jab and some pills to take when she wakes up. They'll get her through the next few days, the funeral, the inquest, he says. 'And what about you, Miss Webster?'

'Yes, I'd like some too, thank you, Doctor.'

'I meant –' He taps his heart.

'Oh, it's still beating.'

'Take a couple of pills, get some rest.'

'Yes, I will. Thank you.'

It's three o'clock. I feel very alone. Mother's fast asleep, Rob is lying next to her. He opens his eyes and looks at me mournfully when I stroke him. Does he know, can he sense death?

I phone Ian. When I hear his voice all I can do is cry.

'What's wrong, love? Your mother . . .'

'It's Kitty. She . . . She's . . .' I can't say it.

'Is she dead?'

'She killed herself.'

'I'll be right over.'

It will take him hours to get here but I don't care if he walks all the way from Hampstead as long as he comes. I need him more than I've needed anyone in my whole life.

I wander round the house from room to room. Kitty's bedroom, all that remains of her now, the beads and bracelets, the little glass animals . . . I'd like to smash the lot. Damn her! Why did she have to kill herself? Couldn't she have faced up to it, shown some guts? Why am I always the one who's left to clean up the mess? Why, Daddy, why?

Daddy? Why did I suddenly think of him? It's Kitty's death that has . . . No, it was my father's. It was his death that balked me of my happiness all those years ago. He was the one who left me to clean up the mess.

Either the undertaker or the police have done a very efficient job of cleaning the bathroom. You'd never know a woman had slashed her wrists in here only a few hours ago. I look in the washing basket. It's full of bloodstained towels . . . I feel faint. I sit on the loo and put my head between my knees . . . Oh God, Kitty, poor little wretch, filling the bath, getting in, picking up the knife . . . Kitty, Kitty, I'm so sorry, I should have been here to stop you. I let you down.

He let me down.

It's almost dawn. I think if Ian doesn't come soon I shall go mad. I shall get a knife and – The doorbell! Thank God! I hurtle down the stairs, almost falling. He puts his arms around me and I weep, tears of grief, anger, relief. We go into the kitchen and he makes coffee.

'Tell me.'

Now that he's here I suddenly feel exhausted, all the tension of the past few hours is beginning to take its toll but I must talk, I must tell him.

'Everybody feels guilty when there's a suicide, Ruth.' His voice is like a balm. 'From what you've told me about Kitty I don't think the shoplifting or the court case had much to do with it. She'd have killed herself sooner or later.'

'She couldn't get over Julian's death. She was so helpless, so lonely when he died.'

'Maybe it's better this way then.'

'Do you think so? Do you really think death is better than life?'

'It depends on the quality of life, doesn't it?'

'But she could have lived here with Mother. It wouldn't have been very exciting but . . .'

'But she wanted to be with her husband.'

'Yes. She was a part of him and that part had died. She couldn't go on, crippled.'

'So now she's a part of him again and she's happy.'

'Do you really believe that?'

He smiles. 'Go and lie down. Get some sleep.'

'But Mother might wake up.'

'That jab will put her out for hours. Go on.'

'You must be tired too. How did you get here?'

'Graham lent me one of his cars. He's a good bloke in an emergency.'

We lie on the bed and he takes me in his arms, kisses me gently. I will not think of anything. I will not think of Kitty. I'm safe now, safe with him.

When I wake up he's sitting by the window staring into the garden. For one moment I think all's well with my world and then the memory of last night crashes in.

'I think your mother's up,' he says.

I put on my dressing gown and open the bedroom door. She's coming down the stairs, her long hair straggling down her back, strands of it across her forehead. That shocks me more than her haggard face. Mother's hair is always so neat, gathered into a lovely silver bun in the nape of her neck. She stumbles. I rush to help her.

'Nobody there. I woke . . . Everybody's gone.'

'Come and have some coffee, dear.'

'She called me. Ruthy, we must go and help her.' She pulls away from me and weaves giddily towards the front door crying, 'Kitty! Kitty!'

'Mother, let's go and have some breakfast, shall we?'

Ian comes out of my room. 'Hello, Mrs Webster.'

She turns at the sound of his voice, stares at him in horror and backs away, her mouth working like a mad woman's.

'It's Ian, Mother. You know Ian.'

She's trembling violently.

'He's come to help us, dear.'

'No! No!'

I can't bear the screaming. 'Let's get her back to bed.'

Ian tries to put his arm around her shoulders. He's a big man but she fights him off, lashing out with her fists. Such strength for an old woman, such hatred. 'Don't touch me! Don't let him touch me! Get away! Get away from me!'

'Leave her to me, darling. I can manage her on my own.' I get her up to bed, give her two pills, make her lie down, stroke her cheek. Just as she's drifting off Ian appears in the doorway. 'How is she?'

It's only a whisper but she's heard. The screaming starts again.

'Darling, please go away.' I said it too harshly. He's gone before I can apologise. Every so often Mother comes to with a start and clutches at my arm, holding me so tightly it makes me wince.

'It's all right, dear, I'm here, I'm with you.'

When she finally falls asleep I tuck the duvet around her shoulders the way she did when I was ill, close the door quietly and tiptoe downstairs. Ian's sitting on the sofa with Rob beside him. I can't help smiling at the sight of them huddled together for comfort.

'She's asleep at last.' I slump down next to him. He puts his arms around me, says nothing. What is there to say? I can't think straight. I feel it is I who have died, I who am lying on that cold slab, the pathologist's knife poised to slice me open . . . 'Oh, Kitty.'

Rob tries to lick away my tears.

'Let's take him for a walk.' Ian pulls me up. 'Come on, love, you need to get away from here for a bit.'

I feel unreal, nodding to neighbours, exchanging greetings with them as if it was just a normal day, as if nobody had just lobbed a grenade into my life. They don't know about Kitty yet. Soon it will be all over the village but for the moment all they're interested in is the tall young man I'm clinging to.

'I'll stay as long as you want me to, Ruth.'

'I want you to stay for ever, darling, you know that, but I don't think it would be fair on you or her.'

'She certainly hates my guts.'

'No, it's the shock, she doesn't know what she's doing. She's terrified that I'm going to die as well.'

'She's terrified that she'll lose you to me, you mean. You must get away, Ruth. You must leave.'

'Now? I couldn't walk out on her now.'

'I didn't mean this very minute. But you must have it clear in your head that when this is all over you're going to marry me. Don't let anyone or anything make you change your mind.'

'Nothing could.'

He looks at me doubtfully. 'I wish I could believe that.'

'I mean it.'

When we get back Mother's still sleeping.

'I think it would be best if you went now before she wakes up, darling. Would you mind if I didn't see you off at the door? I couldn't bear it.'

Later, when I have pulled myself together again, I phone Matthew. A man answers. Matt has gone up to the Nottingham Playhouse for an audition, he says, he'll be gone for a few days. No, he doesn't know where Matt can be reached, why don't I phone the theatre? I phone. They're not holding auditions and they've never heard of Matthew Webster. Either my informant has got the theatre wrong or the city or Matthew lied.

The inquest is brief. The doctor who certified

Kitty's death is there, the two policemen, the pathologist, Peter Turner, Mother and me. I think the coroner would like to say it was an accidental death, suicide seems to stick in his throat, but there's nothing accidental about stepping into a hot bath and running a razor-sharp knife across your arteries. Even Kitty wasn't that vague.

'– while the balance of her mind was disturbed,' he says, looking at Mother and me sympathetically, as if that makes it easier for us to bear. I would have thought deranged or demented were more appropriate words to describe Kitty's state of mind when she stepped into that bath.

A reporter is scribbling furiously, a young girl. She'll squeeze all the pathos out of this story, it'll make quite a splash in the local rag. Oddly enough I don't feel as if we've been talking about Kitty. It's as if the coroner were questioning us about someone we used to know.

I think it's wiser if Ian doesn't come to the funeral. I want him there, God knows I do, but I don't want a grave-side scene with him pulling me one way and Mother the other. She's still sedated but she cries a lot, the tears pouring down her cheeks although no sound is coming out of her throat. It's heartbreaking to see. The arthritis is affecting her badly too, crippling her fingers. She'll never sew silver thread on blue satin cushions again.

I'm dreading tomorrow. The weather has turned so cold, a biting wind from the east. I remember standing by Daddy's grave in weather like this. I held Matthew's hand, he was such a little boy. He kept saying, 'Why isn't Daddy here? When is he coming?'

He let us all down.

Our friends and neighbours are very kind, there's always someone in the house with Mother trying to comfort her. She says the same thing over and over again, blaming herself for her sister's death.

Ian phones, begging me to meet him if only for an afternoon, an hour, but when I tried to leave yesterday Mother went berserk. The Cookmans were here at the time, old friends, Mother went to school with Dorothy, but she doesn't want anyone with her but me. I think if there were a hundred people in the house it wouldn't matter. She only wants me.

There'll be a dozen or so at the funeral, mostly relatives. We've invited them back to the house afterwards. I've tried to persuade Mother to do some cooking, she used to say it was therapeutic – 'Why don't you make some scones, dear, or your lovely coffee and rum cake?' – but she shows no interest.

God knows where Matthew is. I've tried to track him down but it's hopeless. Tasha might know, if they're still together, which I doubt, but I don't know where to find her either. Which theatre did she say she was working for? I daren't ask Ian . . . Anyway, it's probably better if Matthew isn't at the funeral. I can't forgive him for what he's done.

Why did he have to tell Mother about Ian? Why couldn't he have come directly to me with his poisoned chalice?

If Mother and I hadn't had such a row that day we might have paid more attention to Kitty . . . No, I can't lay the blame on someone else. I knew what a terrible state she was in, I should have stayed awake, watched over her.

'She would have killed herself anyway.'

Perhaps Ian's right.

CHAPTER 32

Now that the funeral's over Mother's much quieter. She has also become very vague, doing foolish, dangerous things. She lights a match and forgets she's holding it until it burns her fingers, she turns the taps full on and walks out of the kitchen. She won't go into the first-floor bathroom at all. Sometimes I think it would be a good idea if we moved out of this house. There are too many sad memories.

Ian phones. 'I've got to see you.'

'I can't, Ian. I can't leave her. Not yet.'

'I'll drive over and park in that lane near your house. Surely you can escape for a few minutes? Take the dog for a walk.'

She sleeps in the afternoon, sometimes for three or four hours. Even so I feel uneasy as I close the front door quietly, grabbing Rob's muzzle to stop him barking.

Ian gets out of the car and runs towards me, arms outstretched. I wish to God I could stop crying, it's such a stupid waste of precious time.

'Now it's all over, love, we can get married. I'll

get the licence. We don't have to make a great fuss about it, just you, me and –'

'But it isn't over, darling.'

'Oh come on, Ruth, we can't wait for ever.'

'No, not for ever, I'm not saying that. Just till she's a little better. She'd burn the house down if I wasn't there. I don't know if she wants to kill herself or if she really doesn't know what she's doing. I can't get through to her.'

'It's shock. She'll get over it.'

'Of course she will, that's what I'm saying. She'll get over it in time . . . Oh darling I'm sorry, I must get back now in case she wakes up early.'

Matthew phones. He was in Birmingham. His agent has got him a small part in a television commercial. 'I told Phil where I was going, the silly sod. He must have been high again.'

'It doesn't matter.'

'How's Mother?'

'Terrible. She's got it into her head that she's to blame for Kitty's death.'

'Oh shit, she did the same when Dad died, didn't she.'

'Did she?'

'Sure. She kept saying it was her fault, Christ knows why. His heart packed up, end of story.' How can he remember that when he was such a little boy and yet I can't? 'Look, I'll be over this evening. Keep some dinner for me.'

There's no dinner to keep, we don't eat in this house any more. Mother sleeps or sits in her chair staring into space and I only live for those brief moments in the afternoon with Ian.

'How much longer, Ruth?'

'I don't know, darling.'

We've been over this so many times, sitting in Graham's car, parked half-way up the lane.

'Don't you see what you're doing to yourself? It's the same old story all over again. What are you, a human sacrifice?'

'Give me time, Ian. I can't leave her, not yet. How can I leave her like this?'

'Then get someone to look after her.'

Simpson gives me the name of an agency, assures me they employ good people with some kind of medical background. I arrange for a carer to come every afternoon, Mrs Tindall, a pleasant woman, not at all the martinet I'd dreaded.

'Mother sleeps most of the time,' I explain to her, 'but I won't be away for long anyway.'

Ian's waiting for me in the lane. We've arranged to go to a hotel. It's such a long time since we lay naked, his hands and mouth caressing my body . . . I can't believe it's possible to love someone so much, to want them so much, and yet feel nothing.

'Don't worry,' he strokes my face like a fond father with a troubled child, 'it'll be all right when we're together again.'

When I get home Mrs Tindall assures me that everything went well, there were no problems at all, but when I go in to Mother she clings to me, sobbing. I phone Ian. We can't go to the hotel tomorrow, I can't leave her. I'm sorry, I'm so sorry, please understand . . .

I go to Simpson for a check up.

'You're not eating properly, are you? From the look of you I'd say you weren't eating at all.' He waits for my reply but I've nothing to say. 'Are you sleeping?'

'Not very well.'

'Do you still have that nightmare, the one about the train going into the tunnel?'

'Now and then.' Every night. But I'm not going to tell him, it sounds so childish.

'What are your plans for the future? Have you found another job yet?' He consults his notes. 'Ah yes, you're going on a cruise. That'll pick you up.'

'Well no, actually I cancelled it because I'm . . . I was going to get married.'

If he's surprised he doesn't show it. 'When?'

'Well it's difficult, with Mother I mean. I'll have to put it off until she's a bit better.'

'Couldn't your mother live with you?'

'No, you see my fiancé,' that's the first time I've called him that, 'doesn't have the room to –'

'She doesn't have to live in the same house as you. Lots of mothers live in granny flats at the bottom of the garden.' He makes her sound like a rabbit in a hutch. Throw her a carrot now and then and the dear old thing will be quite content.

'It isn't that simple. Mother doesn't like my

fiancé . . . well,' might as well call a spade a spade, 'she hates him.'

'So put her in a home.'

'Oh, I couldn't do that.'

'Why not?'

'It's so selfish. I owe her something after all she's done for me.'

He leans back in his chair, steepling his fingers. 'Of course you owe her something, you owe her love and loyalty and some of your time but you don't owe her your life – No, no, hear me out. And you certainly don't owe her your future happiness. Look at it this way, if you had a daughter would you want her to give up everything to look after you?'

'I . . . I don't know, I'll think it over.'

'Yes, you do that.' He gets to his feet, my ten minutes is up. 'But don't take too long. Life goes on, Ruth, parent to child, parent to child, not the other way around. She left her mother to marry the man she wanted. You have the right to do the same.'

When I get home Mother's sitting in an armchair in front of the fire dozing. The carer is with her.

'How is she?'

'We've had a long chat. She's been telling me all about her childhood in Norfolk. Well,' she rolls up her knitting and puts it in her bag, 'I'll be on my way then.'

Mother wakes and smiles at me, a sad little smile, like a lost child with kind strangers.

'Mother . . .' I put my arms around her.

'Poor Ruthy,' she murmurs, stroking my hair. 'Poor Ruthy.'

Mrs Tindall is waiting for me in the hall.

'I've been thinking . . .'

'Yes, I know what you've been thinking, Miss Webster. You don't want me to come any more.'

'It's just that Mother is . . .'

'Miss Webster, your mother is elderly and she's grieving. There's nothing we can do about the first but she will come to terms with her grief if you let her.'

'If I *let* her? I don't know what you mean.'

'She isn't your child, she isn't a baby to be molly-coddled, and you have a life of your own to lead. Do you work?'

I should be annoyed about this, I should tell her to mind her own business but she's a kind woman. And frankly I haven't the energy. 'I was made redundant just before Christmas.'

'Do you have any interests? My dear,' she puts a hand on my arm, 'please don't be offended. I know you think I'm an interfering old woman but you must get away from this house if only for a short while. I can look after your mother. She'll come to accept me, if she has to.'

When she's gone I phone Matthew. 'Could you come over this evening? I'd like to talk to you about Mother.'

'Not a hope, old love, I'm packing.' He's on the move again. Yet another landlady has shown him the door. 'No, not Ealing, Birmingham. I met a director from the Rep when I was up there and did an audition for him. I've just heard I'm in. It's a brilliant company, Ruth, loads of big names have used it as a springboard. A couple of years with them and . . . Christ, I can't tell you how excited I am. I was beginning to think I'd never make it. I've just been piddling around all this time. I suppose I've been waiting for them to come to me. Well, now I know that ain't about to happen so the mountain's going to Mahomet.'

'When are you leaving?'

'Tomorrow morning, soon as the cock crows. I've got to find digs and get settled in asap.'

'Matthew, we need to talk about Mother before you go.'

'So talk.'

'I'm getting married.' I rush on, I don't want to hear his thoughts or comments and he's certainly not about to congratulate me, not after the way he rubbished Ian to Mother. 'I can't have her living with me.'

'Well, you do what you think best.'

'No, it isn't up to me, Matthew. It's our decision, yours and mine. What do you think we should do about her?'

'Why can't she live with you after you're married? Ian's got a big place . . . well, his uncle has.'

'Because she doesn't like Ian.' It's on the tip of my tongue to say it's your fault she doesn't like him but if we get into that he'll start shouting and so will I and nothing will be resolved.

'She'll come round.'

'Maybe she will but what do we do in the meantime?'

'Leave her where she is, I suppose. She's happy enough in her own home, isn't she?'

'Oh Matthew, she can't be left alone for one minute.'

'Then get a nurse or a companion or someone for her.'

'But she won't let anyone look after her except me.'

'Sounds as if you're stuck with it then.'

'I'm damned if I'm going to be stuck with it.'

'Look, don't lose your fucking rag. What the hell d'you expect me to do, drag her up to Birmingham and stash her in my lodgings while I'm at the theatre all day and half the night?'

He's right, of course. There's nothing he can do. When I tell Ian he shrugs. 'What did you expect him to say? If it were up to your brother he'd take off and leave your mother to sort herself out. But that doesn't help you, does it? Good old reliable Ruth.' He pats my shoulder. 'Faithful unto death.'

'You make me sound like a dull old workhorse.'

'Of course not. You're the salt of the earth, love.'

Somehow it doesn't sound like a compliment.

CHAPTER 33

I look for an interest, something that will get me out of the house, flower arranging, marquetry, aromatherapy, yoga. But it's no use. Mrs Tindall's disappointed when I tell her.

'I'll get my life back in shape. I just need a bit of time. But thanks for everything, Mother really enjoyed your company.' A lie. And we both know it. Mother resented her and made no effort to hide it.

The phone rings just after eleven that evening, jolting me awake. 'Sorry, love, were you asleep?'

'What's wrong?'

'Nothing's wrong. In fact, everything's right, couldn't be better. We've got our angel at last, all signed and sealed.'

'Oh, Ian!'

'And he's no back-street operator either. This one's got a bit of class and he's in with all the right people too. That means we'll have no trouble getting Council approval. *And* he's going to con his mates into putting up some cash.'

'I'm so happy for you, darling.'

'This is it, Ruth. This is it!' He's flying. 'There's

only one more thing I want – for Christ's sake stop messing about, marry me.' If only I could say yes. 'I'll be up to my eyeballs in this for months, years. It means I won't have any spare time. Not much of a life for you, love, being on your own.' I won't be on my own. I'll shift scenery, sew costumes, sell programmes, work in the bar . . . anything to be near him. That's as close to heaven as I'll come on this earth. 'Look, I'm tossing the ball into your court,' he says. 'If you want me, I'm here. If not . . .'

Every day I watch for signs of improvement in Mother. If only she weren't so listless. She lies in bed or sits in the living room staring at her hands, those hands that used to be so active. I've tried to persuade her to cook, to sew but it's hopeless. The Henshaws come to see her often, Major Fordham, Mrs Fussel. They've all tried to get her interested in bridge again. They're so patient with her.

'The effect of shock takes a long time to wear off,' people keep telling me, 'but she'll get better. It may take months, even years, but she'll get better.'

Months. Even years.

I dial Ian's number a dozen times a day but he's hardly ever there. When I do manage to catch him he's usually asleep and I feel guilty about waking him. Anyway we only say the same old things to each other . . .

'When, Ruth, when?'

'Give me a little time, darling, a little more time.'

'Oh, Ruth . . .'

He's losing patience, I can hear it in his voice. But I don't blame him. His time is precious and I'm only wasting it with my dreary chatter. The cruise I was going on leaves tomorrow. Once it was a red-letter day, now it's just another day to be crossed off my calendar.

Simpson calls in one morning after surgery.

'Mother's sleeping.'

'It's you I've come to see.' He opens his case and pulls out a brochure. 'This is one of the nursing homes I was telling you about, Beverley Manor.' It looks very elegant, a stately home. Prices to match. 'They've converted it well,' he says, flipping through the pages. 'Everybody has their own flat but there are communal rooms where they can get together if they want a bit of company. Your mother will be able to play bridge to her heart's content. And there are doctors and nurses on call day and –'

'No, I'm sorry, Dr Simpson, I couldn't put my mother in a home. It would kill her.'

'Ruth.' Curt voice, tightening of lips. 'Moving into a home would not kill your mother nor would it kill you. However, if you're adamant about it I suggest you get a live-in carer, someone who will release you to get on with your life. It isn't good for you being cooped up here, moping around. I'm thinking about your health, both mental and –'

'Thank you, Doctor.' It was kind of him to come.

There is obviously a heart under all that chain-mail. 'I'll think about it.'

I seem to have said that once or twice before. Maybe more, judging by the expression on his face as I show him to the door.

I was going to spend the day washing and ironing all the net curtains in the house. Mrs Humphreys could do it, of course, but it's something I enjoy. It gives me a lot of pleasure to see how bright and crisp they look when I hang them up. And it keeps my hands occupied. But not my brain. I keep churning over and over the things that Simpson said. He's right, I must do something, I must. I can't ask Ian to wait for ever.

I put Mother to bed, tuck her in and kiss her good night. She falls asleep almost immediately. The worried frown is beginning to leave her face at last. She's regaining some of her old serenity, I think. Or am I fooling myself?

I might as well go to bed too. I'm forty-four years old . . . No, almost forty-five. It's my birthday next month. A June baby, I might have been a June bride. Forty-five and I'm practically bedridden.

I read for a while, doze for a while, watch television for a while, get up, pour myself a large Scotch and stand by the window sipping it. It's so dark outside, an impenetrable blackness, no moon, no stars, as if the whole world is covered in a shroud.

'May has disappointed us,' said Major Fordham

yesterday, rather poetically for him, I thought. 'Let's hope June will bring some sunshine.'

I pull the curtains and block out the night. But I'm blocked in now, I'm suffocating. It will be like this for the rest of my life if I don't do something.

It's almost two o'clock. He'll be asleep, exhausted after another day of negotiations, discussions, arguments . . . I don't care, I've got to tell him. I've made my decision at last. Darling, oh my darling, my love, let's get married now, now!

With trembling hands I dial his number. It rings seven or eight times – Ian, please be there, please! A woman answers. I recognise the voice immediately. It's a beautiful voice, very low, smoky.

I hang up. Not a nice thing to do but what could I say . . . 'No, don't wake him. It's nothing important. I was only going to tell him I'll marry him.'

At the back of my chest of drawers, buried deep under all the sweaters, is a packet of cigarettes I bought just after Kitty died. I meant to burn it. Thank God I didn't. This is my first cigarette for months. I'd forgotten the sheer pleasure of inhaling smoke deep, deep into the lungs.

I sit on the bed, lighting one cigarette from the other, staring at the carpet, following the pattern to the edge of the room and back again, counting every leaf, every petal. I study that pattern for hours as if my life depended on it.

It isn't his fault. It wasn't fair asking him to live like that waiting, waiting in vain . . .

'When, Ruth, when?'

'This year, next year, sometime . . .'

Never.

He'd given up hope. And Tasha is right for him, young, beautiful, clever. She fits into his world.

The wind's dying down now, the rain has stopped. Odd how the weather can change so suddenly. A boisterous night often gives way to a gentle dawn. Rob is curled up on the duvet giving little yelps, his eyelids twitching furiously as he dreams of rabbits. I can hear cars swishing by on the wet street, footsteps hurrying. The first commuters are on their way. I must go and see to Mother. She's always confused when she wakes up. I walk stiffly to her room, my body numb from the long night's vigil, and open the door a crack. She's still sleeping.

CHAPTER 34

All the days seem the same now. There is something soothing about the monotony of my existence. I get up, do what has to be done, take some sleeping pills – I'm up to three or four a night – and go back to bed. Only the nightmare has changed. The tunnel has become a wall. I can see it up ahead. We're going to crash into it. We're going to –

'No! Oh God, no!'

I wake up screaming, my body clammy with sweat.

My room stinks of cigarette smoke. I open the French doors, wrapping my dressing gown around me but it does little to keep out the chilly dampness of an indifferent June. The long, wet grass feels cold to my bare feet.

After Daddy died Mother and I used to do all the gardening ourselves, mowing the lawn, trimming the hedges, digging, planting, pruning, potting. Now we have a gardener, more interested in boosting his meagre pension than making our garden beautiful. Daddy used to grow orchids in the greenhouse, he was so proud of them, now there's nothing in here but broken pots filled with withered plants. Most of the windows are cracked, letting in the rain and cold air.

A shard of glass has pierced my foot but if it weren't for the blood on the concrete floor I wouldn't even have noticed. I could slit my wrists now with Kitty's knife and not feel a thing.

As I turn to leave something catches my eye, a brilliant splash of colour in the midst of all this decay. On a shelf in the corner is Graham's bonsai. Kitty must have put it there and forgotten about it. The soil in its pot is dry. This little bush should have died long ago and yet, against all the odds, it's in full bloom. It's magnificently aglow with deep pink flowers.

I drop my cigarette into the water butt, pick up the bonsai and walk quickly back to the house. My foot is leaving bloodstains all over Mother's beautiful pastel carpets and dear old Rob bounding along behind me is adding his fair share of mud.

'What's that, dear?'

Mother is up. She has managed to get herself down the stairs without my help.

'It's the little rhododendron that Ian's uncle gave me for Christmas.'

'It's beautiful.' No reaction to Ian's name, no hysteria. She's forgotten about him or doesn't care any more. 'Put it on the table.'

'No, I'm going to put it in my bedroom.' On the windowsill so that it's the last thing I see before I fall asleep and the first I see when I open my eyes in the morning – my stubborn, brave little bonsai.

CHAPTER 35

Help the aged have put a sack through our letter box. 'Anything you can give will help.' Mother and I have been through our cupboards and wardrobes so often there's nothing left to give but I trawl through one more time . . . A pair of evening shoes, very high heels, one fine strap diagonally across the instep, a little clutch purse that holds nothing except a lipstick, a compact and loose change, the purse of a woman who's used to having a man to look after her . . .

I put them in the sack, pull out the purse again, just in case I've left something in there like a comb or . . . There's a card, Jonathan Martin, Flat 5, The Cedars . . . Who on earth is Jonathan . . . ? Oh, of course, the scenic designer I met at Graham's party.

I dial his number.

'Hello?'

Why on earth am I doing this?

'Hello?'

I'm about to hang up when I hear him swear. He must think I'm one of those heavy breathers.

Oh, for God's sake . . . 'Hello. Is that Jonathan Martin?'

'Speaking.'

'You probably don't remember me . . . Ruth Webster. We met at Graham Ashworth's party.'

'The thimble lady.'

My reputation goes before me.

'What a good memory you have.'

'Not really. You were the only woman I spoke to all evening, apart from Madam Michelangelo and she doesn't count. So how are you?'

'Fine, thank you. I was just wondering . . . I mean, you know we were talking about scenic design. Well . . .'

'You've jacked in your job as an insurance pest and you want to get into the theatre.'

So he talked to Ian about me.

'No . . . Yes, I'm not working any more so I thought it might be fun to . . .'

'Of course it is.'

'The trouble is I don't know where to start.'

'Go along to your nearest theatre and tell them you want to learn about scenic design and in return you're offering your services free, scrubbing, painting, hammering in nails, whatever. They're always glad to have an extra pair of hands, provided they don't have to pay for them.'

'I'm no good at cold calling.' An insurance expression. 'I mean . . .'

'I know what it means. Where d'you live, Ruth?'

'Just outside Guildford.'

318

'Guildford, Guildford, who do I know in . . . ? Of course, Tim Bracknell. Brilliant bloke, works for The Green Room. It's semi-professional.'

'Oh no, no, I don't want . . . I just want something like . . .'

'Don't get panicky, it isn't Stratford. Semi-professional just means a bit more businesslike than the amateur groups. D'you know The Green Room?'

The theatre that Matthew took Ian to. 'Yes.'

'I'll give you Tim's number. If I can find it, that is. Hold on a minute, there's such a load of rubbish on this desk . . . Ah, here we go. Got a pen handy?'

After deliberating for an hour – can I not make a decision about anything any more? – I finally dial the number. Tim Bracknell is very courteous, he suggests we meet for coffee.

'Tuesday evening?'

'Well, I . . .' Perhaps Peter's wife will sit with Mother. She's offered several times. 'Yes, all right.'

I'm in a sweat. Those who can, do. Those who can't, criticise. I've become quite the theatre critic over the years. But it's one thing to sit in the stalls making mental notes about the acting and the direction and the set that no one will ever read, quite another to pour them into the ear of a real scenic designer. The first thing he'll ask me is if I have any qualifications or experience. To which the answer is 'Not a jot. I'm wasting your time. Sorry.'

He's twice my height and half my age . . . No

he's not, I'm not that old! His face splits into a grin when he sees me. He's right, it's a joke. 'Well,' he says when we've ordered coffee, 'do you have any experience in scenic design, Ruth?'

'No, not a jot.'

'Good,' he nods. 'No ideas set in concrete then. Do you sketch, paint?'

I've brought some of my thimbles to show him. Either he's a very good actor or he's genuinely impressed. 'They're brilliant. Such fine work. This,' he holds up one of my favourites, a butterfly in iridescent colours, 'is fabulous.' He laughs. 'I nearly said Fabergé. Do you sell them?'

Is he making fun of me?

'Would you like it?'

'I'd love it. How much?'

'No, have it. Please.'

'Really? Thanks, that's very kind of you.' He takes the napkin from under his saucer, wraps the thimble in it and puts it in his pocket so carefully you would think it was made of finest crystal. 'I'd be interested to see what you can do with a stage set,' he says.

'It's a bit intimidating.'

'At first. But you'll get used to it. Did Jonathon tell you anything about me? Okay, well I have my own company. My dad started it about twenty years ago. I took a course in just about all aspects of theatre at St Martin's –' from the way he says it I'm obviously supposed to know St Martin's. I give a knowing kind of nod. '– and the plan was

320

that I'd work for him for a few years and then go off and do my own thing. But then Dad got –' he makes a trembling movement with his right hand, 'so he had to give up. That just leaves me to run the show. He'd be gutted if I sold it. I can't let him down,' he shrugs. 'You know how it is.'

Join the club.

'So I get involved in the theatre in my spare time. And The Green Room's brilliant. They let me pick and choose what I want to do.' He pulls a slim book out of his pocket and hands it to me. 'We're putting this on in September.'

'Travels with My Aunt.'

'Do you know it?'

'I certainly do. I love it.'

'Great. So take it home, try to erase the memory of any production you've seen and come up with some fresh ideas. How long do you think you'll need, a couple of days?' A couple of months. 'Let's make it this Friday then.'

CHAPTER 36

Mother is playing Bridge again. Major Fordham has finally managed to persuade her. He and Mrs Pryce and Jean are coming this afternoon. I go into the village to buy something for tea. There was a time we wouldn't have allowed a shop-bought cake over the threshold but mother won't bake any more and I can't be bothered. When I get back the game is in progress. I wheel the tea trolley around the table, using it as an excuse to look at all the hands. Mother has made a foolish bid and is floundering but the others are doing their best to help her win a few tricks. Major Fordham catches my eye and gives me a sly smile. Mother is lucky to have such friends.

After tea I leave them discussing whether Jean should have made a jump overcall with so few points, go into my bedroom and get out my notes. I've been working on them day and night. *Travels with my Aunt* is a clever play. There are twenty-four parts all played by just four actors. Even the women, Aunt Augusta, Miss Keene, Hatty are to be played by men. No costumes, no props, apart from a table and chairs. I want my set to be equally clever and simple.

The first act opens with Henry meeting his aunt at his mother's funeral. Since he's mad about dahlias I've used them as a motif, dahlias as wreaths in every shape – pillows, crosses, hearts. For the scene changes – Aunt Augusta's flat, Henry's garden, Brighton, Paris, Istanbul, the Orient Express – I'm going to use a pull-through backdrop, the kind of thing you see in children's books, pull the tab at the side and a different picture or message appears. I don't know if it will work but Tim knows I don't have any technical knowledge, he just wants to find out if I have any ideas.

I've really crunched my brain to come up with something different. It's so easy to fall into the trap of the obvious – Brighton, the pier. Paris, the Eiffel Tower. Istanbul, domes and minarets. I can use sound, of course. For the taxi scene I've got horns blaring and people swearing. My backdrop is just two fingers, the insulting gesture one frustrated driver makes to another. It's a bit naughty but I've seen much worse on the stage. A bellboy with his eye to a bedroom keyhole represents Brighton and a waxed moustache the Orient Express – everyone associates Hercules Poirot with that train, don't they?

I've still got the whole of Act Two to do – Argentina, Panama, Paraguay – and only one more day. Will he like what I've done or will he take one look and tell me to go home and keep painting thimbles?

I've arranged for another carer to sit with Mother for the evening. I couldn't get Mrs Tindall but the agency assures me this one is just as nice. They're right. I warm to her as soon as I meet her. Mother does not.

'I don't need anyone to watch over me, thank you,' she said when I told her. 'I'm quite capable of looking after myself.'

She's quite capable of blowing up the house and herself with it.

'Mrs Ferguson's not going to watch over you, dear, she's just coming to keep you company. Anyway, she's doing it for my sake not yours. I'll feel more comfortable if you're not here on your own.'

'Where are you going?'

'The theatre. The Green Room.'

'Why can't I come with you? It's a long time since I've been to the theatre.'

'I'm not going to see anything, Mother, I'm going to . . .' Work, have fun, make a complete fool of myself? 'I'm just going to help out.'

'Help out?'

'Work on the scenery.'

She frowns. 'Whatever for?'

Matthew has been wasting his time in the theatre for the past ten years but she has never once said to him, 'Whatever for?'

Tim is already in the café when I arrive. He looks as if he's been there some time.

'I'm sorry, am I late?' Of course I'm not, I left the house with half an hour to spare.

'No, I'm early. I had a bite to eat.'

I get out my sketches. 'They're not very good.' I push them towards him hesitantly. I thought they were ingenious when I was working on them but now . . . I watch his face as he goes through them, turning over the pages slowly, narrowing his eyes. He doesn't like them.

'Excellent.' He glances up. 'No, really, you've shown a lot of originality. I'm impressed. Of course, technically . . .' He spends the next two hours explaining why none of my ideas will work. The pull-throughs get the thumbs down. 'Too jokey,' he says. 'This one,' he holds up the two-finger sketch for the taxi driver, 'the actors will have to wait for the audience to stop laughing. They'll hate you for upstaging them and the director won't thank you for holding up the action.'

It's half past ten when I look at my watch. 'Good Lord, I didn't realise it was so late, I must go.'

He looks bemused. 'You'll have a lot of late nights in the theatre, Ruth. Sometimes we work into the early hours if we have to get stuff done.'

Mother is in bed when I get home.

'Was she all right, Mrs Ferguson?'

'She got a bit sulky but it didn't bother me, I've got a skin like a rhino.'

'Will you be able to come again, do you think?'

'Certainly. When do you want me?'

I tell her about Tim and *Travels with my Aunt*. 'I'm just going to shadow him for this production, there's so much to learn . . .' It's gone eleven, the poor woman wants to get home, she probably has a husband waiting up for her, but I'm so excited I have to tell someone. I want to talk and talk and talk all night.

I'm beginning to sound like Ian.

CHAPTER 37

Graham phones. 'Could we meet for lunch?'

'Oh, I'd love to but –'

'You name the day and the place. I'll come over to Guildford if that's more convenient for you. I seem to recall a nice little restaurant there, French I think.'

'I'm so busy . . .'

'Surely you can spare an hour or two, Ruth? I haven't seen you for such a long time.'

I wake next morning to the smell of burning and rush into the kitchen. 'Mother?'

'Oh dear, I put them in the oven and forgot.'

We rescue the scones and open the windows to let out the smoke.

'They're black.' She looks downcast.

'Just the tops, dear. Look, we can cut them off. They're perfect inside.'

They're dry, heavy, but she has made them herself. I'm so pleased I can't stop hugging her. She got up before me, washed and dressed, came down and made scones for breakfast. I don't care if they look and taste like bricks – they're manna from heaven.

She has set the table too, jam, marmalade, honey. And butter, the eighth deadly sin.

'Oh I'm sorry, Ruthy, how silly of me, I quite forgot. I'll get the Flora for you.'

'With lovely, home-made scones? Certainly not.'

The restaurant is one of those pretentious places with enormous menus and prices to match. Graham has reserved a table for us. The maitre d' seats us with a curt nod of the head, shakes out a napkin the size of a table cloth and wafts it in the direction of my lap . . . 'And an aperitif?' I ask for a Scotch. Clearly he doesn't approve of my choice. Graham orders a double just for the pleasure of making him even more disgusted, I suspect. When he's gone Graham leans towards me. 'So, Ruth –'

'How are you, Graham? Have you had any more parties? Do you remember the one at Christmas, I had a terrible cold? I was so bunged up I could hardly hear. I still cringe when I think of that woman, the sculptor, what was her name? I know nothing about sculpture and when she asked me . . .' I rabbit on. I've come with a list of topics. I'm prepared to talk about anything, parties, old cars, travel, food, the weather, anything but –

'Tell me, Ruth,' he interrupts me in the middle of my monologue. This is the moment I've been dreading. I can tell from his expression, the way he's leaning towards me, he's going to ask . . . 'How is Satsuki?'

'Who?'

'The rhododendron I gave you.'

I'm so relieved I burst out laughing. 'It's recovering.' I tell him what happened, the neglect, the rebirth. 'It's getting strong again.'

'Of course,' he nods. 'They're resilient little things. They may look fragile but they're tough, they fight back.'

Yes, Graham, I understand. There's no need to labour the point.

'Actually I'm thinking of buying another one, a Monterey Cypress.' The Daltons have branched out into bonsai, an exotic addition to their range. 'It's a beauty, about twenty years old. I might start a collection.'

'Well, if you need any advice –'

'Oh, I do.' I've come armed with zillions of questions, more than enough to keep us going until I can look at my watch and say, 'Oh Lord, look at the time, I must be on my way.'

He raises his hand and the waiter appears.

'The bill, please.'

I've run out of topics for animated discussion but I can fill in the remaining few minutes with, 'Thank you for lunch . . . So lovely to see you again . . . Do keep in touch . . .' until I'm safely back in my car.

'Ruth,' he reaches out and puts his hand over mine. 'I'm so sorry.' I pull my hand away. I don't want his pity. 'I was hoping that you and Ian would stay together but . . .' But what, Graham? But the best woman won? But I dithered so long that I lost out?

'C'est la vie,' I say with a nonchalant shrug. But I'm a poor actress. He is not fooled.

CHAPTER 38

I can't believe my luck. Mrs Ferguson plays bridge.

'Oh, I could play before I learned to walk,' she laughs. 'My father used to rap my knuckles if I played the wrong card.'

She is to undergo her ordeal by fire this evening. Mother has invited Major Fordham and Mrs Fussel, formidable opponents. I am down on my knees praying for her. Mother has a lot of respect for people who play good bridge. She'd have forgiven Hitler everything if he'd known how to bid and play a slam.

I'm due at the theatre at seven. Tim is having what he calls a 'concept discussion' with the director.

'I've worked with her before, she's pretty open-minded,' he says. 'She'll listen to what I have to say. Not like some of the others. They come with their own ideas and closed minds.'

Egos, egos. I thought the business world was bad enough, all those supervisors, managers, heads of department, little people with big titles, but the theatre . . . I've never been backstage before. It's nothing glamorous, just a maze of dingy corridors and small rooms, but my heart's thudding all the same.

Tim introduces me to Davina. She's in the standard uniform, sweater and jeans, and I'm overdressed. I look as if I'm auditioning for Henry's aunt. Davina greets me cordially enough and she and Tim promptly forget I exist. Why was I so nervous? They're totally engrossed in technical diagrams, prop drawings, scale models, sound, lighting. If I stripped naked and did a wild fandango they wouldn't even glance up.

Tim shows her his design proposals. I notice he hasn't used any of mine. Oh well . . . He has a pencil in his hand the whole time and is for ever sketching. He listens to her, sketches, makes a suggestion, sketches. Slowly, slowly they beging to agree. Davina's saying, 'Yes, I like that, I think we're getting there.' Tim's beaming. There's enough electricity zapping between them to light up Guildford.

'So what do you think?' Tim says, walking with me across the car park.

'Fascinating.'

'Still want to do it?'

More than I've ever wanted anything in my whole life. There's only one problem, it's been nagging me from the beginning, what if Ian comes down to see it? Hardly likely, he's not interested in 'the gin and tonic circuit, Ayckbourne and Stoppard'. I don't suppose Graham Greene turns him on either. No, I'll never bump into Ian in The Green Room.

'Yes,' I nod at Tim eagerly like a kid who's just been invited to the biggest birthday party on the block. 'Yes, I'd love to.'

'See you on Monday then. We've got a tough six weeks ahead of us. If you've made any plans, cancel them.'

Major Fordham and Mrs Fussel have gone by the time I get home. Mother is in her sitting room sipping brandy with Mrs Ferguson. They're in the middle of a postmortem.

'They won,' Mother says before I even ask, 'Sheila and the Major. We didn't stand a chance.'

Sheila?

'I did some stupid things.' Mother shakes her head irritably.

'But you had poor cards, Ann,' says Mrs Ferguson.

'It's kind of you to make excuses for me, Sheila, but the truth is I'm badly out of practice. Can you play on Thursday?' I get into bed, turn out the light, snuggle under the duvet. Sheila and Ann . . . Oh thank you, God.

CHAPTER 39

Matthew has a part, a really big role, he says, in the Rep's next production, *She Stoops to Conquer*. He wants Mother and me to go to the first night.

'When is it, dear?'

'August the sixteenth.'

'August the . . . ?' But that's next Wednesday. 'Oh Matthew, why didn't you tell me before?'

'I didn't know how it would shape up. I wanted to wait until we were well into rehearsals before dragging you up here . . . Why, you're not doing anything, are you?'

'I do have a life, Matthew.'

I expect the usual snort of derision. Instead he tells me it's the break he's been waiting for, all the top producers and directors, the TV talent scouts, will be there.

'You will come, won't you?' Usually it's a command, now he's almost pleading.

'Of course we will.'

Mother perks up when I tell her. 'We'll have to stay overnight, won't we, Ruthy? We couldn't get there and back in a day.'

I resent missing even one evening at The Green Room but we can't let Matthew down, not when it looks as if he might be getting somewhere at last . . . Or has he floated off into cloud cuckoo land again?

'Don't worry,' Tim says when I tell him, 'there'll still be plenty to do when you get back. And we're putting on *The Turn of The Screw* at Christmas so start thinking about sets now. And remember,' he grins, 'you're supposed to be underpinning the production, not undermining it.'

I've booked two single rooms in a hotel in Stratford on Avon. It would be more convenient to stay in Birmingham, of course, but I love Stratford and I haven't been there for years. Mother spends a lot of time looking through her wardrobe, fretting that she has nothing to wear. It's wonderful to see her so animated again. We chatter and giggle together like a couple of schoolgirls.

'What do you think of this, dear?' She holds up a dress in silver brocade, high neck, long sleeves.

'Nice but dull. Remember you'll be mingling with the glitterati.'

'What about this one, then?'

A full-length skirt and top in beige lace over taffeta, one of Major Fordham's favourites. His eyes always mist over when she wears it.

'Mm, not bad. But you'll have to cut the bodice down a couple of inches. Show a bit of cleavage.'

'Oh, Ruthy!' She pretends to be outraged. 'What are you going to wear, dear?'

I should have given all my new, glamorous clothes away. Instead I put them at the back of my wardrobe where I can't see them. What am I keeping them for – a rainy day? That day has come and gone. 'Oh, I don't know.'

'Why don't you wear the black velvet outfit you bought after Christmas?' Now how does she know about that? 'Kitty . . .' at last she can say her name without breaking down, 'Kitty told me about it. She said it was beautiful.'

We leave for Stratford after breakfast.

'Where do all these people come from and where are they going to?' says Mother, closing her window in a vain attempt to keep out the fumes.

'The traffic will quieten down when we get past Oxford. Where would you like to have lunch, dear?'

'Could we stop at Burford?'

Uncle Frank's family used to live there. Mother spent many a happy holiday with them when it was little more than a quiet village deep in the heart of the country. We'll have to make a diversion but it doesn't matter. The sun comes out at last and looks as if it means to stay for a while. We'll have a leisurely lunch and then drive through the Cotswolds.

'When are you playing bridge with Sheila again, Mother?' I ask over lunch.

'Saturday evening. The Henshaws are coming.'

'Poor Sheila.'

'Oh no, she'll make mincemeat of them.'

'Is she that good?'

'She plays upstairs at the Club.' Kneel and wonder. Only the gods play upstairs. 'She's a widow, you know. There's a son in Bristol and one in Newcastle, both married. She doesn't see much of them. That's the trouble with boys, you lose them when they marry.'

'Where does she live?'

'Godalming. She has a small flat. She says she's retiring soon.'

'She doesn't look that old to me.'

'She's only fifty-seven.'

'Can she afford to retire?'

'Well, I don't think she's very well off from what she's said but the constant travelling's getting her down. It must be very tiring going to different houses all the time.' But very relaxing if she were to live in ours.

'It's a pity she lives so far away.' I drop the thought into her mind in a guileless way. 'She'd make a wonderful bridge partner for you, dear.'

'Mm,' she says, pondering it.

We arrive at The Swan just before five. A shower, a rest, a snack, and we set off for Birmingham. It's years since I was there and I've allowed myself plenty of time to get lost in its intestines. Even so we arrive at the theatre with only fifteen minutes to spare.

'Do you think we could go and see Matthew before it starts?' says Mother.

'No I don't, dear. He's probably half dead with

fright. The last thing he'll want to do is entertain us.'

'Poor Matthew,' she murmurs.

For once I agree with her. It must be nerve-racking to walk on stage knowing that hundreds of eyes are watching you. Apparently even Laurence Olivier never got over his fear of corpsing.

Matthew has given us tickets for the dress circle. We 'excuse me, sorry, sorry' our way to the centre of the third row, crushing knees, stumbling over feet – why don't people stand up, it would be so much easier? – and settle into our seats. Mother has forgotten her binoculars. We empty our purses looking in vain for a pound coin. The Samaritan on my left reaches into his pocket, takes out a coin and gives it to me.

'My pleasure,' he says waving aside my handful of small change.

The house lights dim, the excited buzz dies down and the curtain goes up. The set is excellent, Tim would be impressed. He's instructed me to give him a detailed account. There's a round of applause. I can sense that this is an audience that wants to enjoy itself. I'd like to enjoy myself too but I'm so nervous for Matthew my palms are sweating. And there he is, on stage, playing Tony Lumpkin. Not exactly the romantic lead he's always imagined himself to be but whoever cast him in the role has done him a huge favour. He's a natural comedian and within minutes he has the audience at his feet. They love him.

Mother and I take turns looking at him through the binoculars. You'd think we'd never seen him before. During the interval we line up for a drink at the bar and listen to some of the comments.

'That fellow playing Tony Lumpkin's very good, isn't he?'

'Never seen him here before. What's his name?'

'Don't know, I've left my programme on the seat.'

'Matthew Webster,' says Mother. She never butts into other people's conversations, the nuns would have been appalled at such a breach of good manners, but she's so proud she can't keep silent. 'He's my son.'

We bask in Matthew's celebrity.

The second half is even better than the first, Matthew is really in his stride now, and at the final curtain there are cries of 'Bravo!' when he takes his bow.

We sit for a while, discreetly dabbing our cheeks – tears of joy after so many tears of disappointment. There's a cast party. Matthew wants us to go . . . 'You don't have to stay long. I think you'd enjoy it though. They're a good bunch.'

'Do you feel up to it, Mother?'

It's half past ten. Normally she has been in bed for at least an hour by this time but she looks at me as if I've taken leave of my senses. 'Of course I do.'

Several hundred people have got here before us and they've all managed to get a drink. Some of them look as if they're on their second or third.

The noise is deafening, the shrieks as one luvvie greets another.

There's quite a rake on this stage, it must take a lot of getting used to. I can't see Matthew . . . Oh yes, there he is. He's got his make-up on, he's still Tony Lumpkin.

'Hey!' He gives us both rib-cracking hugs.

We are completely out of place in this sea of jeans. Mother looks like a throwback to the fifties in her elegant lace and I look as if I've stepped out of *Private Lives*.

'Matthew, you were brilliant.'

'Wonderful, darling,' says Mother.

'D'you really think so?'

He's heard it a dozen times already but he can't quite believe it. It's strange but now that he's a success, or on the verge of it, he's lost some of his arrogance. He seems overawed, almost humbled by what's happened. I realise now how much all those years of failure, of losing face in front of family and friends time and time again, demoralised him.

'Yes, really. You're a star.'

I didn't think I'd ever say that to my brother.

'Come and meet . . .' He takes Mother's arm and pushes through the crowd. I can't take the heat and the crush of bodies. I think I'll just creep over to the wings and get my breath back before plunging in. Matthew won't miss me, he's too busy telling everyone, 'This is my mum.' And his mum won't miss me either. She's in heaven.

I recognise some of the faces. I don't know if they're actors, directors, playwrights, or just personalities famous for nothing, Oh, that's Derek Jacobi – I remember reading he got his start here. And I'm sure that's Peter Hall. He looks much smaller than I thought. And over there – Oh God!

They say that when something traumatic happens to you, like falling over a cliff or drowning, the action slows right down. A second becomes an hour, a minute becomes eternity. I know now what they mean. Slowly, so slowly, Ian lifts the glass to his mouth, takes a sip, swallows, turns his head, catches sight of someone he knows, smiles, raises his glass in greeting . . . I feel as if I've been standing here watching him for ever.

'Ruth . . .'

I don't know where I am. What's happening?

'Come on, Ruth.' It's Matthew, tugging at my arm. 'Come and meet Dominic, you'll love him. He played the part of . . .'

We weave back through the crowd.

'Are you all right, dear?' Mother looks worried.

'Yes . . . No . . . So hot.'

I feel dizzy. Everything seems to be swirling around me. I'll fall if it doesn't stop. Matthew suggests we go to his dressing room.

Backstage at a big repertory theatre seems to be just as unglamorous as at a small semi-professional. I can understand why the ones who've clawed their way to the top throw a tantrum if there isn't at least a swimming pool and a tennis court in their dressing room. They've had enough of slumming it.

Matthew's is a shoe box he shares with two others. There's a mirror, a table covered in bottles and boxes of make-up, a couple of chairs and a bar for their costumes. He borrows a chair from another room, sits down and reaches under the table.

'Yes?' he says, holding up a bottle of Bell's blended.

'Please.'

'Ruthy, do you think you should?'

'Yes, Mother, she definitely should,' Matt says, pouring me a stiff one.

A young woman pokes her head round the door, sees Matt and throws her arms around him. 'Darling,' she cries, 'you were absolutely marvellous. I've never seen a better . . . Oh, sorry.' She suddenly becomes aware of Mother and me.

Matt introduces us. 'And this is Miranda,' he says, taking her hand. Miranda's obviously his latest bed-warmer. 'She's just landed the part of Ophelia.'

She pulls a face. 'Not one of my favourite roles. All that mooning around – and for a dithery dipstick like Hamlet. I can just imagine him lying in bed all morning, whining, "To get up or not to get up, that is the question".' She isn't beautiful but she has an interesting face, all cheekbones and brows. Matthew's girlfriends are definitely improving. 'If Ophelia'd had any gump she'd have said, "Now look, Ham, piss or get off the pot, okay? Rosencrantz has asked me for a date and frankly he's a lot dishier than you. So either we go up the aisle or you go down the tube." But no, the silly cow has to go and drown herself.'

'Thank you for auditioning, Miss Ross,' says Matt, straight faced. 'Don't call us . . .'

'Oh, I'll get it right on the night,' she protests. 'I'll sigh, I'll weep, I'll go mad beautifully.' She plucks three or four brushes from the dressing table and hands one to Mother and me. '"There's fennel for you, and columbine. There's rue for you",' she presses one against Matt's heart, '"and here's some for me. Hey non nonny, nonny, hey nonny",' she sighs, sinking gracefully to the floor amid applause and laughter.

Over Matt's shoulder I catch sight of myself in the mirror. Good God, no wonder he and Mother were worried. I look as if I've fallen into a vat of white paint. I down my Scotch and stand up.

'Let's go back.'

'I think you should stay here for a little longer, dear. You still look rather drawn.'

'I'm fine, Mother. Truly. I'd like to meet the rest of the cast.'

We fight our way through the crowd again. The smoke stings my eyes and throat. Is there anyone here, except for Mother and me, without a cigarette? Matt introduces us to Sir Charles Marlow and Kate Hardcastle. When nobody notices, they're all too busy complimenting each other on their brilliant performances anyway, I steal away, edging towards the wings. He's still there, in earnest conversation with an ancient gentleman with a grey ponytail. I can't see Tasha, though . . .

I'm going to do this. I'm going to do it even though my heart is pounding like a sledge hammer and my hands are sticky with sweat.

'Ian,' I touch his elbow, 'I'm sorry to interrupt. I just wanted to say hello.' I just wanted to prove to myself that I'm not a total wimp. I can look at him, talk to him, without coming unstuck. But please God don't let Tasha come. I couldn't face the two of them.

His mouth falls open, he blinks. I didn't think anyone could ruffled the composure of this man but I seem to have succeeded. The ancient gentleman gives me a reproving look and turns on his heel.

'How are you?'

'I'm fine. What about you? Need I ask?' he smiles, back in control again. 'You look wonderful. I always liked that outfit.'

Always? I only wore it once – to Graham's party. He makes it sound as if our affair lasted for years instead of months.

'So how is your theatre project coming along?' I know precisely how it's coming along. I go through *The Stage* every week with a fine tooth comb looking for any mention of his name or the Pandora, his theatre. There's a lot of interest in it.

'Couldn't be better. The original angel increased and multiplied and lo, we have received funds in abundance,' he laughs. 'Actually it's hell, this is my first evening off in Christ knows how long, but a heavenly hell, if you see what I mean.' I'd almost forgotten how it felt to be with him, swept along by his enthusiasm. He's like a tidal wave. 'I've moved to Streatham, by the way. I found a small flat close to the theatre. All that ploughing back and forth to Hampstead was a waste of time.' Graham never mentioned it. But then I never gave him the chance to talk about Ian. 'What about you?'

'Oh, I'm doing quite a bit of work for The Green Room.'

He shakes his head. The name means nothing to him.

'It's the theatre you went to with Matthew . . . when you came down, don't you remember? Just before Christmas.'

He seems to have erased it from his memory. And probably me with it. 'Oh . . . Oh, right. What do you mean, work?'

'I'm doing some scenic designing.' That's the second time his mouth has fallen open. 'I'm really enjoying it.'

'I had no idea you were interested, you never said.'

'I'm just getting some hands-on experience at the moment but next year I'm going to get some kind of qualification.' I seem to have developed the habit of announcing plans that I knew nothing about myself until this moment. 'There's quite a good course on all aspects of theatre at St Martin's.' Tim gave me their brochure. 'It's very intense. It goes on for three or four years.' This is beginning to sound like a brilliant idea. 'I won't have a moment to spare.'

You see, Ian, my life will be just as busy, just as exciting as yours. I don't need you any more. I have a life of my own now. I don't need you, I really don't . . . If I say it often enough I'm sure I'll come to believe it. In time.

'Ruth, that's great.' He's genuinely pleased for me. 'You must –'

'Ian!' A Valkyrie in a caftan engulfs him in a bone-breaking embrace. 'Darling,' she booms, 'I haven't seen you in ages.'

I move away.

We shall never see each other again. I shall probably read about him in the papers, see his name in lights but I shall never speak to him, touch him, make love to him again.

My hands are trembling so much I can hardly hold my glass. 'Mother . . .'

She turns, takes one look at me and says, 'I think we should go now, dear.'

The party is in full swing when we leave. Matthew gives Mother a farewell hug, closes the passenger door, comes round to my side, leans in and says, 'You okay to drive, Ruth? If you're not up to it I can . . .'

'No, I'm fine, Matthew, honestly. I'll be —'

I'm interrupted by a booming voice from the other side of the car park. 'Matt! You were fabulous! Stupendous!'

'Oh Christ,' Matt groans. 'It's the prick I used to share digs with. Robin,' he straightens up, 'great to see you again. How are you, you old bastard?' There's a lot of theatrical hugging and back-slapping, then Matthew introduces us.

'Your sister?' Robin bends down, leering at me. He's going to say something cringe-making. 'I don't believe it. Nobody that beautiful could be related to a toad like you, Matt.'

I have to endure a few more minutes of this before he finally takes his leave.

'By the way . . .' Oh no, he's coming back. 'Where's Tasha? I thought she'd be in the front row leading the clack.'

'She's got the flu, bad dose. She's really pissed off about not coming. I told her I'd give her a blow by blow account when I got home.'

'Poor old love. Give her my very best,' says Robin, walking away.

Mother leans over me and says, 'So you and Tasha are still together, darling?'

'Sure.'

'I'm so pleased. She seems such a nice girl.'

'But I thought she was . . . Didn't she . . . ?' I'll get it out in a minute. 'Isn't she with Ian?'

'She was for a while but you know what he's like. They call him the slavedriver,' he grimaces, 'and with good reason. Tasha's no slouch but he kept her going day and night, she was practically dead on her feet. And we never got the chance to see each other. So she quit and came up here. She's getting quite a bit of work with the Rep now.'

I feel as if I've just fallen from a great height and landed flat on my back. I'm so winded I can't speak.

'Well, I'm glad things are going well for both of you, darling, and please give Tasha my . . . Ruthy, where are you going?' Mother frowns as I get out of the car.

'I'll be back in a minute, dear.'

'Have you forgotten something?'

'Yes. My brains.'

She and Matt look at me, perplexed. I'll explain later. I'll explain everything later.

'You fool!' I mutter as I run through the foyer, down the aisle and up onto the stage. Sister Anne wrote on one of my end of year reports 'When faced with a problem Ruth has an unfortunate tendency to panic which all too often results in her leaping to the wrong conclusion.' After thirty years I'm still doing it.

'You fool!'

He's still there, standing by the makeshift bar. The Valkyrie is talking to him earnestly. He's bored stiff but doing his best to hide it. I but in. No excuses, no apologies. The Valkyrie looks at me aghast. Nobody interrupts her, nobody has ever dared.

'Ian, do you need a scenic designer at the Pandora?' I ask, ignoring the dagger the Valkyrie has just stuck in my ribs. 'I come cheap. I'm not asking for any money . . . Well, not yet, anyway, not till I'm qualified. All I need is somewhere to live. Do you have a spare room in your flat?'

He gives me a long, thoughtful look . . . Then shakes his head.

'I'm sorry, Ruth, I only have one bedroom.' Oh God, he doesn't want me. I've made a fool of myself. I start to back away, pretending to make light of it, only a joke . . . 'But I'm willing to share it,' he says, 'with the right woman.' I phone Simpson and tell him.

'Good,' he says. 'So you finally pulled the emergency cord. Make sure you get on the right train next time.'

No, Doctor, I'm not getting on any more trains. From now on I'll travel how I want, I'll go at my speed. There may be hazards ahead, I may not even be going in the right direction. But for better or worse, for richer or poorer, I'm on my way. At last.